THE DEVIL'S COUNTDOWN

Dedication

Remembering Frank, Patricia, Con and Andrew.

Is Jeff Bourke a prophet or a pawn?

THE DEVIL'S COUNTDOWN

MARTIN HAND

First published in 2023 by ETC Publishing
Dublin
Ireland
https://www.facebook.com/profile.php?id=100067375265305

Paperback	ISBN: 978 1 78846 293 8
eBook	ISBN: 978 1 78846 294 5
Amazon paperback	ISBN: 978 1 78846 295 2

Produced by Kazoo Independent Publishing Services
222 Beech Park, Lucan, Co. Dublin
kazoopublishing.com

Kazoo Independent Publishing Services is not the publisher of this work. All rights and responsibilities pertaining to this work remain with ETC Publishing.

Cover design by Andrew Brown
Printed in the EU

GIZA
Taylor 2023

Part 1

EGYPT

1945/46

1

Three hundred and forty miles south of Cairo, the village of Nag Hammadi was defined by the Nile. When the river was not delivering fish, it was further defined by supporting subsistence farming. Four camels were laden with the digging tools and storage jars for the toil of *sabakh*: natural fertiliser collection. The earnings would sustain this party of fellahin at least until the Coptic Christmas on 6 January. They had followed a well-worn track for fifteen miles before reaching this place. An overnight fire and makeshift camp would shelter the group before they made their laden return journey.

The Egyptian winter sun still needed full Arabian robes to afford protection. A fire would be made from the sparse kindling that was available in a desert. Dry camel dung burns well; no water is wasted within those ships.

The group was made up of six young and fit Arab men including three brothers: Muhammad, Khalifah and Abu al-Magd – all Alis of the al-Samman clan. The signs of tooth decay would not be upon them for a decade yet – that is, if the drinking of molasses was kept to moderation.

The toil was backbreaking. The brothers watched the others and one another carefully. Not doing your share could easily earn you an unannounced clatter to the mouth. Abu's mattock glanced off the soil with a hollow reverberating echo that loudly bounced off the surrounding cliff. Now the digging party instantly had their gazes drawn into this new hole. They gathered around. The two younger brothers obscured the others' view while they hand-dug out the top of what appeared to be an earthenware jar, a foot below the surface. The sun had already disappeared behind the massive rock face called Jabal al-Tarif.

'Is it a burial, Abu?' asked the eldest brother, Muhammad.

Any of the six men knew about the others' prowess for grave robbing. Such things were not spoken of but were known. The gold merchant of their village knew well the route to the antiquity dealers in Cairo.

There were many stories of finding graves close against the cliff wall. Now the six glowed with either expectation or gold lust.

'Is it a coffin, Abu?' asked Muhammad again, dismissive of the others. 'Brother, we will build our fire here and dig in its light.'

The fellahin proved that sweating was possible in the cold of the Egyptian night. All six were eager to take their turn in the toil.

By dawn, a six-foot-tall water jar was exposed by a one-foot circular ring dug out around it. The mound of soil was to have been the fruits of their labour.

Instead, for today, this was just waste. All eyes were on the jar as a rope and pulley system was used, along with the two strongest camels, to extract the find vertically from its tomb. The jar was sealed on top – but how long ago? And why? The hope was that this was an ancient seal.

'Let us break it open here now,' said one of the fellahin.

The eldest brother spoke without hesitation.

'We will not.'

The three brothers stood united, shoulder to shoulder. A stream of Arabic expletives disturbed the early morning stillness. There would be no honour among these thieves while exhaustion and the smell of gold were infectious. Muhammad stayed silent while Khalifah Ali spat out his own Arabic tirade. Instead, Muhammad placed his hand upon a scabbarded knife. The fellahin shut up, leaderless. If it was time to fight, one of them must make a lunge. Would the others follow? That blade had seen use before, and the fertiliser diggers knew it.

'Do we want a Jinn released upon us here, in this desolation of a place?' said Muhammad. 'The place of Seth's red land, only fit for burying the dead. My mother will advise us. Now we depart.'

There were some mumblings from the trio of fellahin. The Ali brothers were watching.

As the eldest, Muhammad Ali was always the self-appointed leader. It wasn't any village secret that the required vengeance for the murder of his father had been recent and extreme. The war had been a shield for crimes like grave-robbing, but murder still attracted the attention of Cairo. The authorities would be more watchful now.

The widow Ali sensed the arrival of her sons even though they were coming into the village earlier than expected, and from a direction that was less likely to attract attention. The matriarch went outside into her courtyard. Standing beside her bread oven, her intention was to prevent her home from being overrun.

'God be with you, our mother. We found this jar and knew you would have understanding, God willing.'

She observed the furtive behaviour of the three men who accompanied her sons, and the man-sized jar that was the reason for it. No Arabian politeness was observed as four of the men bundled the jar into the woman's only family room, passing through the courtyard. Abu, the younger, hobbled the camels and proceeded behind them.

The matriarch of the family, Umm-Ahmad, was already hunched over for her fifty-five years. The room was claustrophobic. She raised her two hands to reach around the neck of the standing vase and closed her eyes as if she was straining to feel for a pulse. The group watched in a silent minute of expectation; their exhaustion suspended.

'I can see a view of many hundreds of years ago,' she said. 'Christians in their robes. Their incense rising as a protection from the stench of an evil cradling.

There is fear in the toil of building a grave for the pure and the impure.'

'But is it gold, blessed Mother?' asked Muhammad. His eyes were gaping wide in lustful anticipation. His mother was squinting as if the light in the crammed room hurt.

'You must not open this thing, my son. It will release a demon that will create a storm. A storm great enough to see the Nile dry up and the black lands become red. In the name of Allah, do not open this thing.'

With a gaze downwards, as if he was taking in some distraction from the beauty in a swept dirt floor, Abu waited. But along with Muhammad, he knew that doing his mother's bidding could be his end. Agitation grew like an odour in this claustrophobic, meagre room. The three fellahin made a synchronous lunge at the brothers. A mattock swung to cleave the head off something – either the head of an Ali or the head of the jar. The jar was struck at its neck, but the sheer weight of the find saved it from toppling. Umm-Ahmad was not so lucky. She was not struck directly, but the ceramic explosion knocked her over, stumbling over two male bodies already on the floor. The second mattock blow struck the belly of the jar. Whether by nature or by design, the jar split symmetrically down the centre like an alien creature revealing its chrysalis. A five-and-a-half-foot high column of books – codices, not gold. Papyrus.

The fellah, demonic in his disappointment, swung the weapon one more time. Although Muhammad attempted to stop him, the strike was enough to send the meticulously ordered library into a new entangled mess.

Seeing their mother languishing on the ground should have sent the brothers into a murderous frenzy. It did not. A golden filigree plume rose from the smashed-open mound of the jar. The shaft of sunlight in the room was perfectly aligned to illuminate the moment. All were watching, frozen combatants, some from wrestling positions on the floor. Three of the men were still standing.

'A Jinn, a Jinn!' screeched the stricken mother from the floor. The golden mist continued to rise and glisten. 'Allah, Allah be merciful, the Devil has come among us.'

The standing fellahin bolted to the door in unison without casting a glance back. Those on the floor couldn't move their cramped, intertwined limbs. Fear in the base of the stomach. Abu and his assailant rose from the ground, scuffled and shuffled their way past Muhammad to get out. Muhammad himself wanted to bolt, but would not, with his mother still languishing on the floor. Mother and son were left alone with the new silence, more frozen than calm.

'If the Jinn had been released, it would have possessed us all already.' Umm-Ahmad was speaking through her sobs. There was nowhere to turn to, and she was yet unsure if she had broken bones. 'My son, I cannot run from my own home. Where would I go?'

Some of the filigree had landed around them.

'This mist is the possession,' she said.

It became still. Muhammad was speechless. Time must have passed, because the sun seemed to be illuminating the abnormal dust in the room from its evening direction. How strange. His mother was crying softly in the corner. Maybe waiting on her end. At the very noon of that day, Muhammad had been hoping to have uncovered a ransom of gold. The weight of the jar had, for a while, lent itself to the possibility.

'Do you not feel it, the presence?' Umm-Ahmad was speaking to her son. 'There, in the corner – do you see it? Do you feel it, my son? This will end us all.'

'How do we kill it – destroy it?' murmured a shaking Muhammad, unable to disguise his terror.

'A Jinn can only be destroyed by an amulet and its spell.'

'Please, Mother, please help me, help us.'

'The Jinn protects the amulet that has control over it. That secret was locked in that jar. But the presence will not leave until the spell is broken.'

Muhammad did not answer her.

'Can you see it?' said Umm-Ahmad. 'There in the corner, in the dark corner of my home – my home. Allah, Allah be merciful.'

2

'What was it all about?' George Cavendish asked himself, looking out of his office window. Below, the street pulsed with life: men and women of all ages, swathed in robes and veils, thronged the crowded marketplace of old Cairo; half-naked children chased stray dogs into narrow alleyways; the call to midday prayers rose from a hundred minarets. It seemed that normal life had asserted itself remarkably quickly after the unprecedented destruction of the past six years. Some things still stayed the same, though. The *Sunday Times* on his desk was dated January 6 1946, and it had taken nearly six weeks to arrive from London.

A war – an anti-Semitic war – had ended a few short months earlier. The last war, the 'Great War', had ended with a pandemic. The Spanish flu of 1919 had killed more people than the bloody war itself.

The Brits were all over Egypt. They'd fought for it, fought for the Suez Canal. But what were to be the spoils of war? What could they plunder? Word had reached the Foreign Office in London about a find. A find that could make Carter's diggings look like scratchings on the annals of history.

Ecclesiastical England was irked. The Protestant denominations had no place, no foothold in the holy city of Jerusalem, the centre of religion for the three Abrahamic faiths. The bloody Armenians … The even bloodier Copts owned the Church of the Holy Sepulchre: the final – no, *temporary* – resting place for a deceased Jesus. What intrigue would be – could be – orchestrated?

George Cavendish was the Foreign Office's man in Cairo. He was getting on in years, and the last of those years had seen him worn down, overshadowed and overruled by the military types. Second in rank to the ambassador, he occupied a spacious colonial-style office in the red dust-filled streets of Cairo. Everywhere in old Cairo afforded you a view of the magnificent trio of pyramids at Giza. That only heightened Cavendish's worries that all great empires come to an end. At least he had plenty of fez-wearing civil servants to run around after him, achieving … what?

'Tell me, Ahmed, please,' said Cavendish to the office underling he had summoned, 'when you could possibly attempt a telephone connection to London, undersecretary Rupert Graves at the Foreign Office? Rather urgent, chop chop.'

The telephone rang some fifty minutes later, and Cavendish picked up the receiver and momentarily listened to the crackle on the line.

'Cavendish speaking.'

'*Delighted to hear from you, old boy,*' said Graves. '*You survived the war, that's a start.*'

'Yes indeed, sir. Tell me, how's Marjorie?'

'As well as can be expected. She survived the war also.'

'Splendid, splendid, delighted to hear it.'

'Tell me, Cavendish, what's all this "find" nonsense? I'm hearing chatter in the corridors here.'

'I most certainly wanted to brief you, sir. It appears some peasant or other found a jar of old biblical texts near enough to some ghastly Coptic monastery.'

'Why should we be interested?'

'Could be two thousand years old, they say, sir. Quite explosive stuff, really – our chance to put England's name on it. Even the names … Saint Thomas, Saint Philip, Judas – and he's no saint … Even Mary Magdalene – no saintess.'

'We're just after beating the Boche. Should we be bothering with Bible books?'

'Well, that depends upon what these books say, does it not, sir?' Cavendish hesitated; had he been overly familiar – impertinent, even? He breathed deeply but silently, and recovered himself. 'Indeed, it certainly raises a question, sir. If these books aren't in the Bible, then why not? Do they support, repeat or condemn the narrative?'

'When you put it like that … Interesting stuff, right enough. Have you got these books, then?'

Cavendish withdrew a white handkerchief from his trouser pocket and wiped his sweating brow. 'Well, we are in possession of some of the find, even though those upstarts at the Cairo Museum have been kicking up quite an Arab rumpus. You see, they claim they have translators and all that … Foreigners – Germans, no less. Should have been off fighting, if you ask me. Bloody academics.'

'*You're not wrong there, old boy.*' Graves's chuckle went a little more of the way to helping Cavendish relax. '*So, what is it you need from me?*'

'We need our own translators. Oxford or Cambridge types. Let's be in charge of which genies are allowed out of the bottle.'

'*Good idea. But that will take weeks. You play your part now, Cavendish. Make sure you take possession.*'

'Well, the problem is, sir, that the thirteen books have been seen by the Cairo Museum curator chappie. Can you imagine – Germans …? The museum types are saying they are the help they need. Bloody loyalty … Bloody ingratitude, I'd say.'

'*For God's sake, man, use our military, why don't you?*' Cavendish, even over the crackle, heard the thud of a fist upon the wooden surface of his superior's desk. '*It's not the bloody Elgin Marbles, Cavendish, it's a few dusty books. If the Egyptians think they have had enough of imperialism, we'll show them, what?*'

'Yes, sir,' Cavendish protested, 'but what if this *is* the word of God? Or, at least, the words of Jesus written down only a single lifetime after his death. That's what we're told.'

'*You're babbling, man.*'

'You see, sir, our military are involved already.' This time Cavendish moved his telephone receiver from one ear to the other in order to allow him to dry his clammy palm. 'A night-time patrol picked up this, what … old woman in the middle of the night, middle of nowhere. Luckily one of our boys spoke the tongue. She had some story about … wait for it … the Devil. Spooked the men, I'm told, even if they had just come through skirmishing with Rommel. Anyhow, our boys brought her home to her dark hovel in a town … em …' Cavendish had to awkwardly stand up and use his free hand to find his hand-written notes. 'Nag Ham—something. The dead of night. The old girl kept going on about burning some pages. Old hags have to bake bread, do they not? She said she needed kindling.'

The telephone line continued to crackle annoyingly. But at least Cavendish had captured the under-secretary's attention.

'*That's more like it, old man.*' Graves's chuckle lifted Cavendish's mood again. '*Our boys came up trumps.*'

'Well, the old girl was happy to surrender her haul – the books. Her bargain was that our boys would take the Devil with them.'

'*Quite the deal,*' said Graves.

'Well, there was a slight snag, regrettably.' Cavendish had been hoping to omit this part of the story. 'The jeep crashed on the way to Cairo. Survived the bloody war, but one of the privates was killed. Worse still, bloody Egyptian authorities got involved cleaning up the mess. It wasn't helpful that our sergeant was babbling on about an evil presence.'

'*I'll send the academics over, no delay. It's finders keepers as far as I'm concerned. If these locals think we fought for them for nothing, they will have to be educated, will they not?'*

'Some greedy antiquities dealers must have greased the palms of the local constabulary. The Cairo police force played a role in delivering some of the books to a dealer – a chap called … I have it here …' Cavendish was shuffling papers across his desk again. 'Phokion J. Tano, no less. That is of no matter. As you say, I can send in our military, with the ambassador's permission. Should show them who is in charge, I'd say.'

'*Cavendish, it's time to offer a simple choice to that Tano individual. Either deliver the books to us, or find himself delivered to a Cairo jail. Yes, and if there are Germans involved, lock them up as well, I say.*'

'The story I'm getting, sir, is that the Germans indeed already had a finger in this damn pie.'

'*Disgraceful,*' boomed Graves, who was now growing exasperated by the disjointed twists and turns in Cavendish's story.

'Yes, way before the war. It seems they do more than eat those ghastly sausage meats and start wars. Some fragment of text found on a rubbish tip in … Wait, I have it here on the desk somewhere …Yes, here it is – Oxyrhynchus, an old Roman settlement.'

'*Get to it, man.*'

'Look, sir, these German scholar types translated a fragment of papyrus found there. It said … no, I have it here … My notes, my notes … Yes, here it is. "Whoever reads and understands the secret teachings of Jesus, written down by Didymus Judas Thomas, shall never know death." Quite a statement, and this was from the only piece of this so-called Gospel of Thomas ever found before now. The trail went a bit cold with the First War intervening. If that wasn't enough … wait for it … a water pipe burst, destroying the Oxyrhynchus fragment altogether.'

'*Sounds like the whole bloody thing is cursed.*'

'So, your instructions, sir, are that we should grab this thing … this manuscript, this Gospel of Thomas, at least?'

'*Yes, yes, exactly. Take the lot as a spoil of war. God knows we've sacrificed enough for these Egyptians. I'll get Canterbury interested into the bargain.*'

'And what to do with these stories of curses and devils?'

'*Nonsense, poppycock and coincidence.*'

'Very good, send me our academics. I'll do the rest, sir.'

Cavendish did something uncharacteristic after he hung the telephone receiver back into its holder. He left his desk and proceeded to the drinks cabinet. He poured himself a large brandy. The small things that were uncharacteristic for him were that he normally summoned Ahmed, and he normally called for a scotch and soda. Cavendish was doing his best to disguise an unease within himself. He had put the wheels in motion. A smash and grab of an ancient set of manuscripts. If he didn't, or couldn't, pull it off – if he couldn't get the ambassador on board – a black mark would appear on his career copybook for sure. He just couldn't let himself think about failure, drawing towards the end of a forty-year diplomatic career. Still, he couldn't stop himself thinking that there might be something, something else in play here.

Part 2
TIMEBOX

3

Jeff Bourke arrived in the States in the summer of 2003 after finishing college in Ireland. His mother, Anne, had encouraged him to grab a J1 visa. It was his last chance. He hadn't availed himself of it the previous summer. It wasn't right. His father Liam recently deceased. His mother still distressed after the death.

International Business was his major, as he explained it to Americans. The business world itself was still a little burnt at that point after the dotcom bubble burst. Too much blind faith had been invested in too many pimple-faced kids who liked playing with computers. Jeff had been bumming around with an old Irish girlfriend, Emily Steward. They had started uni in Dublin together. Emily had moved on, with her father's funds, to finish college in Berkeley. A chance invitation to something called a 'recruitment blast' that started at 10 p.m. on campus was to set up a serendipitous encounter for Jeff with 'the Zimmer'.

David Zimmerman was looking for recruits – more 'followers', really. He couldn't pay, but that didn't matter to most of the Berkeleyan gang. It mattered to Jeff, though, because he hadn't a bean.

Zimmerman set the party a task, and only the winner was guaranteed to be offered a job. On the night Jeff happened to be there, Zimmerman explained the task in these words.

'Ladies and gentlemen, you have two hours, now till midnight.'

He held up an A0 size white cardboard sheet on which was written the mathematical equation for Fermat's Last Theorem. In italics was written *Proven in 1993 by Andrew Wiles*.

'Grab a sheet and tell me how we are going to make a buck out of Mr. Wiles's hard work,' said Zimmerman.

IBM ThinkPads had been the laptop of choice back then. They were flipped open with abandon, and the sound of frenetic keyboard tapping reminded Jeff of old black and white movies where a large pool of young women went clattering away on typewriters.

Jeff didn't have a laptop. His old clunker of a Dell was gathering dust in faraway Dublin. Even if he had processing power at his disposal, he was tuned in enough to think that Zimmerman was looking for a different type of answer.

Jeff grabbed two bottles of beer from Zimmerman's refreshments table and took himself off into a corner. He was discerning enough to know that a couple of beers were not going to dull any creative juices. Maybe they would enhance them. In any event, he was suspicious as to whether American beer had alcohol in it at all. Jeff toyed with the idea of walking out into the still warm Californian night and ditching the nerd fest. *This was meant to be a holiday, wasn't it?* Emily, likewise, was not showing a great interest in the process. But Zimmerman had charisma. He could nearly sense when he was losing even a single audience member. A sustained piece of eye contact between Jeff and 'the Zimmer' established something.

Emily spotted a girlfriend waving from the far side of the gathering.

'There's AJ.' Jeff could make out a tall, good-looking blonde girl. 'I'll introduce you later.'

She left Jeff to his own devices.

With a slug of beer and a blank page in front of him, Jeff began to doodle. The room was buzzing. They were in one of the college dorms, all of which had a ground floor communal area in which this mini nerd community was now congregated.

The Zimmer worked the room. He was looking over shoulders, offering guidance, words of wisdom. Supreme confidence for a man of twenty-five. He was, of course, suiting himself. If he could see the ideas as they evolved, he would be better able to call in the winner.

Zimmerman approached Jeff from behind.

'Fairly blank-looking sheet, my man. Are you freeloading a few beers?'

Jeff was one of those people who picked up an American twang quickly. He had only landed in LA a week before.

'No, bud, it's all under control,' he replied. 'Does

this "my man" thing stem from looking at too many old Sherlock Holmes movies?'

'Call me if you need me is all,' said an unruffled Zimmerman as he shuffled off.

When the clock struck twelve, it was time for some of the nerds to turn into pumpkins. The Zimmer was ruthless. If you wanted to pitch you got your go, but some of them only lasted twenty seconds. Zimmerman would simply shout 'no' and move on. It didn't, of course, bother him that he might frighten off a good idea. He'd already seen what he needed to see. Maybe except for Jeff. The various computer heads had gone after Fermat with a vengeance. They didn't need their whiteboards at all. Sixty or seventy screens of code on the ThinkPad was enough. Zimmerman definitely frightened off a few when he declared, 'If you hadn't got the brain cells enough to write it down on the presentation sheets, well …?'

Emily and her friend Annie Jo – AJ – were egging him on.

'Jeff, come on, piss or get off the pot,' said Emily. 'Make the pitch, will ye, so we can blow this joint.'

There were no males of interest in the room, and Emily was vibing that she had been in this and other dorms for long enough. AJ was perhaps a little less interested in moving on. The male Irish accent had maybe struck a chord. *The looks weren't bad either – a bit thin, maybe – reddish blond.* AJ stayed schtum even while her Irish girlfriend was trying to make Jeff a smidgen uncomfortable. Whether he was bowing to the subtle female pressure or not, Jeff took to the floor – a deep breath being a willing substitute for confidence.

He turned his board to the audience and gave them time to read and digest:

Fuck Fermat

Let's de-geek computers.

Social Connection
is
where
we
are
going!

'Look, guys,' Jeff said. 'Very admirable and all that, but nobody has been stopped from making money just because there is a dusty math algorithm that is proven, not proven, I don't know, I don't care. What does it matter? Now, if your ThinkPads were in touch with each other, then look how small the problem becomes. Larry, Bill and Jane are all sharing their energy, their ideas, their time in real time. You have all gone off, half-cocked, in a race which, even if you can win, there will only be one winner. Lots of losers, so reject that bullshit, get collaborative, get connected. In short, get with the programme, not programming.'

Maybe the couple of beers had loosened Jeff's vocal cords. He did his presentation in acting mode. Sure, what the hell, he didn't know any of these guys from Adam.

The Zimmer was impressed. He liked dramatics, like Jeff pointing at his fictitious Larry, a Bill, and some random Jane. Zimmerman closed the formal session there and then.

'Unless somebody has something to add,' he said, 'I declare the fair-haired gentleman from the Emerald Isle winner of tonight's proceedings. Now grab a beer and let's get this party started.'

Zimmerman joined Emily, AJ and Jeff. Emily was no longer as keen to be away as she had been. The Zimmer was a good-looking guy in the sense that Abe Lincoln was handsome. 'Handsome' might have been stretching it, but charismatic for sure.

'Nice speech, my man,' said Zimmerman. 'Will you take the job?'

'How much does it pay?' asked Jeff.

'Nothing right now, but it's what it will pay when we pull this thing off.'

'What thing is that, exactly?'

'That's the point,' said Zimmerman. 'You tell me – or at least you were telling me during your pitch.'

'Yeah, Jeff, your idea was really slick,' said Emily. 'What was it again?'

Zimmerman got the joke but, just in case, he elaborated.

'Our boy here summed it up nicely. The newbie generation now don't want computers to solve problems, they want them to be connected. That's what our product is going to be. Not technical connectivity – the internet gave us that already – but social connectivity for sure.'

A meeting of minds: Zimmerman knew he had the lieutenant that he wanted.

4

Work, when it started, was out of a garage – literally – in San Jose. A lot more industrial than Berkeley was. There were two banks of six workstations on either side of the garage wall, all wired for rapid internet. The centre of the back wall had a box-like annex attached: the location of the single basic bathroom.

Zimmerman's mantra was, 'If you're going to get going in tech, then you have to have the corporate customers you need on your doorstep.'

Living the American dream was getting off to a slow start. The twelve garage inhabitants needed the odd well-timed pep talk from the Zimmer.

'My men and women, these are the early stages of an engineering revolution – the new social media. The media of the future. The future of the media.'

Zimmerman was playing it by the book. He had done twelve recruitment drives, and that's the number who occupied the lab on Sunnyvale Boulevard. Nine guys and three gals. Jeff was making the job come together as best he could. His Jungian red personality was called into play. The team knew Jeff called them geeks and nerds, and they kind of liked it. His own business qualification, at least, had set him a bit apart from the IT tribe. There was no malice, no put-down. *Craic* – Jeff hated the Gaelic word but liked the idea. A few of the guys just got into it, calling him a weird Irish mick. It was a way of building up a bit of camaraderie. Showing a bit of leadership. Every time he checked in, it was with the same mantra: 'Can you turn us a buck?'

'Monetise, my good man, monetise,' to quote the Zimmer.

Jeff's personality and his business techniques meant that he drove the IT talent crazy.

'Jeff, you mean we have to stop coding to help you and your process maps? Ah, heck.'

'Yeah, guys, but I promise I'll make it up to you with a few pints on Friday night – sorry … *beers*. I forgot you nerds didn't speak English.'

That summer was Jeff's summer to man up. He had his first qualification behind him, and a new American girlfriend – AJ. Sitting in a bar waiting for her to arrive, he had eyes only on the door. Infatuation mode. That euphoric feeling that you think will never go away because you're lucky enough to be paired up with perfection. The trick in life would be that when infatuation stopped, would love be left in its place? Would he have the maturity for love? The stamina for it? All the hormones would have you chasing around. It usually took an aberration of nature for a young guy to keep his dick in his trousers. He'd soon know if he was on the right track. She would either agree to move up to the Bay Area or she wouldn't.

Two members of the fledgling team always seemed to be in short supply. Zimmerman himself wasn't much for hanging out in the garage. Other fish to fry, and bigger wigs to hang with. Martin Gabrielle was one of the twelve, but not one of them at the same time. There was something of the night about the guy, as far as Jeff was concerned. Dark, wavy and slightly oily hair, dark complexion, slender wiry build. He had a way of moving – a shiftiness, a turn of expression that jarred. Gabrielle had taken on the role of the ideas vetting man.

It was a kind of production line. Jeff worked out and workshopped the team's ideas. Gabrielle got to see all the potential products, but had the final word on which were approved for further development. The only time Jeff saw Zimmerman get exercised during that first fall was when Jeff questioned Gabrielle's role. Zimmerman wasn't having any of it. It wasn't any lack of insight, or backbone, it was just a signal.

'Jeffrey, Jeffrey, Jeffrey, I need my knights to fight our good fight. You can even be a bishop if you want. But please, please, let's be clear. There is only one person setting out the board strategy and that is me.'

Only the Zimmer was allowed to move the chess players and Gabrielle was going to be his black knight, so Jeff cracked on.

San Jose's main claim to fame was that it was close to San Francisco and housed some very big IT players in very big offices. Zimmerman's twelve-person company, TimeBox, had a cramped but airy – when the door was open – garage as a HQ. It didn't take much time for some of the troops to ebb and flow into the adjacent four-bedroom house. It might have originally been assumed that this was Zimmerman's residence. As it turned out, he was seldom there and when he did show, he generally took up a single room for a single night.

Jeff's upbringing would have made him baulk at entering the main house proper without permission. The American team seemed to have no such qualms.

There were practicalities here. The bathroom at the back of the garage did nothing for privacy. Anyway, you had to enter the house to use the kitchen. The house was from the 1960s: two storeys, clean and frugal, certainly never remodelled. The colour beige seemed very much in evidence on the inside furnishings. The outside was a pale blue lateral wood-panelled finish.

There were plenty of trees around to block you off from the neighbours. Plenty of critters and wildlife, too – typical suburban America. Chances were that the mosquitoes would be out come the following summer. So would the raccoons, if it wasn't for Jeff imposing a strict garbage disposal regime.

'Put the lids back on the bins, guys, will ye. It can't be that difficult.'

There wasn't much to be seen of Martin Gabrielle occupying a workstation. That at least meant a bit more space in the garage. It also meant that Jeff, for no apparent reason other than personality, seemed to be asked for direction a lot – that is, direction in the matters of social media screen content. In the matter of people gravitating into the house, and then the bedrooms, he wasn't asked. A little bit of coupling up was going on.

'AJ, is this mixing business and pleasure going to work?' asked Jeff. 'Should I say something … intervene?'

'I think you should focus on your own love life and let others focus on theirs,' answered AJ.

'Yeah, but what about fights and rows, and maybe jealousies and break-ups?'

'Honey, do you not think Zimmerman has all this figured out? If there's a domestic flashpoint that causes you a production problem, wait and see. Martin Gabrielle will appear like magic.'

'You're making a few jumps there, AJ, no?'

'Jeff, stick to business, will ya? When it comes to the business of love and relationships, I'll call the shots.'

AJ moved up and in with Jeff just before Thanksgiving. She got a job as a pharmacist in an established drugstore chain in San Jose. Moving in showed commitment, but it was also a way of not wasting time. If it didn't work out, you would soon know.

Her father, Colonel Mike Maher, was invited up for the turkey dinner. 'No-Nonsense Mike', as Jeff called him, was exactly that – a big bulk of a man ingrained in the military. AJ was close to her dad. Her mother,

Catherine, wasn't. After the divorce Catherine had become less and less involved, until it was just a case of AJ and her dad. Mike had adjusted his military career accordingly. He got himself desk-bound in San Diego, maybe a bit of reward for his Desert Storm service. Mike's role – Chief Liaison Officer to the Navy, a colonel's lapels – meant his daughter would get a good shot at stability.

It didn't take much insight on Jeff's part to see that he was dealing with a man who wouldn't suffer fools gladly.

'Jeff, hope you ain't lookin for a dowry,' said Mike, 'but I will ask you to treat my girl – your girl, now – right. All actions have consequences. I don't travel much and I don't plan on living in your ear in the Bay either. But if there's trouble and I have to visit ... well, you'll know about it.'

'There'll be no trouble,' said Jeff. He knew already that he loved his daughter.

In their early days living together, AJ got tired of listening to the anti-Gabrielle harangue coming out of Jeff. That seemed to be part of his letting-off-steam mechanism. When she finally got tired of it, she let rip.

'You sorry mick,' she said one time. 'Bullet-headed, unemancipated Irish Catholic dick,' she said making a fairly explicit phallic gesticulation.

'OK,' Jeff countered, 'so what would one of you Bible-bashing, evangelical, holier-than-thou US types have me do?'

'Build up a rapport, idiot. Change the direction, change the relationship. Talk to the guy, get going on a human, personal level. Get out for R and R. What about a one-on-one dinner?'

'I've a better idea – what about a two-on-two event?'

'Yeah, why not?' AJ answered. 'What's Gabrielle's partner's name?'

'Simone Haddad.'

The two couples met up on an arranged Thursday evening. Jeff didn't know what the protocol was for picking up the tab, but a trip to Jammet's sure was going to clock up a nice bill. This was the Brown Derby of San Jose.

'Don't be a tight-ass, honey,' said AJ. 'You asked, you pay.'

'Well, actually, you asked.'

'Jeff, shut up,' AJ said, passing through the restaurant door. She knew that her partner was nervous. Jeff spotted Martin Gabrielle, already seated with Simone.

He walked straight over and popped up with an icebreaker.

'You order any wine yet?'

'Why would I do that?' Gabrielle replied. 'We don't drink alcohol.'

'OK,' said Jeff, looking awkward. 'Well, I guess I should have known that.'

'There are perhaps many more things that you should know,' said Simone.

AJ was seeing this exquisite-looking young woman

for the first time. Brown skin and beautiful, bottomless, deep hazel eyes. Her elbows were resting on the cotton tablecloth with her chin resting upon her clasped hands. Her nails were painted with a deep green gloss varnish.

A black-tie waiter appeared before AJ could take her own seat. He took her coat and she was gently guided into the chair.

'Could I ask if you wish to order wine?' the waiter asked. 'I'll alert our sommelier.'

'No need,' said Jeff. 'I'll take the house's recommendation. Red, please.'

AJ wasn't exactly sure that Jeff knew what a sommelier was.

'Where are you guys from?' asked AJ.

'My parents are from Lebanon originally,' Simone replied. 'They were grateful to escape the war and be accepted into America. Is your story similar, Jeff?'

'Em … not quite. The war – conflict – in Ireland was mostly up in the northern part of the country. Thankfully – and, by the way, with a lot of support from the US – it was just over, a couple of years anyway, before I came over and met AJ.'

'It's funny to think you are both migrants from war-torn countries' said Gabrielle. 'Both supported by the great US democracy. This is the only right place to control the world.'

'Wow, that's a big statement,' said Jeff.

'Martin, where do you hail from?' asked AJ.

'Gabrielle, please, I prefer it to Martin. Too many

Martins in the world. Like you, AJ, I suspect, I'm a homegrown American. All the way from Great Falls, Montana, but of Serbian extraction.'

'Well, while we're all laying our cards on the table …' AJ began. 'My name is Annie Jo Maher. So, I guess, with that name, the Irish are over-represented at this table. Don't worry, though, I'm third generation. You'll only have to put up with one sorry mick at this table. I'm a California girl first and foremost, and call me AJ, please.'

Jeff was glad to see how skilfully his girl was steering the conversation, while he was sipping wine at a rate that seemed to cause Gabrielle's eyebrows to rise.

'Did you ever think that the cut-throat murderers who wandered the streets of either Belfast or Beirut are still wandering around those streets today?' Gabrielle asked. 'The battles may be over, but are the wars won?'

'I didn't really think about it,' Jeff replied. 'I guess that we're all just so glad of the peace. Anyway, could the same not be said of your part of the world? The Balkans, the old Yugoslavia, was always the tinderbox for European conflict. Never mind the world wars. What about the recent war – the Serbs, the Croats? Bloodthirsty animals would park their work-week suits on the Friday, don the khaki uniform, and do this surreal weekend warrior thing … I mean killing.'

'Now we're getting into heavy country here.' AJ felt it was time to steer the conversation in a different direction. 'Maybe we could get back to more mundane stuff, like menus and work.'

'No, thanks' said Simone, displaying a beautiful but expressionless face.

AJ joined the 'expression through eyebrow-raising' group.

'Surely, AJ, this is an important thing. These boys can talk about work any time.'

'My woman is correct,' said Gabrielle. 'It was you that brought up the question of lineage, and it turns out we're all from dirty little places with dirty little secrets.'

'Is this one of these – and I hate the analogy – glass half full, glass half empty things?' Jeff countered. 'I'd prefer to be singing the praises of our ethnicities. But you're telling me we're all from a long line of murdering bastards.'

AJ was wondering if her partner had taken a few too many sips, too quickly. She knew Jeff was edgy about the meeting. Except it wasn't a meeting; it was at least meant to be a relaxing, get to know you better, dinner.

'No, these are important societal issues,' said Gabrielle. 'Is this not why the United States has the moral authority to be the world's policeman? It doesn't have a track record of genocide – well, let's leave the Civil War out of it – and slavery, of course.'

Jeff was hating this. Gabrielle was making too much sense with his throwaway comments: shining his torch on the world's dark underbelly.

'Your own race, Jeff – the Irish – have remarkably reinvented themselves in this great country of ours. I suppose it was Kennedy that made it OK to be Irish. Up to then, the Protestants held all the cards.'

'Thanks for that observation,' was all Jeff could muster at short notice.

AJ's mouth was hanging open.

'Gabrielle is correct,' said Simone. 'There's more evil in the world than good.'

'What about our jobs?' Jeff responded. 'Our role …? Us, our new social media – TimeBox? A force for good, surely?'

'For sure, Bourke, until it's hijacked – and it will be.'

'Ah, please don't rain on the parade,' said Jeff. 'There's a real feel-good factor about the whole simple connectivity of TimeBox. That's the culture I'm trying to build in that little garage factory of ours – "You're never alone" kind of message.'

'Soon they'll be wishing they were.' Gabrielle was quick to respond. 'It's not that human nature will lean toward evil. It's just that there's bad in us all, and in the future, at any given point in time, there'll be more TimeBox users looking to take a swipe at you than promoting you.'

'Then why do it?' asked AJ.

'It's a means to an end,' Gabrielle responded. 'It will lead to bigger things.'

'According to your Mr Zimmerman, this *is* the big thing,' said AJ.

'Well, that depends on what your agenda is, does

it not? You, for example, might be one of these world peace hippies. Zimmerman is driven by ego and all that goes with it – money, et cetera.'

'Jeff, what are you driven by?' asked Simone.

'My upbringing. My mother, Anne, and my father, Liam – when he was alive. I'm a slave to it and I can't change my path. I just can't piss on the little guy, just because he is a little guy. I'm a fucking little guy at heart.'

'Language, please, honey,' said AJ.

'Then how do you expect to get far?' asked Gabrielle.

'By working damned hard and by sticking to my own moral compass. Traits which I hope have attracted this beauty towards me.' He turned his head to look directly at AJ. 'When I was growing up, it was under the influence of two parents who would have to strain themselves to say a bad word about anyone.'

Jeff placed his hand on AJ's. She might have known this to be true sentiment from her partner, but she knew Jeff was leaving himself wide open to attack.

'You're not long for this world, Jeff,' said Simone. 'This commercial world, that is, if that's your ammunition.'

'Each to their own, I guess. Look, I don't feel particularly hungry anymore. Maybe another time.'

As Jeff got up to leave, he was secretly delighted that AJ stood up in unison with him.

'Maybe,' said Gabrielle. 'Maybe.'

'Not one of your best ideas, AJ,' said Jeff after they

had emerged on to a cool street. 'I told you he was a strange bastard.'

'Look, I'm not apologising for trying, but now that we've tried … Well, I don't know where to go.' AJ faced him and took his hands to hold. 'I'm guessing you're well pissed off?'

'Let's go get something to eat. What about McNally's on Irvine? We can walk, it's not that cold.'

'I thought you said you weren't hungry.'

'Depends on the company, my love, depends on the company.'

In the initial hungry years, Jeff still had to acknowledge that Gabrielle's product vetting system was effective. TimeBox was making money – small money. The company's processes – Jeff's processes – were working. It was all the better for him if Gabrielle was not around a lot of the time. Jeff picked his time to have one more go at changing the company dynamic.

'Again, no, no and no again.' With three fist thumps of the table between them, Zimmerman spelt it out. 'You're getting the picture, right?'

'Look, David, I'm not doing ego here. I don't have one. I just don't think that our structure, our way of working, is the best we can do.'

'Which part of *no frigging way* are you not getting? You said yourself the production line for ideas and the change processes are working. Might not be making me as much money as I'd like, but it's working.'

'Yeah, but is it working optimally? You already

know there's a personality clash – to say the least. Why would you want to keep us so tightly linked when you know we can't stick each other?'

'Jeffrey, Jeffrey, Jeffrey, I've already given you the answer, my man. Because it works. Look, he stays out of your hair … most of the time. You told me that yourself. I'm guessing your team, your grunts, are equally glad to see as little of our Martin G as possible, yeah?'

'You got that straight,' answered Jeff.

'Then you're in the happy zone, no?' Zimmerman was smiling.

'So, you're telling me I should rejoice? Gabrielle pops in now and then in some kind of part-time role to tell my team *Yes* or *No* to work and ideas that people have broken their arses working on?'

'Less of the attitude, Jeff, please, less of the attitude.' Zimmerman offered him a less placatory smile this time. 'There's room for both my knights, but there's only room for one king. And you're looking at him. In cases like this, I'm a great believer in decision by committee. That's if it's a committee of one – me. Now keep up the good work, will you, and get on with it.'

Jeff did get on with it. The company had a hundred plus employees by the end of 2005, still in San Jose, but no more garages. Their first real office space was a Microsoft leftover: a four-storey fixer-upper. The people were state-of-the-art; Zimmerman still did most of the recruiting. Thankfully for Jeff, if Gabrielle hadn't liked visiting the garage much, he equally made himself a rare visitor to the new Palo Alto office. Jeff was de facto in charge.

5

By the spring of 2007, Jeff's workshops had taken on a degree of notoriety in TimeBox. He generally started with a mantra along the lines of: 'Look, people, the trick is to allow the news feeds to flow, and you pick the right time to insert your message, your advertisement, your whatever. No, we don't pay for news content – we're just borrowing it. Why, the very thought …'

He had been driving on the recruits with his enthusiasm and using them to recharge his own mental and physical batteries.

TimeBox was still waiting for the breakthrough, and whatever it was, it wasn't going to be a small leap. How do you turn half a million users into two million? The number-crunchers were gone, dead and buried. Accountancy was for back office. The new breed were data analysts – DAs – and the new gospel was artificial intelligence – AI.

Two million TimeBox users was the magic number. Why? Because these new nerds – the DAs – said so. Because mathematics, the language of the universe, doesn't lie. The algorithms showed that if you could reach a customer base of one million, nine hundred thousand, then there was no losing the race. Even if Yahoo, Google or Microsoft wanted to diversify and get into the game, they would be just too far behind. What would that mean? Bonanza! The big players would know not to piss away investment dollars taking on TimeBox. Instead, they'd be in collaboration mode, or takeover mode, and that would mean more dollars – big ones. Even Jobs over at the holier-than-thou Apple Inc. would have to take note.

Jeff knew he was on to a winner because Gabrielle was on board with his technical strategy, and that meant Zimmerman was happy. But the real breakthrough still needed a killer insight – a key idea.

Jeff and AJ had their apartment, a small one in the flats of San Jose. They both wanted to cement things, maybe, by buying a house together, somewhere closer to the bay. Just like the rest of the Joe and Jane combinations, they had to head towards the bank. The couple met Janis Smyth sitting behind the manager's sign on the desk, out on the bank floor, not hidden away in some back room.

They had all their ducks lined up for the 11 a.m. appointment – the ducks being reams of paperwork, IRS returns, earnings, outgoings and so on.

'Mr Bourke, Ms Maher, right on time,' said Janis. 'Thank you indeed for your punctuality.'

'No problem,' replied Jeff.

Janis's eyes rose from her paper work in response to the Irish accent.

'So, Mr Bourke, Ms Maher, you have a joint mortgage of five hundred thousand dollars taken out, what ... two years ago? Now you want to sign up for an increase to nine hundred thousand?'

'Exactly right, ma'am,' replied AJ.

The Americans did that *sir, ma'am* thing better than anyone. Respectful, not subservient.

'Look, let me cut to the chase. You've furnished us with all the necessary documentation. It won't, however, be possible for the bank to meet your request at this time. But wait ... Before you say anything ... Our bank is willing to advance you a term loan in lieu of a mortgage extension. The amount will be the four hundred thousand, as requested. The interest rate will be ...'

Janis pushed a sheet of paper, face down, in the direction of the couple. Jeff couldn't help but smirk. The niceties of writing and not saying the rate of interest ... Well, it wouldn't have been an Irish thing.

He picked it up, turned it over, and made sure AJ got to look at it at the same time.

'Is this a mistake, Janis?' asked Jeff.

'Five point five per cent,' said AJ. 'But our current mortgage is running at two point three per cent. That sure is a lot of additional repayments.'

'I'm afraid that's as good as the bank can offer at this time,' replied the manager.

Jeff was uncharacteristically dumbstruck. AJ did the talking.

'Thanks for your time, Janis. To be honest, I'm not

sure we can afford it.' AJ was the first to stand up. She shook hands. Jeff didn't. He was already walking towards the door and AJ had to quicken her step to catch up.

'Honey, a bit rude, don't ye think?' AJ had placed her hand on the back of his shoulder to slow him down. He looked mad as hell.

'What a dim-witted woman,' said Jeff.

'I don't think so, Jeff.' She found herself nearly breaking into a trot to keep up with her irked partner 'She was just following bank policy to the letter, is all. Slow down, will ye.'

He stopped dead in the street to face her.

'Janis hadn't even taken a look at our paperwork, that's my guess.'

Jeff and AJ were holed up in the nearest coffee shop they could find. Jeff wanted a double espresso to counter a hand that was mildly shaking – either with shock or rage, he wasn't sure. AJ wanted a glass of something with a shot of alcohol in it, to unravel what had just happened.

'Well, she didn't say no. That's something, right?' asked AJ. Jeff couldn't say anything, so she continued. 'You see, you get TimeBox – but the middle-agers?'

'Yeah, you're right.' Jeff managed a wry smile. 'That bitch sounded to me like something from the Middle Ages all right. No, AJ, there's something else going on. Something worth paying attention to.'

'Ah, honey, we were asking for four hundred thou

on an existing mortgage of half a mil from someone who probably doesn't believe you have a real job.'

'Well, how then did we get half a mil, as you call it, just over eighteen months ago?'

'Because they liked my prospects as a pharmacist, where we sell real things, called drugs, to real people with real money. I'm telling you, middle-aged middle managers don't get your digital world.' AJ sipped her Napa chardonnay and sat back to gaze at her sullen partner.

'But I earn four, five times what you cool pharmacists earn.'

'Honey, if you're planning on playing a boys' game of "my penis is bigger than yours", then you can play it – and a few other games as well – on your own.'

'Sorry, my love, I swear I'm not playing games. I'm seething. It's our plans – *our* plans – that are put on hold.' Jeff inclined sideways on his stool to kiss her. 'Now, back to my train of thought. You said it yourself – the bank will give us the money, but not as a mortgage extension, only as a new term loan. What gives?'

'That's business,' AJ said simply, shrugging her shoulders. 'Why lend at two point three per cent when you can try and squeeze five point five out of the poor slobs in front of you?'

'But why run the risk of frightening us off?' Jeff objected. 'Either pushing us into abandoning the investment altogether, or worse, pushing us towards a new lender.'

He paused at this point to grab the barista's attention.

'Want another one?'

'Give us a chance to wet my lips, will you?' AJ grinned. 'I'm not Irish, you know. Anyway, since when are you a double, double espresso fiend?'

'Stop, will ye, I'm not letting this go. No, we really are on to something here, AJ. Wherever we were being pushed, it was away from a mortgage extension.' Jeff knew where he was going with this. 'I already see the make-up of my research group. I'm getting the band back together, you could say. I'm going to let them loose on a deep screen scraper investigation into what is going on with domestic housing and mortgage lending. We'll start in the States. Hopefully without Gabrielle sticking his unwelcome nose into it. What do you think?'

AJ looked into his eyes. 'You and me against the world.'

6

By the autumn of 2007, TimeBox had a staff pool of 196 to choose from. But for this hunch, Jeff wanted the garage originals to use their own sub-teams to drive at an answer. It wasn't a group of twelve; two of the originals had moved on, and Gabrielle wasn't invited. Jeff had known these guys for four years, and he knew what made them tick. Equally, they knew that dealing with him meant you had to be bright, be brief and be gone. Still, Jeff was aware he'd have to call in old favours. He worked the floors of HQ, deliberately bumping into his old team at watercoolers and in coffee break rooms. Stan Labronski, known in the company as 'Red Stan', was the guy who hung with the data analysts.

'Stan, fancy popping over to ours for a bite to eat?' asked Jeff. 'Bring Melissa, of course.'

Stan would be a key member of the project team. So would his partner, Melissa Steward. She liked to fire the odd shot across Jeff's bow.

'Melissa, I'm going to need your help on something.'

Jeff spent a week sowing the seeds, suggesting that he needed an important contribution from the guys he viewed as important.

After two months of background meetings and base touching, Jeff was ready. It had been a while since he'd assembled Zimmerman's original garage dwellers. Still, eight in the room was enough. You weren't mandated to attend; only Zimmerman had that level of control and he never bothered to exercise it. Everyone assembled into their underused fourth-floor boardroom. It had a panoramic view of other drab, dated office buildings.

Red Stan had already used the data analysts to trawl the domestic mortgage financial market on the net. Answers had to be backed up by a separate independent source. Melissa had interrogated the subscriber community. Fifty thousand TimeBox users gave up their secrets easily. You asked them the dreaded survey questions, starting with: 'We so value your input.' TimeBox surveys, multiples of surveys, plenty of shitty rewards – *we all like something for nothing*. No rules broken, no intrusion, plenty of lies, plenty of jerks, plenty of decency, plenty of life, plenty of math for Melissa to get at the message under the lies.

Empowered with the information, Jeff had enough to call the "originals" together. He told them he wanted to get them all on the same page. But really, he needed them to devise an artificial intelligence strategy. He was in a street fighting mood. Even so – and he liked it – there wasn't going to be any reverence shown to him. He ran his strategy sessions with boundaries.

'Now, ladies and gents, nobody gets out of this room. I don't care if it takes till nine tonight or nine in the morning. We're getting an answer before we leave. I'm not interested in any flimflam. Answers, direction, open mic, fire when ready.'

A room of beanbags, whiteboards, coffee, jellybeans. He had learned a few tricks from Zimmerman.

'Well, it's simple, really.' Muhammad Bajaj volunteered the first contribution. 'Our customers must like us, because our data set was statistically twice the size it needs to be to give us an accuracy of between one point five and two point five per cent.'

'Yeah,' Norah Buggy interjected, 'it's amazing what a few crappy prizewinning possibilities will get you.'

'Yes, righteous Norah, righteous,' said Jonathon South.

A bit of a giggle from the gang.

Norah and Jonathon had been another one of the couples occupying a bedroom in the original TimeBox house. Norah was the only one who didn't call Jonathon by his nickname, 'the Hippie'. Jeff wasn't getting it, anyway; he called it 'nerd humour' and let it go over his head. Likewise, they didn't like the fact that he called Muhammad 'the Prophet'.

'It's only because he keeps coming up with maths predictions.'

He wanted to steer them back on course.

Satisfied that he had their attention, Jeff continued. 'We're here to answer the question, what's with the domestic mortgage market? I've been rabbiting on about. What are the messages, and what is the strategy? What do you think, Megan?'

Logical Megan Regan was next up.

'The messages are simple.' She ticked them off on her fingers. 'Message One. Any amount of home starters, first-timers, have been sucked into a quagmire of debt. Jonathon, if this had been the hippy era, then the vibe would have been, "Hey, man, what does it all mean? Buy a house, buy two. No dude ever said anything about paying money back."'

Megan smiled, but nobody was laughing. So she continued, a little red in the face.

'Message Two. If you are in the re-mortgage business, then the answer is, "No, and please feel free to take out a term loan." And before you ask for a reason – it's the *Titanic*. The banks already know they're holed below the waterline. They're sinking. You could nearly set your watch by it.' She confidently tapped her wrist with a finger.

'By what?' asked Jeff.

'One financial crash or other per decade,' Megan replied, 'with every second one being a rocket, and this one is going to be a rocket.'

'One of my old sayings was—'

Jeff wasn't quick enough, and Marti Obamaji completed his sentence for him.

'"What could possibly go wrong?" Yeah, we know.'

'OK, fair, Marti.' Jeff grinned. 'Good work. Right, guys, let's get back on track.'

'Sure thing, Jeff,' said Melissa, 'but it's you that's gone off on a tangent here.'

She and Stan were the other couple formed out of

the original TimeBoxers. She commanded respect because she had a reputation for challenging Jeff.

Back in Ireland, there was a Dublin word for the developing atmosphere. It was called *cheek*. They had done Friday night bar sessions in McNally's, for sure, but they hadn't done a workshop together in an age. These guys didn't do respect. They didn't do disrespect, either. It wasn't in them, and it wasn't privilege, Jeff thought. You just had to pick the right people, and Zimmerman was good at that.

'If the findings were right,' Melissa continued, 'then an opportunity presents itself. This is enormous, and nobody is talking about it. Strange, the entire media intelligentsia acting like a universal ostrich.' Melissa always had a moody look on her as if she could never be happy.

'Is it?' asked Jeff. 'Come on, guys, your coffee cups are full enough. Nobody gets out of here until we're finished. Who here speaks for artificial intelligence?'

'You know I do,' said a slightly twitchy Stan. His dollop of red hair and eastern European pallor set him apart from the other skin colours in the room.

'Over to our chief of AI, so.' Jeff looked in Stan's direction. 'Tell me, Stan, how we turn this mess to our advantage.'

'We'll hashtag it. It's a new technique.' Stan made the sign of the # with his finger, a bit like a priest making the sign of the cross. 'Hashtag words like "finance", "loan", "mortgage", "lend" – you get it?'

'No.' Jeff shook his head. 'But it's probably just me, is it?'

'Tag is the key word,' Stan continued. 'Everyone is on the web. So, we detect their searches, based upon hashtag keywords, and offer our own little snippet of wisdom, like "an important message from TimeBox". You know the kind of thing – you're about to be ripped off. That's for you guys. Tell me the message and I'll code it.'

Melissa had a look on her face that told everyone: this guy is worth paying attention to. However, Janet Hewson from 'New Business' spoke up before anyone else could. As the person who had to work most closely with Gabrielle, she'd recognised her cue.

'If what you're saying about tagging is righteous,' she was looking at Jonathon, 'then I start to see we might have a shot at getting the by-product we're looking for.'

'Attract more subscribers?'

'Well, we all know about Jeff's "magic number",' said Janet

'I'm loving it,' Jeff enthused. 'When the market and the tech come together … beautiful.'

'If it works.' Stan popped that one in, maybe not anticipating the ensuing silence.

'Are you saying that hashtagging might turn out to be as useful as a fart in a spacesuit?' asked Jeff. That raised Melissa's eyebrows.

'Just saying, we want to be technical leaders, don't we?' Stan countered. 'A flop wouldn't look good on TimeBox's résumé.'

'If we ever needed to take the chance, now's the time,' said Jeff. 'I've every confidence, so … to summarise. We look at the searches, we pounce on keywords. We give our message. If our message gets traction, then we know we get to be the good guys.'

'A note of caution, Jeff,' said Melissa. 'You've heard the phrase "Don't shoot the messenger". That doesn't mean the messenger won't be shot.'

'So, your advice …?'

'Maybe a toned-down message, not "the end is nigh" kind of stuff.'

There was a mumble of chitchat in the room. The workshop was energised by the realisation that this could be the moment for TimeBox – if they could act in unison, and quickly. Melissa's moody face was a visual cue that there were risks.

Jeff stood up and addressed his colleagues in a changed, serious tone of voice.

'You know, guys, we're forgetting that there are huge casualties out there already, and we might only be able to help a few sorry Joes from falling off a ledge, maybe literally. So, I'm not watering down the message. "Is Your Lender Trying to Sucker You? A message from TimeBox that you must read." That will be the tone.'

'Better lawyer up so,' said Melissa.

'So be it,' said Jeff. 'We have the tech solution joined up with our marketing strategy, and we're going to use it as a force to knock it out of the park or die trying.'

'So,' said Melissa, 'next step is to head to your buddies Mr Z and Mr G. Good luck with that.'

Funnily enough, that was a phrase that AJ had also started to use.

'Let's do McNally's Friday night, on me,' said Jeff.

You always let the Irish guy organise the drinks get-togethers. It was great to be a stereotype, sometimes. McNally's was a standard American design: long bar, with high stools for solos and couples. The TimeBox gang normally soaked up a couple of the booths which lined the side walls. Pitchers and wings were the norm. The wings were the speciality of the house.

Jeff's Dublin friend and college buddy Aidan Mulcahy was visiting that weekend. Aidan, over a couple of years of gym attendance, had turned himself from a spindly thin guy, like Jeff, into a physically big man. These days he gave out an aura: 'not to be messed with'. The spots were gone, and a sharp cut of his black mane had left him looking as if he wouldn't be out of place on an American football field.

Marti Obamaji was a bit drunk and a bit messy. He'd struck up a conversation – if you could call it that – with a duo of American girls who were sitting at the bar. When their boyfriends came in later, Marti was told, 'Buddy, you're bothering the girls. Why not disappear now, while you're still being asked?'

'If I wanted to be called your buddy, I'd ask for it,' said Marti, slurrily.

The discussion now had the attention of that full end of the bar.

'You're asking for it all right,' said one of the newcomers.

He was just about to lay hands on Marti when Aidan appeared.

'Is there a problem here, men?' he asked.

'No, no problem.'

The boyfriend withdrew his hand to a non-confrontational position. Aidan used his bulk to remove Marti from the scene and point him in the direction of the safety of the TimeBox table.

'Could I get a pitcher for these lads and their lovely partners?' Aidan asked the bartender.

'Marti, now sit the fuck down and stop causing trouble for a change,' hissed a slightly irate Melissa.

Megan and Jonathon similarly pitched in to get on his case. No one wanted to be barred from McNally's.

'Stop acting like a fuck,' said Jonathon.

'No, we can't use the F-word on these Friday night outings,' Jeff said. 'Keep that passion for the office. Try our word, "feck" – that's a good alternative. That right, Aidan?'

'Fucking dead right,' replied Aidan. 'Fucking dead right.'

When his friend sat down again, Jeff asked him how the housing market was in Ireland.

'I ask the mother and the uncle all the time,' he added, 'but I don't get much back.'

'Look, it's like the Wild West,' Aidan told him. 'One hundred and ten percent, twenty per cent, mortgages on offer. Ridiculously low interest rates on overpriced stock. What's your phrase again? "What could possibly go wrong?"'

'Look, that's interesting. We've been diving into this stuff and pretty much seeing that a lot will go wrong – and soon. I'll keep you posted. How's the lovely Libby? I haven't succeeded in getting her using TimeBox – yet, anyway.'

'I miss her,' Aidan said. Jeff saw his face drop. 'She's hiding in Brussels.'

'Anything stirring romantically?'

'Yeah, she has a girlfriend.'

7

When the crash came in September 2008, it was biblical in scale: Lehman Brothers gone; Freddie Mac and Fannie Mae heading to the wall; a $300 billion bailout approved by Congress just to keep the stinking edifices alive. Too many greedy people were drinking from the same trough. People were dying by their own hands, wiped out financially.

TimeBox was growing its balance sheet while financial institutions were burning their own. Jeff's hunch had paid off, and the product of human connectivity – social media – had proven even more important for keeping in touch with an out of control financial roller coaster.

Jeff was never picked by Zimmerman to be a typical IT hack. The Zimmer wanted him managing people and ideas. A crisis in the economy got TimeBox growing and social media recognised. But it was still a fledgling experiment. It was time to recruit – and in big numbers.

'Crush the competitors as they emerge,' said Zimmerman. 'Make it happen, Jeff.'

*

There were interns everywhere, populating the new building. Some were a bit overawed by the experience: 'Me – part of a flagship business.' Other kids treated it without any reverence.

Jeff had an intern PA called Kerri. She was eighteen. He liked her name and warmed to her work ethic.

'Bourke,' Gabrielle said without preamble. 'Not sure I like attractive young girls having access to senior executives.' He had just walked into Jeff's open-door office. 'Know where I'm coming from? Distraction, scandal, Clinton ... Not nouns I want to see in any sentence accompanied with the name TimeBox.'

'I think you might be jumping the gun a bit, Martin,' Jeff answered.

'Damn sure he is,' Kerri snapped, 'and for your information, my boyfriend plays college football.'

'Girl, please only speak when spoken to. I was addressing myself to Mr Bourke.'

Jeff decided to try and defuse the situation.

'Kerri, allow me to introduce Martin Gabrielle, our head of Production to Market.'

'Thank Christ,' Kerri muttered. 'Imagine if he was head of HR.'

'Close the door on your way out, girl.' Gabrielle's tone hadn't softened one bit. 'I wish to have a word with your master.'

Kerri threw him a look and proceeded deliberately but slowly out of the door.

'Close the door!' Gabrielle shouted.

She ignored him. He closed it himself and turned

towards Jeff, but remained standing.

'Exactly the problem, Bourke – rapid expansion of staff, not enough vetting. You keep going at this rate and we'll need yet another new premises.'

'I'm glad you mentioned that, Martin.' Jeff forced a smile. 'I'm bringing to the next board meeting the concept of a European office in Dublin. That's Dublin, Ireland,' he added.

'I know where it is, thank you. What's this? Looking after the old sod, are we?'

'The opposite, in fact.' Jeff's smile didn't waver. 'The "Paddies" maintain the lowest corporate tax rate in Europe. Do you really want to pay Obama forty per cent of our profits?'

'Oh, for the days when such talk could be wrapped up as a treason against the state.'

'God, that must have been a long time ago. Anyway, I've two good contacts from old on the case.'

'I think that might be putting your finger on the problem – nepotism. That's not what we want the glowing face of TimeBox to look like.'

'Get over yourself, Martin, will you?' Jeff stood up to face Gabrielle from across his desk. 'It's common knowledge you and Zimmerman have been all over Capitol Hill, pressing the flesh. So don't chastise me for taking a legit political sounding in Dublin.' Jeff delivered his "don't chastise me" line while digging his finger into Gabrielle's shoulder three times. 'There's a new headman in town there – Kenny. Might just be the right time to strike, be part of the recovery. Now that's the kind of soundbite you want, isn't it?

Gabrielle just turned and walked out, brushing his shoulder with the back of his hand.

When the board met in June 2009, to discuss a European HQ, Jeff had enough influence to swing it for Dublin. That got him a bit of political notice from Ireland. It was good optics to see a new, young, vibrant outfit hit a Dublin that was, just like the rest of the European capitals, still reeling from the banking crash.

If Jeff couldn't get back to Ireland much, he was relentless in trying to get two old and close college buddies on board: Aidan and Libby. The TimeBox original team had already met Aidan. Jeff knew they were in for a surprise when they got to meet Libby.

During the college years in Dublin, Jeff had formed a friendship – a bond – with his two classmates 'L and A' – Libby and Aidan. Libby was a slightly built young woman, brown hair, blue eyes, as tough as nails. Back then, Aidan was a tall, gangly, spotty youth. A desperately hard worker.

Jeff had been a driver of recruitment diversification – not with an agenda, but simply recognising that a whole load of computer wizards would only get you so far. Doing business in eighty-odd countries needed linguists, psychologists, and specialists in other fields, just to get the right perspective.

He had looked to recruit Aidan after the 2008

crash. When he got him, Aidan had sown the seeds with Jeff: 'Why not go after Libby and complete our old gang?'

Of course, Jeff was in touch with her, often to the annoyance of AJ. That's what TimeBox was about: contact. Libby maybe wasn't an exact fit for the company, because she was more an advocate for privacy than social media sharing – a girl who preferred output to input. After a few rejections, Libby gave up and responded, 'Why not?' Even so, it took about six months to wind up her gig in Brussels before heading back to the new TimeBox Dublin. Jeff knew it would be worth the wait.

Back in the day, the Dublin trio had planned a night out about a week before finals. Nothing heavy – just soothing that bit of exam tension with alcohol. The guys had come back into town after college ended, a few loosening-up drinks being on the agenda as a launch pad before heading into a heavy week of pre-exam study.

Dublin city centre always had a sense to it, at night, that trouble would never be far away. Too few policemen, and too many looking in the wrong direction. Maybe, it had something to do with not carrying guns.

This was a mini pub crawl, but not to get blasted – just to grab a drink in three or four of their student haunts.

They had just emerged from Mooney's, on the

Liffey, right into a couple of lads feeling the need to form an obstruction. These guys had the aura of trouble about them, and Jeff's senses told him '*fuck*'. The knees were a bit unsteady suddenly: fight or flight, and the fear pulsing from knowing he was out of his depth. Two bulky members of the scum of the city were saying something, but the something was of no consequence. It was shit talk. Filling in time until the strike came. Jeff was trying hard not to believe that a concealed bottle might be flashing through the air at any point. You always know what is coming. You just humour these punks because you're trying to believe your body is lying to you. You're not in danger. But, deep down, you know you are.

A smaller Aidan, in those days, did the decent thing by pushing the slight frame of Libby sideways through the small gap that separated the bulk of the two blobs. No great objection. These real men wanted to deal man on man.

Jeff took a slap straight into the mouth. It wasn't designed to rattle teeth, just to warm things up for a bit of fun and carnage. The language of scum.

Big mistake. Libby had removed her right shoe from her black-stockinged foot. This wasn't a stiletto type of night, but there was a fairly sharp heel all the same. She buried it with a blow that got its momentum from the size of the arc she spun her arm through. A beautifully horrific spurt of blood hit the side wall of the entrance portal of the pub. Libby, still facing the backs of the two assailants, switched the right-hand shoe to her left hand and recreated the arc of the swing. This time, the little bit of movement, and with slightly less co-ordination from her left side, meant that the heel contacted more with the eye socket than the temple of her intended target.

Very effective, though. Second man down.

'Jesus, Libby, have you killed this one?'

Aidan was looking at victim number one, still bleeding from his new position on the ground. Victim number two was crouched with his hands holding his wounded eye. A further kerfuffle came about as an innocent patron tried to leave the premises and found that the door wouldn't open with Jeff's back in the way.

'Time to exit, boys,' said Libby.

Jeff and Aidan stepped over and to the side of the stricken pair. Libby grabbed Aidan's shoulder for balance as she replaced her shoe. A final murmur from the floor prompted a straightforward reply from Libby.

'Scumbags! Now, what about Mulligan's for a decent pint?'

'Fuck, Libby!' Aidan cried. 'Is that first fucker dead? Like, the one who wasn't moving?'

'Well,' she said calmly, 'if he is, then whoever was trying to get out of Mooney's can deal with it. I'm thirsty.'

'Jesus,' said Aidan. 'If anyone seen us, we're fucked.'

'I'd want to do something with this mouth full of blood,' mumbled Jeff.

'Easily solved,' she said. 'Spit it out and wash it

down with a large gulp of cold Guinness. Come on, boys, I'm brave, not stupid. Let's get a move on.'

They shuffled along quickly towards their new destination. A bit of pace, furtive looks behind. Jeff's mouth had become too full with the effort of containing his bloody spittle. He picked as private a spot on the street as he could, and just spat it out, hoping that he wouldn't have to go searching for a tooth on the ground. The thought of an ice-cold drink adding an antiseptic aid was increasing in appeal.

There was no further chat till they had their drinks served. They were probably lucky to get them – the two boys looked dishevelled. The barman in Mulligan's had looked them up and down. Libby was glowing. Confidence from the beauty of action.

'Boys,' she said, 'if you're ever feeling a bit unsure before you go into a place, walk in with an air about you that says "I own the place".'

'Libby, what the fuck?' said Aidan. 'If we're arrested for assault, the exams are screwed up.'

'Aidan, I'm telling you ... First – you see any policemen around here?'

'Libby, you left those guys in bits ... in shite, like.'

'Lads, you're my friends, and you're a bit rattled and so am I.' She took a large swig of her drink. 'But I grew up in Finglas with the best and the worst. I'm telling you, take a lesson out of tonight. We don't go looking for trouble, but when it presents itself, act first and we'll do the autopsy later, preferably over a pint. I'm telling you, never give a scumbag an even break.'

No better woman to have the last word.

Looking back, Jeff knew Libby Hendrick was the right choice for TimeBox Ireland.

8

The first sign for Jeff that his roller coaster was derailing began to appear just before Christmas in 2010. There had been a lot of pain following the financial crash two years earlier. It couldn't be denied. There was a rise in suicide statistics – some very ordinary Joes.

What was a source of troubled conversation between Jeff and AJ was the number of kids – young adults – buried in the suicide numbers.

The couple had inherited a fifteen-foot-tall fir in the front garden of their new Willow Glen home. They had just come in from the garden after decorating it with Christmas lights.

'What's with your mood, honey?' AJ asked. 'You seem down.'

'Where did that all come from – these young suicides?'

'I guess these kids aren't totally insulated from the pain of losing everything,' AJ offered. 'You see maybe your dad is destroyed after a lifetime of work. Maybe then you go off the deep end yourself. The bankers were able to walk away, scot-free. That alone might drive you crazy.'

'Sure, but getting back to those kids ... Is that what you'd consider doing if it were you in their shoes?'

'Well, no, but that's maybe because I have resilience built in and I'm not a kid. You know – military dad and all that.'

'So, you're jumping to conclusions that this bunch of kids are killing themselves because they're not as resilient as you?'

'Honey, I'm going to let that one go because I know you're genuinely upset.' AJ took his hand in hers. 'It's nice you care for folks you don't even know. But come on – getting mad at me ...?'

'Sorry, my love, you're right, I'm being a dick. Sorry.'

'So, what's really bugging you?'

'What if we're part of it, or I'm part of it?'

'Jeff, you've barely had time to deal with the kudos you—' She put a finger to his lips. A gesture to say *shush, I've something to say. No need to interrupt*. 'Yes, *you* earned for the company, not to mention the growth. Even Bloomberg used their favourite words in the same sentence as your name – "exponential growth". So, explain, please – where's your head at?'

'Well, have you been following *USA Today*?' Jeff waved vaguely to his laptop screen. 'I'm nearly getting sick of it. The latest ...' He paused; his lip was quivering. 'This beautiful girl in Seattle, Ruth Huberman, is dead. They showed a picture of her. Another one. Another overdose. Her mother went through her daughter's TimeBox pages and puts the blame squarely on us. And I think that means me.'

'What does Zimmerman say about this? Have you asked him?'

'"Take it up with Gabrielle."' AJ found herself counting the lines on a brow she had never noticed as furrowed before. 'That's the stock answer to anything that could uncomfortably take away from his bottom line. Gabrielle has long since turned himself into quite the henchman.'

'By "bottom line", you mean the bottom line as in money?' she asked.

'I don't know.' Jeff shrugged. 'There's so much of that. He's thinking about reputation, legacy and that shit.'

'Very regal of him.' AJ was doing that raised eyebrow thing of hers.

'Look, David and I used to have dinner all the time, you know that, like to discuss how things are going – strategy and stuff. It's all dried up now. You make your appointment through his man, Gabrielle.'

'The engine – the social media engine …' AJ shrugged. 'When you think about it, it has no regulation at all.'

'Well, we saw what a lack of banking regulation looks like, and where that got us.'

'But where would you be going with that idea? Who would regulate social media? The power class are all fifty-plus-year-old men. Sure, they don't get it, so where would you start to control it? You're right, though.' AJ grinned. 'Social media – SM to some of these guys, without the "and", would conjure up images of whips and gags.'

She could see that her man was upset. Maybe unjustifiably so, by assuming too much responsibility. It was a bright Saturday afternoon; he took her hand and kissed it.

Later, they chatted from the comfort of their own warm bed. She was still trying to make sense of Jeff's worries, but at least all the tetchiness was gone. The power of sexual contact.

'I suppose when you're an adult you forget the vulnerability of being young. I remember being seventeen, that was a tough year,' AJ was thinking out loud. 'You forget the way you thought … It's a funny thing. Adults with a certain kind of disposition – it might be too strong to call it evil – can exploit that.'

'I don't think it was adults in Ruth Huberman's case.' Jeff rustled a little bit uncomfortably under the bedclothes. 'More like young teenage girls. We give people such an intimate platform. Straight into your bedroom. Might just be an uncaring attitude, a word that was chosen well enough to hit home, to kill a growing spirit. I've added to my old mantra – house sales and car crashes bring out the worst in people. And now social media as well.'

'It depends … and you could look at it through the lenses of different human beings.' AJ placed her hand on his chest as she rested on her side beside him. 'You and Gabrielle – what a clash. You'd nearly treat your interns like equals. Gabrielle would treat them as inconsequential. Kindness just wouldn't be on his agenda.'

'What are you getting at, love?'

'That there's still something different about being inconsequential and being wounded. Maybe the definition of evil is that you devote your nurtured talents to hurting people. And the worst hurt is the one that stings to the very core of the youngest and most vulnerable, knowing it's sowing the seeds of self-destruction in a kid. Look, if you're thinking about bringing … I don't know … regulation to the table, Gabrielle is going to be let loose to scupper the party. There will be blood.'

Jeff thought for a few moments about what AJ had said. She was right: Gabrielle was just a henchman, really. Zimmerman was a different animal. Instead of one-on-one interactions, his genius was to create a platform where one on one became one on many – and better still, many on many. There had never been a platform for real-time social experimentation on such a large scale.

'AJ,' Jeff said quietly, 'have I been part of creating a monster?'

Jeff had made his journey to knowing the whole TimeBox engine was a masterclass in exposing teenage vulnerability. You could suck a youngster into a vortex of mental turmoil. You couldn't release yourself from the very media source that was destroying you. You might miss something that would kill you.

9

The second Saturday morning of January 2011 was a bleak experience – not when Jeff left San Francisco International Airport at 7.30 a.m., but certainly when he arrived alone in a miserably sleety Seattle two and half hours later. Was there anything bleaker than the first weeks after Christmas in dismal weather? Jeff had a pain in his stomach. He was going to make a cold call to the Huberman household – a grieving household. Jeff had seven years' worth of cold calling for business behind him. But this wasn't about getting traction and sales. What was it about? Forgiveness, maybe – or maybe just decency. In memory of his own deceased father. This wasn't going to be easy.

No need for a private investigator to track down the Hubermans' house. This was the age when people freely shared everything about themselves on their TimeBox profile. Ruth's account was still live – another bit of process gone haywire. Maybe the only time he'd ever knocked on a door and hoped nobody would answer was on that Saturday morning. But there was someone in: a barrel-chested man with a slightly greying crew cut opened the door.

'Good morning, sir.' Jeff's feeling of unease was bordering on fear. He'd never been in a situation like this. He was an alien. 'My name is Jeff Bourke, I'm an executive with the social media company TimeBox. I apologise for the unannounced call, but maybe putting stock in my partner's advice ...' Jeff knew he was bumbling and stumbling. 'I didn't know if you'd admit me.'

'Son, it's not about admitting you,' Daniel Huberman replied. 'We – my wife and I ... We were told to expect you. That has been, maybe, the only thing that has been getting Carmel through this time of ours.'

A dressing-gowned Carmel Huberman joined them at the front door.

'Is that him, husband? Has the Christian come?' Carmel already knew the answer and began to cry.

'Can I come in?'

Jeff's stomach tension wasn't easing, but was being joined by a trembling sensation; he wouldn't like to be asked to show how steady his hand was. As AJ was prone to telling him, 'Honey, you don't have to tell me your emotional state – your body shows me.'

Jeff was right to be feeling tense. Daniel grabbed him with one massive hand around the front collar of his shirt and bundled him over the threshold. Jeff had the sensation that his sixty kilograms had been lifted clearly off the ground, but it was more that the toes of his shoes were being dragged along the floor. The man's clenched fist was digging hard against his Adam's apple.

'Son, if you think you're getting a free ride because some pastor told us you were coming, think again.'

Jeff couldn't answer even if he wanted to. Daniel deposited him on the sofa closest to the front door. Carmel gently closed it.

'Daniel, at least he has a pair,' she said.

'Darling, don't be dishing out any compliments before we even know why Mr Bourke is here.'

"Darling" seemed to Jeff like a strange word to use just at a moment of violence.

'Why are you here, Mr Bourke?' asked Carmel.

Jeff was trying not to shake visibly from his sitting position, while a giant of a man and a diminutive lady stood over him. Then they decided to sit down together on the sofa opposite.

'Can you talk, Mr Bourke?' asked Carmel, without any tone of concern. She had stopped crying.

Jeff's brain had restarted – a bit, at least – dazzled, maybe, by a shot of survival adrenaline. His hazy guess was that Daniel Huberman was a military man, or maybe retired. Just like AJ's dad, he certainly had a gruff side.

'Yes, I think I can talk.' Jeff proved the point to himself.

'So enough already ...' Carmel said. 'Why are you here?'

'To find out a little more about your daughter, Ruth,' said Jeff.

'I'm at least glad you didn't say "to offer my condolences".' Daniel Huberman was sitting, was speaking calmly, but noticeably he had his right fist clenched. 'And I'll tell you, son, that's because for you and your kind, I'd happily live out my grief by inflicting bodily harm. There's no line you would not cross when you've lost your only child.'

'I'm with you on that, darling,' Carmel said soothingly, 'but let Mr Bourke carry on. You've got your wind back? What is it you wanted to ask?'

Jeff shuffled a little in his seat to get further comfort. He used his right hand to massage his throat, checking to see if he could swallow spit without pain.

'When you spoke to *USA Today*, can you tell me how that went?' Jeff realised that the couple would never know how much effort that sentence had taken.

'The newspaper people helped us to decipher this alien thing …' Daniel groped for the words. 'Ruth's TimeBox account.'

'It must be the work of the Devil.' Carmel's words were combined with new tears. 'That is what we believed when the journalists agreed to read Ruth's account, or profile, whatever it's called.'

'A litany of abuse and insults from a bunch of anonymous swine,' said Daniel.

'In the end, Ruth said goodbye to your and our world on TimeBox.' Jeff was looking at Carmel. He had never seen someone shedding so many heartfelt tears without it affecting her voice, her words. 'We loved her, but she was lost in your evil, Mr Bourke. We asked the paper to write it up and fully expose TimeBox as an agent provocateur for young adult suicide.'

'Bring the whole shithouse down!' said Daniel, with a fist thump of the table that made the coasters jump in the air.

Jeff was learning about grief. *Was I like this when Dad died, angry?*

'They said maybe it would have been possible a couple of years back,' Carmel said softly. 'But now you people have too much money, too many lawyers.'

'A world without justice,' Daniel said, calm again – for the moment, anyway. 'You Christians, who love Jesus. That man wanted to build a world based on justice. Now we can see – there's no justice. Your thing will go on and on killing people with, it seems, impunity. It's really, and bizarrely, a validation of our Torah and our Jewish faith. There will only be justice when the Messiah comes upon Jerusalem.'

Jeff wondered, *Am I expected to contribute to … what? A debate on Jesus.*

'Can I ask you a question?'

There was no reply, so he went for it.

'You said you were expecting me, or someone … and a pastor you mentioned?' Jeff knew he was a bit muddled.

'That was our rabbi, Max,' Daniel said, 'giving us a message from his Christian friend, or contact, or whatever. The new breed talk to Gentiles. Maybe it's no harm.'

'But in our bottomless grief, of course we turned to our rabbi. He has been so good and a very great comfort, Daniel, has he not?'

A recovering Jeff couldn't help himself. He wanted to get back to the message.

'I'm really sorry, I'm getting lost,' he said. 'Where did I come in?'

'Because Rabbi Max asked if he could bring a message to us from a friend,' said Carmel. 'The friend, when he came to our home, was a … I think it's called a "charismatic", a type of Christian pastor. Just like our faith, there are many sects in your Christianity.'

Daniel was equally keen to take up the story. Jeff needed to get at the story and was being enthusiastically met by the Hubermans. They wanted to tell him about Ruth – maybe because it kept her alive in their hearts.

'Our prophets are from the Hebrew bible,' Carmel explained. 'Some of your tribes, Rabbi Max tells us, speak in tongues and make prophecies. But where there are prophets, there are also false prophets. So, yes, we were told you would come.'

'But, ma'am, sir,' Jeff protested, 'I came to you with compassion for your loss. I wanted to know what role TimeBox played in that loss. I don't know anything about prophets, or religions, really. If TimeBox contributed to Ruth's suicide, then I wouldn't be human if I didn't try to make … well, first an apology and then a difference. That is why I have come.'

'But you can't bring her back for us, Mr Bourke,' said Carmel.

'No, I can't.' He couldn't maintain the intensity of her eye contact and looked at the ground for a moment. 'But I've made policy changes in the company before, and I wouldn't hesitate to do it again. We all have lords and masters, but I'll willingly take mine on if there's a right thing to do.'

'Yes, we know about your Jewish and Arab masters.' Daniel gave Jeff another one of his stern 'I might be about to blow' looks.

'Sorry, I don't follow you?'

'Your Zimmerman and Gabrielle,' said Daniel. 'A Jew and an Arab.'

'I know David Zimmerman is a Jew, but he doesn't practise. Martin Gabrielle is a Montana man.'

'Look, you at least took some trouble to come here.' Carmel poured some oil on the waters. 'We were told you would come.'

'We may have frightened you with talk of our faith,' Daniel added.

'The pastor was not a frightening man,' his wife continued. 'He was decent and confident. That's what I liked about him – he believed in what he was saying.'

'OK … but what was it he said?' Jeff was still unconsciously feeling his neck.

'That he had, I suppose, a vision, or whatever which way he saw things.'

'A man will come,' Daniel added solemnly. 'He has

been chosen to bring you, and some others, salvation. He is from within the virus but will be recognised as a vessel.'

'Is that it?'

Given their obvious grief, Jeff was immediately embarrassed by his bewilderment.

'Son, when my wife went upstairs that day, after we got home, she saw our girl and I'll tell you, the crazed shrill cry she let out told me in advance what to expect. Ruth got a terrible death. She had foamed at the mouth as her body tried to reject the concoction of drugs she had swallowed. A permanent solution to the hurt dished out to her on your social media.'

'But Mr Bourke, it's not just the words or the message we got.' Carmel now looked to get away from that terrible image remembered by her husband. 'This man came looking for us – and, it seems, for you. I talk of his confidence. He wanted nothing.'

'What was his name?' Jeff asked urgently. 'Did he know my name?'

'You should know that even our prophets spoke in riddles.' Daniel sighed with annoyance. 'It's not a trick – it is that God does not reveal every detail when he talks, I guess. Those made in his image must figure it out.'

'Sorry, I'm a bit deflated,' said Jeff.

Daniel sat forward in his seat, giving Jeff the distinct impression that he had said the wrong thing – again.

'Listen, son. That man – not even one of our own

– gave us hope when we were empty. Mock him at your peril.'

'You've been chosen, it seems to me, Mr Bourke.' Carmel sighed, but at least she'd stopped crying 'My heart sinks when I hear you are deflated. Does this mean there'll be no justice for my Ruth?'

'Sorry, sorry, I didn't mean that, Mrs Huberman. I just meant that I don't know what to do with the message.'

Daniel relaxed back into the sofa.

'I do not think, in either of our religions, the prophecies came with a manual.' Jeff was surprised to see a smile – a faint smile. 'All we ask is that you take a course of action that would give you – us – the hope of justice and maybe the salvation of others.'

'Before you leave us for your busy, busy world,' Carmel added, 'something else the pastor told us. What was it, David? Wasn't Egypt mentioned?'

'No, wife, what he said was along the lines that "salvation must be fought for in the cradle of the Christ". It was me and you talking that mentioned Egypt. Remember, the family of Jesus fled from Judaea.'

'Yes, you're right, that was it,' Carmel agreed. 'Egypt and Arabs.'

*

'Well, tell me what you think of that tale.'

Jeff was asking AJ from his Seattle hotel room, later that afternoon.

'Like I said, I was so wound up waiting for your call. I'm

not sure I've taken it all in. Look, these people up north keep guns, you know.'

'AJ, Mr Huberman had a build on him like your old man. He wouldn't have needed a gun to hurt me. You'll see the marks on my throat when I'm home.'

'*Look, the main thing is that you're safe and well and coming home.*'

'Yes, but what do I do with this crazy story?' asked Jeff.

'*Digest it, and if it creates a fog, you'll just have to wait for the fog to clear.*'

'AJ, I devised a policy and strategy that kept TimeBox from investing in Africa and the Middle East. Remember, we like Europe and Australasia, where the big bucks are. I did that based upon data analytics, not prophecies.'

'*Look, Jeff, you wanted their story and you got more than you bargained for. What about this poor girl, Ruth? What's to be her justice? And the other Ruths?*'

'Jesus, at least I understand that bit. We have to put a cloak of moderation on TimeBox accounts.'

'*Self-regulation? Wasn't that where we came in, Jeff?*'

'Yep, but at least I got to start with that answer. I'll organise a face-to-face with the gang of two.'

'*Good luck with that, honey,*' said AJ.

'Is my new mission to be putting manners on TimeBox?'

'*Be careful you're not seen as someone with a score to settle against the big boss. Americans don't like that.*'

'Funny, it's a spectator sport in Ireland.'

'*I thought you had a good Catholic upbringing, yeah?*' AJ managed a playful laugh, just to break the mood. Her man must have been in some sort of danger, and maybe he was playing it down. '*You should be well versed in all that Bible talk anyway.*'

'In one ear and out the other, I have to say.'

'*How violent was he, Jeff?*'

'I've never experienced anything much like it. That was a good roughing up, military style. He knew how not to crush my larynx while holding my collar so tight that I couldn't get a breath.'

'*Did you think about calling the cops?*'

'No. I just thought your dad would have done the same thing to me in the same situation.'

Jeff was home early on Sunday morning. He kissed AJ, who then backed off to take a closer look.

'Now there's a phrase I've heard your buddy Libby use – "the neck on ye."' She grinned. 'You weren't lying, that looks sore. You'll have to up your dress sense with an ascot.'

'No thanks!'

'I told you, honey, grief is a powerful emotion – maybe the most powerful of them all, because anger is part of it. So, I guess losing your only child is going to lead to powerful anger. Now that I think of it, I maybe shouldn't have let you go.' She had her hands on his shoulders.

'I've a few bruises. I'll live, but Ruth Huberman

will stay dead. Look, AJ, the story they had for me blew my mind. They are Jews, but a Christian pastor is part of the story. Their rabbi introduced him because he had … Well, I'm struggling to describe it. He, this pastor guy, had a vision that Ruth's death would not go unpunished, or something.' Jeff grimaced.

'You know, honey, I'm not going to recoil at that. Everything … Everything we see and do is governed by the world we see around us. What about the world we don't see?'

'Yeah, but this is out there – I mean, way out there.'

'We'll see,' answered AJ.

'The Hubermans were told I'd be calling,' he said.

'What? You – by name?'

'No, not by name – anyway, anyone could have googled me. They were told to expect justice, with me providing it. I am a vessel.'

'Hold on …' AJ paused to think for a moment 'What does "a vessel" mean?'

'You know – a container, a carrier of something,' answered Jeff.

'Ye, but what is the "something"?'

'I don't know, but there was something else that was really weird.' Jeff shook his head. 'Hold on, I have to get my thoughts straight and this goddamn throat still hurts. This will all end in "the cradle of Christ", I think they called it.'

'Honey, you did at least warn me it was out there.'

'At least you haven't told me to shut up.' Jeff managed a weak smile, but it didn't disguise a face that was troubled.

'Come on, you were brave enough to go.' AJ cupped her hands gently around his swollen neck. 'I'm proud of you. Sleep on it tonight and we can talk more. For now, we'll enjoy a glass of wine tonight. See if you can recall any more of the details and write them down. It might be important. It might come to you in your dreams.'

10

Jeff Bourke was a TimeBox man. More by luck than by design, he'd got in at the start – one of the twelve – and headed upwards. By the time February 2011 rolled around he had driven his way through the company, and maybe driven the company as well. Jeff liked to rib the media types; 'No, his left-hand man' was his answer to claims that he was David Zimmerman's right-hand man. Editorially, Fox didn't like Jeff's Irish wit. It was off-putting. They couldn't gauge what he might say next.

TimeBox had invented social media and had made David Zimmerman wealthy beyond wealth. He didn't pay his people megabucks and, paradoxically, that kind of earned him more kudos. The detractors, of course, were on hand to declare him 'a miserable Polack'. Strange, because he had no Polish roots.

Jeff had a work ethic that was driven along by something that wasn't about money – maybe something in his upbringing, something from his mother, Anne. But in the years since 2008, after five years trying to get the rocket into orbit, there was a lot of lucre swishing around – a strange benefit of the banking collapse. He'd long since given up worrying about mortgages and loans. He did more than all right, and poachers from the new competitors that had grown up didn't waste their time chasing him. Jeff's niggling doubt was something he wouldn't share, even with AJ: he wondered if he was just happy to be a number two in the organisation. Now, another more pronounced niggle had arisen.

Zimmerman had a new type of business model. If you had a pulse and a credit card, you qualified as a customer. Better still if you, as a customer, thought you were getting something for nothing. It didn't cost anything to open a TimeBox account. He didn't feel the need to like little people, and the product's place in the market meant he didn't have to. Jeff rocked up whenever it was necessary to tone down the boss's rhetoric. He was good at it, and comfortable with the media.

From the original TimeBox twelve, only Norah and Melissa, together with Jeff and Gabrielle, had made it to the board. Zimmerman kept the numbers tight and Jeff had needed the women's support to land Dublin as their European HQ. Making the assumption that he could rely on their continued support was exactly that: an assumption.

At the February 2011 board meeting, Jeff had finished reporting the financial results from TimeBox's European operation. An effective tax rate of 2.25 per cent was good for the P&L account.

'Libby and Aidan have done a good job in TimeBox

Dublin,' he concluded. 'Faith justified.'

'Good, Jeff,' said Zimmerman, 'but why do you insist on heaping praise on others for your good efforts?'

'You've spent a lot of time over there in the last eighteen months, yes?' asked Gabrielle. 'If it was down to others, then what was it? Were you on holidays with your mother?'

Norah and Melissa shifted uncomfortably in their chairs in unison

'I'd rather move on to "Any other business",' said Jeff.

'Yep, carry on,' said Zimmerman. 'You have the floor.'

'Well, it's like this, David. I've had my data analytics guys look into a hunch I had—'

Jeff was halted by Zimmerman putting up the open palm of his hand.

'Stop there, Jeffrey, my man. *Your* data analytics guys? Surely, they're *ours*. I doubt if our Melissa likes to hear her Stan is yours.' Zimmerman smiled at his own cleverness and looked around the table. Melissa kept her head down. 'But if you're on to a new initiative, yes, we will listen.'

Not for the first time, Jeff was seeing the visible enforcement of some societal rules. Two people at the top constituted a relationship, three transformed it into politics.

'But we have a new direction to propose, also,' Zimmerman continued. 'You don't have a complete monopoly on this company's resources. Methinks that we can't fight on too many fronts. Remember Hitler – too big for his boots and would not be told. That's the way you describe it, Martin, yes?'

'I'm lost,' Jeff admitted. 'How come I'm not aware of your initiative, whatever it is?'

'I could just as easily ask how come we're only hearing now of your new proposal, whatever it is,' said Gabrielle.

'Because I'm the ideas man,' Jeff replied. 'You vet the ideas. Has there been a change?'

'Touché, well said, sir.' Zimmerman applauded briefly, but nobody followed his lead. 'Now, before you boys go knocking seven bells out of each other again, remember – these are the best of times. Martin, how many subscribers?'

'We passed one billion on New Year's Day.' Gabrielle allowed himself the smuggest of smiles. 'Fools were enjoying the fix of cementing their pathetic new year resolutions by publishing them. False backbone, I'd call it.'

'That's what I like!' Zimmerman gave him a warm smile. 'Finger on the pulse, and nice incoming revenue streams. Take a minute, take a minute – we're together so infrequently these days. We've come a long, long way in a mere seven years. Got stronger because of the banks, methinks. A long way from that night in Berkeley, Jeff, remember? Now, ladies and gentlemen, let's get back to business. Jeff, you fire first.'

'We've put together a data set that makes a prima

facie case for TimeBox being implicated in the suicides of multiple young people. We're always on, always invasive. Remember, we're a social experiment.'

'Talk about raining on a parade.' Gabrielle's sarcasm was in his tone. 'More like pissing on it. How can we sell that pearl of wisdom, even if it's true?'

'We can't,' said Jeff, 'but we can take positive action. Something that can make us winners long before the point in time when the LA or New York *Times* gets hold of this – and they will.'

'Is that a threat?' asked Norah.

Jeff was feeling very friendless suddenly.

'Of course not,' he answered. 'For God's sake, outside IT wizards can churn up the numbers as well as we can, predict what volume of deaths will occur. A story is likely to break, and sooner than you might think. But this can be win-win stuff – of course it can. People's lives matter. If we've done wrong, let's put it right.'

'Yes, Martin, Norah, please,' said Zimmerman, 'we haven't even heard the idea yet. Jeff, I must say, for a man who didn't like Fermat's theorem, you sure have taken to mathematics. Go on, bamboozle us more, please.'

'Regulation and site moderation.'

Both David Zimmerman and Martin Gabrielle were staring directly at Jeff as if he had invented a new expletive. Melissa had been uncharacteristically quiet.

'This is a joke, right?' she asked. 'Where's the money in that?'

'Has he lost it?' Gabrielle was looking directly at Zimmerman and continued. 'Two words, one location – North Africa.'

If Jeff was feeling anything, it was relief that the four versus one attack was paused.

'Egypt,' said Zimmerman. 'A Cairo office is already being staffed up. We don't rest on our laurels, you know, in this company of ours.' He couldn't resist another smirk. It was time to put this Irish boy back in his box.

Jeff's head was spinning: Egypt; the Hubermans; predictions; prophets; stabs in the back.

Zimmerman and Gabrielle could see their news had a better-than-expected shock value.

'Gabrielle will be spending a lot of time with the new office,' said Zimmerman. 'So, I'll need you here, Jeff, minding the shop. Look, just say we're putting your new stuff on hold for a while. This is exciting. We've become aware that there's a wave of anti-regime sentiment cutting across North Africa. It might even extend to the Middle Eastern states. Gabrielle has picked up on some chatter calling it the "Arab Spring". It's time to support a social conscience – you're right, Jeff.'

'Since when does the leading social media platform get involved in politics?' asked Jeff.

'When it's a perfect opportunity for business growth, is all,' answered Gabrielle.

'You see, Jeff, we've become a plaything for privileged First Worlders,' said Zimmerman. 'We've got to bring our product to the underprivileged masses, the downtrodden.'

'Men, men, please – where's the market research? Is there any analysis done on unintended consequences?'

'Jeff, Jeff, come on,' said Zimmerman. 'You've forgotten how we got to where we are. Entrepreneurialism, not data nerdism. We have enough of those grunts on the payroll. Surely the number two in the organisation doesn't need to join the ranks of the "undead".'

Somewhere in himself, Jeff knew he was being handed a masterclass in being outflanked, outwitted, and generally fucked. He had got as far as the words *regulation* and *moderation* and no further. Explaining this to AJ was going to be fun … not. He hadn't seen Zimmerman in this maverick mode for a long time. He'd forgotten that was what had made him his millions.

If Jeff was a politician, he would already have been looking for angles as to how to distance himself from this new proposed involvement.

By 2011, TimeBox employed more than nineteen hundred people globally. On two of them – Libby Hendrick and Aidan Mulcahy – Jeff had staked his reputation by parachuting them into key positions in TimeBox Ireland. He realised why Melissa and Norah had attacked him at the meeting. It was called payback.

11

Jeff had invited Libby and Aidan to a FaceBox meeting. He said he wanted to discuss the board's view on their Dublin operation. When the connection was made, it linked up a boardroom in Dublin with Jeff and AJ's dining room.

'Well,' Jeff began, 'it's only four months ago that Zimmerman and Gabrielle told us Egypt was where it was at, and, by God, has the place kicked off or what?'

'Hope you're not being flippant about it, Jeff,' said Libby. 'There's an awful lot of blood being spilt, and more to come, I suspect. They're calling it a spring now, but let's wait and see.'

'Libby, I'm sure Jeff didn't mean anything,' said AJ.

'Sure, love,' said Jeff, 'but let me speak for myself, particularly when you know what I'm about to ask the guys to do.' He paused for a moment. 'I might as well come out with it. If TimeBox is being used the way I think it's being used, then I need to build a case – I mean, like, collect testimony … evidence. I can't do that without boots on the ground. That means going to North Africa. Before you even digest that, I do at least mean with trained security agents. AJ's dad's personally recommended two people, ex-military, he would swear by. I'm interviewing them this weekend. A husband and wife team – Beth and Dale. Maybe a bit unusual, but definitely recommended.'

'Jesus, Jeff,' Libby protested, 'this is a bit out of the blue.'

'Libby, I need to know what the heck is this Egypt thing with TimeBox.'

'We're heading to Egypt?' A simpler question from Aidan.

'No. Libya first,' he said, 'because there's a chance to link in with Gaddafi.'

'This gets stranger by the minute.' Libby didn't like surprise agendas. Her face on the video call told you that.

'Oh, I get it,' said Aidan. 'The single guys will make for less collateral damage if we get topped.'

'I know black humour when I hear it, especially from you.' Jeff shook his head. 'I will be going. Colonel Gaddafi has had a lot of dealings with the Irish over the years, and we have good contacts now that can get us an audience.'

Libby gave him a quizzical look. 'Given the move from Zimmerman and Gabrielle, I thought your prize was to find out what is going on in TimeBox Egypt.'

'It is, and I'll ask you to go there if it's safe. We'll deal with Cairo when the demonstrations calm down. That will be our security's call. Besides, I want to see if we survive Gaddafi first.'

Aidan laughed. Libby didn't.

'This is a big ask, Jeff,' Libby cautioned. 'From a desk job to a war zone.'

'Look, some part of TimeBox setting up in Egypt is about keeping me in the States.' Jeff shuffled uncomfortably in his seat, with AJ standing at his shoulder. 'If I go walkabout in Egypt, it starts to look obvious that I'm up to something. We'll know more after we visit their neighbour. Gaddafi will be interesting. My contact guarantees it.'

'I don't know.' A glum looking Libby concluded. 'Watching the news, I don't know.'

'Look, will you at least meet the security team?' Jeff asked.

'What did you say their names were – Bett and Dylan?' asked Aidan.

'It's Beth and Dale. I've checked your calendars and you have availability early next week.'

The doorbell rang.

'That's them, I guess,' said AJ.

'Will you get it, love?' asked Jeff.

'What did your last slave die of?' replied AJ, joking, as she headed down the hall. 'Hi, Dad,' she said, throwing her arms around her father's neck.

'Hi, honey,' Mike replied as he held his daughter's embrace. 'Let me introduce you to Dale and Beth Longworth,' he continued. 'Mr and Mrs Longworth, formerly of the 5th Airborne and recently returned from Iraq. They come highly recommended from an old friend, Admiral Davies.'

The handshakes were awkwardly conducted while AJ heralded the guests into the dining room. She switched off the news channel playing on the wall-mounted TV.

'Jeff, you still saving on office energy bills?' asked Mike.

'Now, Mike, you know me well enough. There'll be a few stragglers in the office, even on a Sunday morning. I like a bit of privacy. Don't you?'

AJ was doing that imperceptible female thing, looking over the new people – the female, especially. Beth was a pretty-looking woman. Maybe late twenties. Her mid-length hair was trained through the back strap of a baseball cap with a US Marine Corps crest on the front. She didn't remove it as she took her seat at the polished mahogany table – a sure sign that Beth had been travelling, and a hair wash would take up too much time. Her husband dwarfed her: a big, physical man, crew cut, no cap, handsome, AJ thought.

AJ was thinking, *If Jeff employs this guy, then there must be something Freudian in a skinny guy latching on to big burly men*. Her father included.

'What's the brief?' Mike asked. 'I couldn't get anything out of my daughter.'

'That's good, isn't it?' Jeff replied. 'You must have bred loyalty into AJ.'

'Oh, I guess.'

'Look, it's sensitive, that's for sure.' Jeff ushered the visitors to sit and AJ distributed three new coffee cups. 'You know from the news – and maybe your own sources – the Middle East may have gone quiet, but North Africa has kicked off, big time.'

'There's no oil for us there, son, so the military won't be going.'

'That's what I wanted to bring up.' Jeff took an opportunity to pour the coffee and grab a moment. 'I want to go. We have— Not me, but TimeBox has opened an office in Cairo. We have … you'd call it intelligence, that TimeBox is being used to stir up the trouble.'

'Listen, son, from what I learned in Iraq the first time, and I think these soldiers would back me up, the Arabs don't need much help in stirring up trouble.'

'Well, I have to tell you, Colonel,' said Beth, 'I found the opposite to be the case.'

'The Arabs just want to be traders, workers, dealers,' Dale backed up his wife's statement. 'They'll fight only if they have to.'

'So, who goes first?' asked Beth directly. 'We're here why?'

'Well,' Mike began, 'from my point of view because you're proven to be damn good soldiers.'

'Yes, we did our tours.' Dale sat upright, almost to attention as he spoke. 'Served our country. Glad to be back in one piece.'

'Don't forget … got married along the way,' Beth added.

'Interested in going back?' Jeff asked her. 'Private contracting?'

'Well, that's what we're here to discuss.'

'What I have in mind is two options,' said Jeff. 'You do piecemeal security work for us – you know … including going abroad. We'll talk about the destinations in a while.'

'OK, that's what we were expecting, I guess,' said Beth.

'So, what's the other option?' her husband asked.

'We'll take you on in full-time TimeBox employment.' Even AJ hadn't seen her partner look this serious for the longest time. 'Now that's a different gig. There would be training and upskilling, cybersecurity. Not all bad guys come shooting at you with bullets. This option would depend on aptitude assessment.'

'The second option means moving to Palo Alto?' asked Beth.

'Well, San Jose at least,' said AJ, 'but, yes, we're not a remote working org. Where are you guys based now?'

'Portland, Oregon,' answered Dale.

'OK, so that's the logistics,' Mike said firmly. 'What I want to know is what you're up to.'

'Yep,' Jeff agreed. 'That's where we should go next. I want to interview Colonel Gaddafi in Libya. Obviously, I want to do it before the place gets too hot to handle, too dangerous.'

'That guy would give the rank of colonel a bad name,' said Mike.

'Maybe so …' Jeff hesitated. 'But I know we can

get an audience. Cairo seems already too dangerous a place to visit, but I admit that's where I think we would get our best intel.'

'AJ, please tell me you're not part of these travel arrangements,' said Mike.

Jeff wanted to answer that one. 'No, Mike, but you've met my Irish friends, Aidan and Libby. They'll go with me.' He made eye contact with Beth.

'Jeff, look, I admire your bravery, but what's going on?' One thing about Mike's crew cut: it couldn't hide a furrowed brow. 'You guys are on the crest of a wave. Your company is going places. Where did this fly in the ointment come from?'

'Mike, all I can tell you is that our office in Egypt is spending money – big money. Something is well off. If I don't act, I will be culpable.'

Mike placed a firm hand on Jeff's shoulder. 'Son, these good people and I have been to places where real people have had no tomorrow. You think this out long and hard. You want to make sure you have a tomorrow.'

12

Getting access to the Irish government jet to get into Tripoli, under the radar, was going to cause one hell of a public outcry if it ever came to light. Jeff Bourke's commercial sponsorship of Dublin as a European HQ for TimeBox was having unforeseen benefits. Transport, security and an invitation to meet the regime leader.

'My friends …' Colonel Muammar Gaddafi gave them a warm smile. 'I welcome you, Mr Jeff and Mr Aidan, to my humble home. Your bodyguards must remain outside. My personal guard will look after them. Have no fear.'

If Aidan wasn't thinking it, then Jeff was: *Humble? This place is a fucking palace.* Beautiful carpets, scented aromas, bowls of figs adding to the aroma.

'I do, yes, I do acknowledge your bravery in coming here, in troubled times, as knights for the cursed BoxTime. My advisors had suggested to me to execute you, and I do admit to having given it some consideration. It would send your devil Jew Zimmerman a message, yes?'

The Libyan leader was talking about life and death as if they were nothing. Of course, to him, they were nothing. You would have to have a vat available to hold all the blood on this man's hands.

Strangely, though, the colonel's calmness put Jeff and Aidan at a kind of ease. That must have come in handy for pacifying the poor bastards he was about to kill.

'I must suggest to you, Colonel, that our boss is not a practising Jew,' said Aidan.

Jeff didn't think that it was wise to carry on with the 'play down Zimmerman' rhetoric. It didn't matter, as it turned out. The colonel continued the conversation.

'When my men told me you were two Irish boys, I immediately decided no violence would be required. I have had much dealing with your politicians and your IRA. I found the terrorists more honourable to deal with.'

The two 'boys' had grown up and become politically aware in an Ireland that was trying to recover itself in the post-Haughey era – which really meant the authorities were being more discreet about their backhanders. Jeff was, by luck or design, out of Ireland when the financial crisis hit in 2007 and 2008. The political system, as well as the banking system, had imploded. The hope was that a new Ireland would emerge, phoenix-like, from the flames. It hadn't.

'We are not the tribal Arabs of old,' Gaddafi continued, 'though I myself like to spend time in the desert tent. We have universities and scholars and IT professionals. They tell me interesting stories of how your BoxTime has been used to stir the dissenters against me. No mercy will be shown towards Zimmerman once I have the opportunity. Be glad you are Irish. I like the Irish. They are the Arabs of Europe.'

'Colonel, we have a common interest,' said Jeff. 'I hope you can see that. We want to know who is behind the clandestine use of TimeBox for anti-establishment purposes.'

'My friend, you are number two in BoxTime, yes?' The colonel leaned forward on his cushion suddenly. 'Then how can I believe that you do not know what goes on? My friend General al-Sisi in Cairo will put down his rebellion without mercy, as will I. I have urged him to rout the BoxTime offices out of the ancient city. Any Libyans working there, I have requested their execution.'

'A bit drastic, Colonel?' asked Aidan – maybe unwisely.

'I will judge that, my Irish friends.' Gaddafi raised his voice for the first time. 'We train our medicine professionals here in Tripoli, not anywhere else. We do not like your organisation stealing our pharma— What is the word …? Chemist graduates.'

'Sorry, Colonel,' said Jeff firmly, 'but I myself established the recruitment strategy at TimeBox. We're multidisciplinary, but, no, that doesn't extend to employing medical expertise.'

Gaddafi ignored the answer.

An aide entered the space and made eye contact with the colonel. He then approached and bent to whisper in Gaddafi's ear. He assisted in helping the colonel rise to his feet.

'My Irish friends, I must attend to other matters. I offer you my blessings for safe travel. I will dance upon your Zimmerman's grave.'

They never spoke again.

Jeff called the debriefing when he, Beth and Dale made it home to San Jose and Libby and Aidan were back at their Dublin base.

'Agenda item one,' Beth began without preamble. 'You entered that tent despite our objections. So, chain of command compromised.'

'Beth's right, Jeff,' Dale added. 'We can't work like that. If you pay us to be in operational command, then you've got to take our instruction. It's important, it's called staying alive.'

'Look,' Jeff said apologetically, 'I could reel off a list of excuses, but I won't. We made a call that we weren't in danger. You're right – note to self not to let it happen again.'

'You were at a street protest in Tripoli,' said Beth. 'Jeff, come on … not in danger?'

'Yeah, but that was an unfortunate encounter. You were there and you got us out of trouble fast.' Jeff was eating humble pie by the fistful.

'We advised you not to be on the streets at all,' said Beth. 'Then we find ourselves trying to evacuate you from a mob of maybe a thousand.'

Jeff was getting his ears bashed. There was no AJ

about to rescue him, and Libby hadn't had her go yet.

'I'd like to have heard Gaddafi for myself, like inside the tent,' said Libby.

'That was Gaddafi's call. Like I say, won't happen again,' said Jeff.

Aidan came to his defence. 'The colonel had been acutely aware that TimeBox – he insisted on calling it BoxTime – was being used against him.'

'I can see why.' Libby jumped in. 'If the orchestration is successful in unseating his dictatorship, most likely it will establish a power vacuum, and all the carnage and death that goes with it.

'Seems to me that up to this point,' Beth began, 'the world norm had been that traditional covert organisations like the CIA and the KGB used their own dirty tricks campaigns to destabilise regimes with arms and money. Now the world is being changed by words and messages on social media.'

'We got to turn that into evidence,' answered Libby. 'That's Gaddafi's testimony and our TimeBox analytics.'

'You're right,' said Jeff. 'At the moment it's just the whiff of a case against our own company.'

'I think we just got in and out on time,' said Aidan. 'The spring looks to be well turning into an unpleasant winter.'

'Libya and Tunisia may be the battlegrounds,' said Jeff, 'but Cairo is the nerve centre. That's where we need to get traction. A problem child that TimeBox likes to keep quiet about. The colonel challenged me

– how could I not know what goes on in TimeBox?'

'Jeff, we survived Libya. When do we head to Egypt, so?'

Just like that day outside a bar in Dublin, Libby could still be fearless.

'Because I myself continue to be afraid of any of us dying,' said Jeff. 'Dale and Beth will make that operational call on our proposed visit to Cairo.'

'It's too hot, we have intel.' Beth was quick to respond. 'It seems the military regime is not too crazy about visitors.'

Gaddafi was dead less than two months after Jeff and Aidan's meeting with him. That was a wake-up call, for sure. That event was closely followed by the killing of the US ambassador to Libya in Benghazi.

'Jesus, Jeff, that could have been us,' was Aidan's comment on it.

'Good call not to go to Cairo, you agree?' Jeff asked.

If and when Jeff ever got to use the testimony they'd gathered in Libya, it remained to be seen if anyone would be interested in the views of a dead man.

13

Martin Gabrielle sat with General Abdel Fattah el-Sisi, drinking aromatic tea. The general had swapped whatever military barracks he was used to occupying for the more lavish setting of the Al-Ittihadiya presidential palace and gardens. The setting was new by Egyptian standards, to the east of the Nile. The reason for the meeting was old: another military coup.

'General,' Gabrielle began, 'you are a man who recognises the power of influence which can go so much further than the power of the prison, the gun or the bomb. You do not want this great and ancient kingdom to go the way of Libya and Tunisia. Maybe the way that Syria is heading. My company can help you with that.'

'Exactly how?' asked the general.

'As always, with investment and with people. We have ways of using artificial intelligence that can win the hearts and minds of your people.'

'You, my friend, are walking on … What do you from the West say? Thin ice.' The general had begun the meeting reclining on a luxurious sofa, legs crossed, relaxed, teacup in hand. He was now sitting bolt upright, legs apart and on the edge of the sofa. 'This is a time when bullets are freely available to solve problems. You must tell me why I should not view you as a problem. This most pernicious of media – TimeBox, you know – was used malevolently, to undermine practically all North Africa and some of our Middle Eastern brothers. At whose request was this, if not pro-Israelis?'

'General, you must accept that my company and our product can't be held responsible when manipulated by others.'

'As I was saying, this is a time when bullets can be used liberally to pay back entities that allowed themselves to undermine the state of Egypt.' The general had laid his cup down on the coffee table that separated the two men.

'General, please agree with me, we must look to the future.' Gabrielle took another sip of his tea, calmly. 'Of course, we will make personal reparation to you for any damage caused to Egyptian society. Please look to the confidence we have in your regime. We want to expand offices here in Cairo. People employed in laboratories, set up with specialised equipment.'

'Laboratories? Are you diversifying, Mr Gabrielle?'

'I only mean IT laboratories, to begin with.'

'Strange you should say that, when I know it to be true that your company has been poking around Cairo University, asking about pharmaceutical and biological disciplines.' The general's gaze was boring through an unfazed Gabrielle.

'I can only say that we want to be at the heart of Egypt's recovery, whatever it takes, General – and I mean, whatever it takes.'

David Zimmerman was keeping a mile clear of any involvement with the disastrous aftermath of the Arab Spring. Gabrielle was all over the mop-up operation. The Zimmer had been happy to be the front face of TimeBox's involvement in the emerging positive uprisings. It was another case altogether in the Arab Winter, when everything had fallen to shit. Like any other business, who wants to take on negative publicity – more especially, if you had been hypocritical enough to milk the positivity at the start? It's very hard to harvest positivity when the body count starts mounting, and turmoil, chaos and military coups signal that the party is over.

Egypt had always been at the centre of the Arab world. Whatever characteristics the Egyptians had exhibited to enable them to rule the known world in ancient times had carried them forward into the modern era. In the early 1970s, it had been Prime Minister Anwar Sadat – at least, in between coups – who had brokered the peace with Israel.

It might have made business sense for TimeBox Dublin to be linked to the new Cairo office. But TimeBox Cairo remained a separate entity, funded from a source only Zimmerman was privy to. It was massive compared with the company's other fledgling offices: maybe three hundred people on the payroll, but with a HQ square footage that told Jeff there could only be space for forty-odd employees. Stories had got back to San Jose about military raids on the office in late 2011.

Libby and Jeff had chatted at the time.

'Maybe Gabrielle will be back with his tail between his legs?' said Libby. 'What do you think?'

'Is that something to look forward to?' Jeff put his head in his hands. 'I'm not sure which would be worse. Gabrielle here thwarting us, or us being thwarted by not knowing what he is up to abroad.'

Money was at the heart of the TimeBox relationship with Egypt. Gabrielle didn't care where it was funnelled to. The former general, now president, funnelled the funds into decent humanitarian causes in both Egypt and Jordan – at least, as reported in the press. In a piss-poor country, it can be easier to be seduced by riches easily come by. As 2011 rolled into 2012, the money was rolling in at a momentous rate. The Egyptian president didn't understand TimeBox's product. Social media didn't contribute to the norms of the capitalist world. It didn't make money via commercial breakthroughs in science, technology or medicine. Instead, this product was about being in constant contact and connection with your peers. The president had become happy that if TimeBox wanted to funnel support funding through him, so be it.

14

By the spring of 2013, Martin Gabrielle was pretty much living in Cairo full time. That had its upside for Jeff: his nemesis's very rare attendances in the US, even at board meetings. The rumours of the money being spent were eye-watering. Gabrielle must be building up the office. He certainly always had a forensic accountant tailing him. You didn't want some smart-arse *New York Times* journalist uncovering what would be a very uncomfortable money trail. TimeBox had prided itself on its culture: young, vibrant, 'we're all in this for the good of society' kind of thing. Neither Gabrielle nor Zimmerman wanted to think about the fallout of a good old-fashioned financial scandal.

Gabrielle and his partner Simone dined at the presidential palace regularly. He was adept at laying platitudes upon the president with a trowel. History had provided ample ammunition – from both the ancient and the modern eras – that the geographical position of Egypt was key. Sandwiched as it was between the Arab states of North Africa and those of the Middle East, it was the prime location to influence the whole region.

What bugged Gabrielle was that he hadn't been able to open the US President's door to the former general. This black man was proving difficult to buy. He could not move too fast. World order needed the muppets, the mugs, to still believe that the world was run by decent elected men and women.

'We might need to wait for the right kind of man in the White House. All in good time, all in good time, Zimmer,' as Gabrielle was prone to repeating.

Jeff was in his office in San Jose. Libby and Aidan were eight hours ahead in Dublin. As usual, their meeting was conducted via their own company's secure video link.

'I was more up for it after Libya,' Libby said. 'We've waited two years – why Egypt now?'

'The place has calmed down,' Jeff replied. 'Dale has eyes on the ground there. I think I've said this to you before. It's called not getting anyone killed, Libby, especially my friends.'

'Are you coming, Jeff?' asked Aidan.

'No, I want to get ready to bait our media friends – a charm offensive. We're making feck all progress in getting heard otherwise. Dale and Beth are lined up from this end. You don't move a muscle without them.'

'Funny kind of employment, this,' Libby observed wryly. 'Working for a company *and* trying to undermine it.'

'You're wrong, but you're right,' said Jeff. 'An awful lot of employees do that anyway without even noticing.'

'Cynicism – from you?' asked Aidan.

'Not really,' Jeff countered. 'This is a win-win if we can do the right thing. TimeBox will progress, even if TimeBox Cairo is a casualty.'

'Let's not get too philosophical,' said Aidan. 'What's the brief?'

'Play the game,' replied Jeff. 'You're senior company representatives. You have the right to know where our money is being spent. See if there's anything in the biology, pharma story.'

'What biology story?' asked Libby.

'Remember the Gaddafi story?' said Aidan. 'You know – TimeBox recruiting biology and pharma grads.'

'You might remember, he wouldn't let me into the tent,' said Libby. 'I kept Dale and Beth company.'

'You know well you were briefed,' said an annoyed Aidan, 'except for the part where the crazy colonel wanted al-Sisi – you know, the Egyptian guy … dictator or whatever – to execute the Libyan students involved. Crazy stuff. Anyway, can we bring a few bucks, you know – to grease the palms?'

'Yep, you know the rules,' said Jeff. 'Sign it out and I'll countersign, all above board.'

'Jeff, this playing by the rules will be your undoing,' said Libby.

'Don't you worry, girl. If the gloves need to come off, I'll join you in the trenches.'

'Looking forward to it,' she retorted.

The three friends proved that they could still get tetchy with each other.

'What about Beth's baby?' asked Aidan.

'For sure,' said Jeff. 'Dylan is a little boy these days – but if you think that would stop her, you don't know our Beth.'

'You've had her and Dale desk-bound over there for a while now?' asked Libby.

'I know what you're getting at, and you needn't sweat it. They keep themselves fit. They're still military, and that won't be changing.'

Cairo via business class travel was no ordeal. The winter sun temperature was pretty much on a par with San Jose, and more pleasant than a wintry Dublin, set against the majesty of an Islamic cityscape, with the minarets rising like obelisks into an azure sky. The visual beauty was complemented by the rhythmic, melodic call to prayer. Beautiful, at least from the luxury of a five-star hotel. TimeBox executive expense accounts were good.

The city was quiet, and a far cry from the tumult of two years previously. A safer place to get a story, with Beth and Dale on hand for any unforeseen circumstances. The team had planned a very gentle introduction to their two-day trip: a meeting with the president of Cairo University. The agenda was to question what additional bursaries TimeBox could contribute to the faculty, and in what disciplines – general enough. A pencil-thin Professor al-Ashwari, with a receding hairline, wore a suit that put the casuals of Aidan and Libby in the shade. He greeted them in the foyer of the university's main building and, with his assistant, escorted them directly to his office.

'Somewhat delighted to meet with more honoured TimeBox guests,' he began when everyone was seated. 'Your Mr Gabrielle has been most generous, and a great provider of employment. We have very close ties.'

'For sure, diversification is a credit to our company,' said Aidan.

He and Libby were at least good at supporting each other's probing lies.

'You are so correct, friends. We here in Egypt do not see so many uses for your social media. It was everywhere during the failed uprising. Not so much now.'

'Yeah, I wonder why,' mumbled Aidan, with Libby throwing him a look.

'Do you have an intake of foreign students?' she asked.

'Generally, only our Arab brothers.'

The professor was comfortably sitting with fingers intertwined and hands resting on the desk in front of him. His aide, the larger gentleman who had met them at the entrance, was standing uncomfortably behind and to the right. Aidan's thoughts were along the lines of, *I thought all these Arab guys started their meetings with the hospitality of offering tea.*

'Some are glad to be able to study in a stable environment,' the professor continued. 'Would anyone like to be in Assad's Damascus now? I think not. Of course, many universities specialise, so when your Mr Gabrielle sponsored his funding model to bring R and D to, shall we say, less developed states … Well, this was good for all, was it not?

'Depends on what they're researching.' Aidan couldn't help himself.

Al-Ashwari initiated a pregnant pause which the two TimeBoxers knew spoke volumes. The room took on a new atmosphere. Aidan went for it.

'Perhaps, Professor, as a sign of goodwill, TimeBox would like to offer you an additional contribution to the university – a financial contribution.' He placed his briefcase on the professor's teak table. Al-Ashwari stood up abruptly.

'Regrettably,' their host said, 'I must be away to a further engagement. You must be advised that our research is as directed by TimeBox, here in Cairo.'

Libby thought about salvaging the show, but quickly thought better of it. Aidan had taken a risk. It hadn't paid off. A long journey for a short visit?

The walk out of the administration facility gave them a better chance to observe that Cairo University was a building site, expanding around its periphery. The work was more noticeable as they made their way down stairwells, escorted off the premises by the professor's aide.

The scene outside, where Beth and Dale had parked by arrangement, was less sedate.

'Jesus,' Aidan hissed. 'This thing is turning to shite very quickly.'

'Thanks, Aidan, great observation.'

Libby could see a small crowd of students gathering around the entrance. Dale was spread-eagled against the wall. It wasn't police – or, at least, the uniform looked more like the khaki of soldiers.

'Resistance is futile, it seems,' said Aidan.

'Now might be a good time to stay quiet.'

Beth knew enough not to move suddenly, but was able to fill in the guys when they slowly got close enough to her.

'You were hardly gone through the doors when this unit showed up,' she said. 'No point arguing – they're armed to the teeth. I'm glad we didn't bring sidearms. It wouldn't go down well.'

'What will we do next?' asked Libby.

'Sit tight,' Beth said simply. 'Even if they assault Dale, I won't intervene.'

'Oh,' said Libby.

'Seen it all before.' Beth didn't seem at all alarmed. 'This has been staged. They'd like the situation to escalate. Make a few arrests. Anyway, a few cracks in the ear would do him good.'

Libby was thinking there was a touch of Irish in that woman. A man whose uniform bore an army captain's insignia walked over to the group and relieved Aidan of his briefcase.

'Dear Western visitor, I regret to inform you our government no longer deem your visit here conducive to the national interest. We thank you for your visit. You will now be escorted to Cairo

Airport. Please re-enter your vehicle.'

Dale was already in the process of being manhandled into the back of their jeep.

'You OK, honey?' Beth turned her attention to Dale now that she had their vehicle enroute.

Aidan and Libby looked directly at each other.

'We're being escorted,' said Dale.

'I don't think our Jeff is going to be best pleased,' said Aidan.

'No,' Libby agreed. 'Especially when you left behind a briefcase with a hundred grand in it.'

'I don't think I left it behind,' Aidan protested. 'Let's put it down as a tax expense. A contribution to the Egyptian economy.'

'But it was a military captain who took hold of your briefcase.'

'That's just a detail, Beth.'

If Aidan was worried about the money, he sure wasn't showing it. Libby was relieved they were all still in good shape. Everything had happened so quickly; it was only then that she allowed herself to feel relieved – slightly relieved. They still had to negotiate the airport.

'Just a detail,' Aidan said again.

15

Jack Featherstone was a young old-fashioned journalist with the *Washington Post*. He was around the same vintage as Jeff; he dressed a bit scruffily and liked a drink. He could have been badged as a classic stereotype, but as an African American, he avoided that tag. A competent reporter all the same.

Jeff had been through a few skirmishes with the media – mostly tidying up after Zimmerman, because you couldn't allow Gabrielle to set foot in front of a journalist. Zimmerman had sent Gabrielle in to bat on a slot Bloomberg were doing on the rise of TimeBox's competitors. His use of the word 'exterminate' hadn't gone down well with the American viewing public.

Jack Featherstone had been a junior in the *Post*'s newsroom back when the financial system was imploding. That meant that he was of the right vintage to tune in to the new bleatings coming out of TimeBox. Jack arrived in TimeBox HQ one day in 2008, asking to speak to whoever was undermining the financial stability of the United States.

Jeff was glad of the mainstream media attention. Both men sounded each other out at that first encounter.

'Strange name for a black American?' Jeff asked.

'Yep. I'm guessing some white Englander had a hand in that somewhere, man.'

The two men had kept in touch over the intervening years. Not so much a friendship, but a relationship that meant that if you were asked to travel across the country for a meeting, you knew it was important. You also knew you would be meeting in a bar.

'What gives, Jeff?' Jack began. He was standing beside Jeff's booth and offered him a fist pump. 'You got another Fannie Mae, Freddie Mac story for me?'

He was straight off the plane, and found Jeff in McNally's on 5th and Irvine, as arranged.

'That seems like an age ago now.'

'What gives with this anti-TimeBox jive you gave me over the phone?'

'Jesus, man. Straight down to business, Jacko, sit, sit,' Jeff laughed. 'How's she hangin'?'

'You got me there, man. Lucky you're stinkin rich, 'cause I'll tell you, political correctness is going to wait in the long grass.'

'Yeah,' Jeff replied. 'If there's one thing that kills me, it's this fascination with that thing … that thing. What is it again? Oh, yes, I remember. Be somebody else, not yourself, perfectly natural. Just ask Freud – if you can dig him up.' Jeff awkwardly used his arms to do a mock digging routine.

'No wonder Fox hates you.' Jack yawned mockingly. He was either tired or pissed off after the flight. 'They couldn't interview you, not knowing what cuss would come out of your mouth next. I'm telling you, man, America loves a success story. You're a mick, and if you think you'll rain on blue-eyed boy Zimmerman, your story better be as watertight as a duck's ass.' Now Jack was doing the mimicry. He used his thumb and adjacent right-hand finger to form an O in front of Jeff's face. Then he graphically closed the hole.

'Right, if you're going to take that attitude, buddy, it's your round. I'll summon Myles for you.' Jeff leaned over the edge of the booth with a two-fingered gesture towards the bartender. 'Two beers, Myles. But I'm intrigued. Apart from our little phone parley, what makes you think I'm planning on raining on parades?'

'So don't get caught on a camera at a protest in the centre of Tripoli.' Featherstone was also willing to use two-fingered gestures. But his fingers were reversed in front of Jeff's face. 'At least, not before our ambassador goes and gets himself killed.'

'That's old news,' said Jeff, trying not to show that he was rattled by the reporter's knowledge.

'Look, Jeff, the media will cut you slack while you're still a successful blow-in. But you start to be a threat to our all-American boy, then do I need to spell out who will be left without that chair when the music stops playing? There are already a few knives being readied for you, my friend.'

'Jesus, I thought I was here to do the talking.'

Jack had to know this was serious, or he wouldn't have flown down from DC.

'You're talking like a man who's been hearing stuff,' said Jeff.

'Two more, please?' asked Jack, as Myles was depositing two beers on the table. 'I'm thirsty.' Sitting in a booth in McNally's was a signal: private conversation; do not disturb.

'So, what have you been hearing?' asked Jeff.

'Jeff, you more than maybe anyone on the entire planet don't need to be told we're living in a digital age. Politicians have a new-found interest in social media.'

'So?'

'Look, Obama's well into his second term. You know what that means?'

'Wait – you're going to tell me, yeah?' said Jeff.

Jack lowered his voice. 'There's a lot of Congress guys filling their coffers, waiting for the next run. And word is, you guys in TB are bankrolling Republicans and Democrats already. Talk about hedging your bets.'

'What's the word on who'll be on the ticket?'

'Looks like it's going to be a circus. They're lining up down the sidewalk.'

'Names, I'm interested in. Would I know any of them?'

'If you're moving in the right circles, Jeff, you should be friends with them all. That way, you're always backing a winner. Your media likes "friends", don't it?'

'Come on, humour me.'

'Well, it's like line up twice the number of usual

suspects.' Jack took a slug from the bottle and relaxed his shoulders. 'There's a Bush there, for example – Florida Jeb.'

'Jesus, is there ever not?' It was Jeff's turn to take a slug – a long one – not suddenly feeling as comfortable as he had been. 'When might the great US run out of those guys?'

'Probably never. Old George does have grandkids, you know?'

Jeff took off his jacket and laid it on the seat beside him. He was feeling warm and the beer wasn't cooling him.

'Oh, God, what would a new Bush do? Have a third go at saving the Arabs from themselves?'

'Just be careful about what you don't wish for. Word has it Donald Trump might be interested in having a run.'

'I'm not mocking that one, man,' said Jeff. 'He's a business guy, and that at least would bring a different approach to Washington. If he comes through, I'd be saying "give the guy a chance." He'll have his own money, so why look to TimeBox for a handout?'

'Jeff, did you have gullible pie for lunch?' Jack was looking Jeff right in the eyes. 'None of them will refuse a place at the trough. Leopards, spots, et cetera.'

'Look, Jack, if you're keeping an eye on the TimeBox coffers, you might want to keep an eye on our Egypt office.'

'Jeff, do you ever get jaded talking about that part of the world?' Jack yawned. 'The Middle East. You've yacked on at me before, remember? What about a story based in the mystical Far East? You know – magic carpets and stuff.'

'Jack, don't be joshing me,' said Jeff. 'I'm serious – deadly serious. Not just millions ... Close to a billion has been pumped, or dumped, into TimeBox Cairo. Martin Gabrielle has been pretty much resident there since late 2010.'

'Brave guy, moving in during an uprising.'

'What about moving in to *start* an uprising?'

That got Jack's interest. He sat up from a semi-slouched position.

'I didn't think you needed to spend a billion to get a revolution going in that part of the world.'

'You Americans are always trotting out that line,' said Jeff.

'It's true, man,' said Jack. 'The Arabs seem to be constantly up for a fight. Like you Irish, I suppose. Look, Jeff, the Arab Spring is yesterday's news. Have you something new for me? That was a long journey, and these days we see you social media guys as our competitors, not our buddies. It's not like it was back when the banks were screwing us all.' Jack placed a hand on his crotch, briefly, to be crude.

'Look, the fact that I can't get to the bottom of a huge spend out of TimeBox is telling me something stinks.'

'OK, OK, you're buying the burger.' Jeff remembered how you knew when you got this particular media hack interested. His eyes dropped the sleepy uninterested look and bored straight into your face. 'What gives?'

'Look, I might be starting in the wrong place, but we did … maybe a crazy thing. We got an audience with Gaddafi while he was in the middle of his Arab Spring.'

'Will you go on the record with that? Because if you do, you'll lose a lot of credibility. Still, brave considering that there was a lot of his own trying to kill him. Why were you putting yourself in the firing line, Jeff?'

'I didn't see it like that,' said Jeff. 'He seemed to like the Irish. Had a lot of business dealings with them back in the day. As he said himself, he thought dealing with Irish terrorists was easier than dealing with the Irish administration. He really meant the beef sellers – politicians, I don't know … Maybe he realised that the Irish were as crazy as he was.'

'I'm impressed, but testimony from that "crazy" is a difficult spin.'

'Don't be too impressed, it's out of character for you.' Jeff was serious, but he allowed himself a smile. 'I had my guys with me – Libby and Aidan, from the Dublin office. Not to mention Dale and Beth, our security.'

'Two Irish and two Americans,' said Jack. 'Nice balance of lieutenants.'

'You said it.' Jeff exhaled, trying to untighten himself and knowing that was what he needed the alcohol for. 'Beth and Dale are ex-Marines – a couple.'

'Jesus, Jeff, you're militarised?' Jack continued with his piercing glare. 'You're serious?'

'It wasn't that dramatic.'

Jeff got a break from that journalistic stare by turning to again summon Myles' attention. 'Myles, two plates of wings to start with, yeah?'

'Coming up.'

'Jeff, you mightn't be giving yourself enough credit. So, you have my ear, at least while I'm waiting to eat.'

'Jack, you know this – I'm a TimeBoxer.' Jeff was now meeting Jack's gaze directly. 'We have thousands of employees. I won't turn my back on the company, but if there is illegality – I mean the illegality of getting people killed – I won't be part of it, not even by staying quiet. I can't.'

'Seems like you want to make some serious allegations.'

'Jack, it's the tightest bit of security in the entire business world. Even Putin's finances are more transparent.'

'So, tell me what you know,' said Jack.

Jeff let forth.

Myles appeared to set the cutlery on the table.

'Usual dressing, Jeff?

'Treat us to a selection, Myles, you're only young once.'

When he left, Jeff continued. 'Right, so this is how it looks. You've fallen out with your former buddies. They're doing stuff in Egypt to make up for wreaking havoc in North Africa. A lot going on there, Jeff – I'd need more.' Jack had dropped his piercing glare. 'Now if you want to tell me TimeBox will be used to throw the election, that would be news.' Jack cupped his hand around his right ear in a mock show to accompany a mock smile.

'That's the point, Jack. The manipulation in North Africa was driven, I believe, by TimeBox resources based in Cairo. But now Pandora's box has been opened. The case proven – a bot-driven approach can plunder any message it likes. I think that influencing our election is a very likely scenario, and an unregulated social media platform won't be required to lift a finger to stop it.'

'Now that sounds promising – as a story, I mean. We'll keep the lines of communication open, Jeff. That's all I'm committing to for the minute, anyway. Well, that's apart from drinking a few more.'

'Support me in a closer look at our Cairo operation, Jack.' Jeff was struggling not to sound beaten.

'Jeff, the *Post* isn't interested in Arabs.'

'The carnage is still going on in Syria, remember.'

'What do you want me to do?' Jack Featherstone raised his arms as a gesture of surrender. 'Head off to the desert? Syria? No thanks.'

The wings arrived.

16

Jeff kept up his contact with Featherstone. Jack had made it clear: if there was a story, the US election would be where the story was. He had been right in his earlier hunch that Trump would run for president. The *Post* published the following leaked email correspondence from Donald Trump's office.

> *Tell Mr P from me, if he can pull this off, he will be my new best friend, and you know best friends do favours for each other, don't they? If H gets the job, it will be sanction this and block that. You know how it is.*
>
> *This is the great thing about having a huge country at your disposal, with a whole load of low-paid professionals that you don't let out of the country.*
>
> *TimeBox is all about being happy-clappy and making Zimmerman plenty rich, even plenty richer than P, but I forgot, nobody knows how rich P is.*
>
> *Think about it. The bots take on a persona and make lots and lots of social media friends with real American voters, young and old. Then you subtly bombard your new friends with messages that sow*

the seeds. Like Hillary is not as sweet as apple pie. That's huge. Why? Because deep down a lot of voters remember Hillary taking a swipe at dear old Barbara Bush. Exactly over describing Babs as a sweet old lady who stayed home to mind the stove while her man ran the country.

You don't come out and say "Hey everybody, H is a roaring bitch." You sow seeds like, "Maybe H is a roaring bitch and by the way please feel free to reach your own conclusion, thank you very much." Emotional intelligence, my ass. Yes, you will, or it's at least good that you think you made up your own mind.

Our contact in Cairo will assist with IP addresses. For obvious reasons we don't want to show up with too many "friends" from actual Russia. If you're serious about helping with this thing, our man Mr G will assist, guaranteed. This election will be won again on social media. Just ask Obama.

It was electronically signed: 'From the Offices of Donald Trump.'

'Nice work, Jack,' Jeff said over the phone. 'Only problem being that you published two days after the election.'

'*You don't have to state the obvious, thanks,*' Jack answered, knowing he was on the back foot.

'Published a week ago, that could have made a difference. The CIA might have been less interested in Hillary's laptop. At least you took my advice on investigative journalism, no?'

'Any more of that and I'm hanging up. Look, maybe too little too late for the election, but the "illegal" use of TimeBox is a story that won't go away. That's what you wanted, ain't it?'

'Where did you get your source?' asked Jeff.

'Nice try, wise guy.'

Jack might have wondered why Jeff wasn't sticking it to him harder. The election was over, and President Trump was coming – there was no stopping that train. But there was a reason, and it went back to the previous year.

Beth asked to present her Data Analytics' team results. That signalled a session in the privacy of Jeff and AJ's house, with Libby and Aidan on FaceBox.

'It's all coming from Moscow, we think,' said Beth. 'A huge flow of TimeBox messaging and it's all pro-Trump.'

'If that swings him the Republican nomination, then why not proceed with the same strategy for next year's election?' said Aidan.

'If you've got the metrics, Beth, I'm going to pull the servers in Russia,' said Jeff.

'Jeff, you know the way the internet works,' said Aidan. 'The bloody messaging might start being routed elsewhere – even through Ireland.'

'I don't care,' said Jeff. 'This isn't what our product is meant to be about.'

AJ got up and went over to his chair. She just put

her hand on his shoulder. He was shaking with rage.

'Bourke, what is it I'm hearing?' asked Zimmerman. 'Entire data centres switched off?' Once Zimmerman was calling you by your surname, it wasn't good.

'That's right, David. Do you want our reputation destroyed?'

'Martin, what are the financials?' asked Zimmerman.

Gabrielle was on video call from Cairo.

'Come on, David, he's costing us millions,' said Gabrielle. 'Idle server farms. These messages generate advertising revenue. Did people forget that? Have they become rich? Bourke has to realise he is an employee, and must be disciplined – or better, stopped.'

'Jeff, the servers need to be restored by midnight,' said Zimmerman. 'If not …'

17

'Jack Featherstone – our *Post* guy,' Jeff began. 'You got to give him credit. Relentless editorial pressure and it's paid off. I think he knew he owed me, us, one.'

'Yes, Jeff,' Libby agreed, 'he turned out to be your bitch, all right.'

The large screen in Jeff's office portrayed Libby from seven thousand miles away, as feisty as ever.

'Now, Lib, Jeff called us together for a reason,' said Aidan, sitting across from her. 'It's early morning over there, so let's not get too tetchy.' He waved a finger at her playfully.

'Thanks, Aidan.' Jeff made his own salute at the screen in return. It might have been a bad attempt at relieving the tension associated with what he was about to ask. 'Good news, but big news. Congress has to give the "charges" against TimeBox a hearing. All we're waiting for now is a date from the joint Houses, and I for sure want to have my ducks lined up. So, the single agenda item today is back to Egypt, strike two.' That got their attention alright.

'Jeff, Jeff, why go back?' asked Libby. 'Even without the analytics, the dogs in the street know the election was rigged.'

'*Influenced*, not rigged, Libby,' said Jeff.

'Look, look, there's a case to be answered for sure.' Libby sounded exasperated. 'Russia versus the US. Is that not the ground we fight on?'

'Anyway, would we be let in?' asked Aidan.

'Well, don't tell them you're back looking for the hundred K you lent them, anyway,' said Libby, joshing.

'Ha bloody ha.' Aidan now had a scowl that showed he wasn't in the mood for being on the butt end of the humour.

'There's still a loose end I want to sort out before I ever face the suits in Washington,' said Jeff.

'Which is?' asked Libby.

'Where's all the money going? Pharma research, my ass. No drug could be that expensive.'

'When we were there before, Gabrielle made sure we got the tour of the university, a short one,' said Libby. 'You know all that.'

'That tells me pharma is just a front,' said Aidan.

'They're not manufacturing anything chemical, that's for sure,' said Jeff. 'AJ has done that research for me. If it's just a front for pumping "sorry" money into the regime, can we get real proof? It's been going on a long time now.'

'So, as Lib says, is it worth going back for? It wasn't pleasant the first time.'

'Aidan,' Jeff said patiently, 'I'll be the one standing in front of those ball crunchers on Capitol Hill.' Jeff held out his open palm and closed it slowly to form a clenched fist. It was graphic but he was amongst friends. 'Being sideswiped by a curveball is not where I want to be. Egypt is at the heart of this somehow.'

'Is this that Huberman story cropping up again?' asked Libby.

'No, no.' Jeff shook his head in an unconvincing way. 'That's a long time ago. Your memory is good, Lib, but that's not it, no. Cairo is TimeBox's dirty tricks office. We know it – it's on the record and we have boxes of analytic proof.' Jeff paused; he was feeling lonely. The sensation was strange. 'The good old boys in Congress might just put stock in traditional documented testimony, that's all.' He paused again, wondering if the other end was on mute. 'Look, it's a long shot, I know I'm asking a lot. I still have to have faith.'

Jeff was taking the meeting from his office. He was on his own. The lads were a long way away in Ireland. When Libby saw his eyes had watered, she couldn't take the vulnerability of it. Blurting out the name Huberman had had an effect.

'OK, I'll go,' said Libby. 'You coming, Aidan?'

'When?'

'Next Saturday, don't want your absence flagged. I have your flight booked.'

'Figures,' said Aidan.

Jeff looked brighter now. 'I haven't told you the best part. You're getting a meet and greet session with Gabrielle and the lovely Simone. I think the Zimmer is trying to kiss and make up, that's all.'

'Surely he smells a rat?' asked Libby.

'Maybe he's just lonely, Lib.'

Libby thought back to their college days, using it as a mechanism to get to sleep that night. *Was that tear in Jeff's eye a put on? He sure did recover quickly.*

You just didn't know if the Middle East of 2018 would end up being a place where you had an unfortunate rendezvous – maybe even with a bullet. Americans weren't popular, and by the time you explained your Irish citizenship, you might already be dead. What drove an ordinary Josephine to go from taking a pay cheque all the way to taking these kinds of risks? Was friendship enough to do that? Maybe she wasn't ordinary. How do you measure friendship or love, and how far do you bring it? Was it meant to bring you all the way to the grave, potentially?

She hadn't formed a lasting relationship with a boy or girl, despite trying both. Back in college, a flirtation with Aidan had fizzled out. But the two of them had maintained a bond – maybe as simple a bond as the one that sex ensures always exists between ex-lovers. She and Aidan had done the guts of eight years in TimeBox Dublin. Maybe it was time to move on?

She knew Jeff had used the bond between her and Aidan, knowing they would look out for each other. He left it to adults to respectively either keep their dick in their trousers or keep their panties on. As kids in the college years in Dublin at the turn of the millennium, they could hardly have imagined TimeBox and where it would lead.

*

The team had been through this drill before. Dale and Beth would be waiting at Cairo International with transport. The meeting arrangements were known but they involved splitting up into two groups. What annoyed Libby was that she only became aware of the arrangements once she had landed. Dale and Aidan were dropped at TimeBox HQ. Beth and Libby were off to meet Simone Haddad at a different address.

Beth pulled up outside an antique-looking sandstone building with a medieval-style moat. Definitely old world but the women, whether they realised it or not, were standing in antiquity.

'So, this is Martin Gabrielle's partner? Want me to come in with you?' asked Beth.

'Beth, as per instructions, they want one on ones.'

Libby crossed the bridge and was mesmerised once she entered the foyer. The room was circular. *How come it looked like a box from the outside?* She was facing the reception desk where a middle-aged Egyptian man was sitting. He had a fez on the desk beside him which left Libby wondering: *Is that for show or do these guys still wear those hats*? He addressed her in perfect English.

'You're here to see the Director?'

Before Libby could answer, Simone entered through the exhibition entrance door.

'Ms Hendrick, it might help you to know you are a welcome visitor, both to Cairo and here at our Coptic Museum.'

Libby was thinking quickly: *This place is dripping*

money, and man … the elegance of this creature.

'You know that my partner, Gabrielle, is one of the original twelve TimeBoxers. Only the main players remain. The survivors. Winners and losers, I guess. Attrition – natural, of course.'

'Well, thanks,' said Libby. 'I'm pleasantly surprised, I must admit.'

'Would you like to explore some of our Christian treasures?'

'Yeah, well, I'm from Ireland. We're up to our nuts in ancient texts and books.'

'Very well, please would you join me in my office?'

She didn't wait for an answer. Simone re-entered the exhibition space, veered to the right and ascended a spiral staircase. When they were seated, Simone at her desk and Libby on the far side, she continued.

'So, a book – a gospel, older than all the rest – is of no interest to you?'

'That's about the size of it,' said Libby. 'Look, I'm a bit pissed, to be honest. I came to meet Martin.'

'I'd better correct you.' Simone held up an open palm. 'He prefers to be called Gabrielle. It's that imperious Balkan thing.'

'Look, whatever, but I wanted to meet Gabrielle and the deal seems to be, my colleague Aidan gets into TimeBox Cairo and I get a night at the museum. Come on, you're a professional woman. Do you like playing second fiddle?'

'So, good news. You can lead the orchestra.'

'We want to recruit you and Aidan. Your man

Bourke is running on borrowed time in TimeBox. But it's no matter – it's your talent we're looking to harness. To give Bourke his due, he did recruit good people.'

'Well, yes, in their thousands,' Libby agreed. 'So why me and Aidan? And, to my earlier point, why not talk to us together at TimeBox HQ?'

'Divide and conquer.' Simone gestured with two outstretched closed palms, which she parted.

'You're honest.' Libby smiled the joyless smile of a woman who hated having her time wasted. 'In any event, I'm not a librarian. I'd be no good to you.'

'You're very dismissive of my work here. Minding the Christian equivalent of the Dead Sea Scrolls is worthy of world attention. It doesn't get it, of course. Christianity is a very lukewarm religion. But we digress. No, you'd be using your communication skills within the engine room of TimeBox. Maybe you might like to leave Dublin, for a change. Maybe head up Palo Alto?' Simone's bottomless hazel eyes were open wide, welcoming.

Instead of being shocked by the question, Libby found her own eyes wandering around the walls of her office. There was a beautiful symmetry to the framed stills that ran around the perimeter of the space. Libby's eyes were drawn circularly around the rectangular shape of the room. She took a moment while Simone observed her without blinking.

'What's all this?' asked Libby.

'My life's work.'

'I know you're a director here, TimeBox funding and all that, but still you've been here, what, seven years? That's a short lifetime.'

'These are the pages of the Gospel of Thomas. They are two thousand years old. They are the work of many lifetimes. I see biblical scholarship is not your forte, Elizabeth.'

'Listen,' said Libby. 'Maybe your partner might be having more luck with Aidan, but I guess I'm just an old-fashioned girl. I'll stick with the man Bourke.'

'But you're a lesbian, Elizabeth.'

'Not that kind of sticking,' said Libby.

'I only met Bourke once, I wasn't impressed.'

'I've never met Gabrielle, I'm not impressed either.'

The meeting had been short and not so sweet. Libby said her goodbyes with 'A pleasure to meet you.' She didn't mean it. 'I'll make my own way out.'

'Beth, drive us back to Gabrielle's office,' she said when she returned to the jeep. 'We'll pick up the boys.'

'I'm glad you're out safe and well,' said Beth.

'Thanks, Beth, but I think I was always going to be safe in a dusty old museum. Well, it was quite clean, actually, beautiful really.'

'Sure, sure …' Beth seemed relieved. 'It's just that the place is a fortress. One way in and one way out. A defender's wet dream.'

'Stop, stop! Too many sexual references for one day.'

'What does that mean?' asked Beth.

'Ah, nothing. Just the conversation with Gabrielle's woman. Stupid stuff – a betrayal, disguised as a job offer. She was OK really, a beautiful looking woman.

'You interested?'

'I'll pass, Beth. I never felt threatened. I just think all this "girls talk to girls, boys talk to boys" stuff is ... I don't know ... stupid. You should have let Dale come with me, just to break up the sexual symmetry.'

They were turning a corner in the El Sheikh Mubarak district, within sight of the TimeBox Cairo building. Aidan looked pale, sitting on the small entrance wall outside the modern compact two-storey office building. Dale was standing beside him.

'Oh, this doesn't look good, Beth.'

They pulled up beside them, but Aidan showed no resolve to stand up and enter the comfort of the air-conditioned jeep.

'What gives?' Beth asked Dale through the window.

'He's been roughed up for sure,' said Dale.

'What's the situation?' asked Beth.

'It's strange,' her husband replied. 'I've been in and there's not a soul around. I had a cam on the rear entrance. I've already reviewed it. Gabrielle never came out.'

'Well, then, he's still in there.'

'Beth, I know how to recon a building.' Dale squinted at her. 'Neither Gabrielle nor anybody else is in there, and no one came out.'

'Aidan? You OK?' asked Libby.

Aidan didn't answer.

'Look,' Dale said, 'I couldn't get anything out of him, so I did leave him to do the recce of the building.'

'You shouldn't have,' Beth said in a tone that didn't need much interpretation, She was well pissed off. 'Now do another one, just to humour me. You OK with that, Lib?' She had turned to Libby and now returned to her husband again. 'I told you we should have been in there with them. We were stupid to let Gabrielle dictate the terms.'

Dale re-entered the building with the ease of a soldier that knew he wasn't going to meet anybody. He knew his job.

The remaining trio were quiet for a short time. Then Aidan broke the silence.

'It's not all bad. He'll get us an interview with Assad if we want it.'

'Jesus,' Libby swore. 'The way you look, do you want to trek into Syria, or is it here – the meeting?'

Aidan paused. 'No, it's a trek all right.' Aidan was getting it together, but he was like a man recovering from a winding; he was taking his time.

'Well, if that's what our boss wants, well done,' said Libby. 'Look, Simone already told me that you'd be offered … Well, you could say a job, but really a bribe. So how did we go from that to a godforsaken trip to a war zone?'

Aidan remained sitting on the wall, still recovering himself. It was Saturday evening, beginning to grow dark.

'I can't really remember,' he said.

Dale was now re-emerging through the office front door.

'Not a sign.'

'Sorry we let you down, Aidan,' said Beth.

'Well,' Libby countered, 'it looks like you could make it up to him by keeping us alive in Syria.'

'When did that come up?' asked Dale.

'You can ask Aidan, now that he's talking again,' said Libby.

The road to Damascus was never going to be an easy one. It was simple for Jeff to encourage the team to make it. 'Wow, if we're getting blanked in Cairo, getting intel out of Bashar al-Assad would be a prize alright.' But he didn't have to make the two-day drive with two border crossings with Israel. Aidan had an abundance of time on the journey to curse him. And he did.

Beth seemed to feel that she and Dale owed them after what had happened in Cairo. They both shared the driving with stops only for fuel, toilet breaks and food on the run. Libby was glad to see Aidan moaning. It wasn't his norm, but at least he was lively again.

Assad might have been fighting a civil war since 2011, but it didn't stop him welcoming the arranged guests into his palace on Mount Mezzah.

'But of course, why would you be thinking that you'd be anything other than welcome guests to Damascus? Senior team of TimeBox. Now yes, I seem to attract more detractors than friends on your platform, but it is a battleground. Gabrielle has assured me of his support, and my government is grateful for such American-based support. Maybe I am an unwitting uniting force for both America and Russia. Imagine this,' said the president.

Libby was imagining it while Aidan's jaw dropped. This was either proper and extreme narcissism, or this man needed to use some form of Arab wit to keep himself afloat.

'What a success your company is, and you might acknowledge that is an Arab complimenting a Jewish CEO. I like to deal with Gabrielle simply because he likes to live in this piece of the world.'

Assad clapped his hands loudly and a male waiter entered the reception room. A beautiful aroma of coffee filled the nostrils of the Irish duo. The doors that TimeBox opened were impressive. They were not always pleasant. Libby knew about leaders. She had met a few in her time in Europe. Just enough, mind you, to ensure that you could tell the real thing.

This guy led his country by force and money, and he needed and used lots of both. In bed with Putin – *well, if you lie with dogs?* Their journey to Damascus from Egypt had left them dusty and dishevelled. At least they had got an audience with the president of Syria; who else was doing that? The duo had never felt particularly in danger, with vigilant Dale and Beth in control. Assad ruled the airspace with his Russian buddies. You could rail at the hypocrisy, the evil of the regime. However, when your mission was to visit and assess the situation, you were glad your neck was protected – even by a guy who you wouldn't be able to justify pissing on if he was on fire. The Irish team's new information was the revelation that this man was happy to be on Gabrielle's payroll.

Assad ushered the delegation to be seated in a luxurious sofa away from his desk, on the casual side of his thickly carpeted office. His two aides remained standing by his side while he sat in an adjoining armchair. Libby felt the need to explain.

'Our guides encouraged us not to keep you waiting, Mister President. A road trip through the Golan Heights would leave you a little dusty. Our apologies.'

Assad went straight into it. 'Obviously your company has made reparations to us to compensate for your earlier meddling in our affairs. This is what I mean – I'm bringing you Americans and the Russians back closer together. Who would have thought it? My doors are always open to Gabrielle's people. I have never met your Mr Zimmerman.'

Aidan felt the ground shift from under him. Libby showed through her eye contact with him that she was on edge. They had taken on this difficult assignment at Jeff's request: 'Yes, great, go find out how deep we're in with the Assad Regime.' They had only taken a first sip of the coffee and Assad had already spilled the beans. TimeBox had got the uprising going, and the greasy till was open for reparations.

Libby got a thought flashing through her brain: *It*

would be nothing for this guy to just poison us and move on if that's what Gabrielle wanted.

The thought dissipated with the reasoning that Assad could have had them disappear long before they got their dusty asses plonked on his Arabian sofa. The penny was going to drop some time or other that this was the Bourke versus Gabrielle show. Assad – if he didn't know it already – wouldn't take long to work out that he was talking to the opposition.

Libby and Aidan made their report back to Jeff after their return to Dublin. In the end they flew out of Tel Aviv. The jeep was abandoned.

The report for Egypt was as strange as their one for Damascus, but for completely different reasons. There was no possibility of meeting President al-Sisi. TimeBox Cairo had no labs, no factories, no apparent pharma connections except for Cairo University. Jeff's theory was that a TimeBox outfit had spent more than a billion dollars … on what? The new useful information had come from Syria: that Assad, through his own testimony, was a recipient of TimeBox funding.

'Gabrielle seems to spend time in the university,' said Libby. 'I got that from his partner, Simone, who … wait for it … is director of the Coptic Museum, whatever that is. These people are in Cairo for the long haul.'

'Aidan, what did you get out of Gabrielle?' asked Jeff.

'Firstly, we learnt one thing from Assad that we should have known from Gaddafi.'

'And that was?'

'That you have a habit of sending us on huge journeys to attend very short meetings. And as regards what I got out of Gabrielle. Fuck all, Jeff, except that he is one dangerous bastard.'

Jeff was, for a moment, rocked back in his seat. 'Look, you're back safe. Maybe that's the main thing.'

'Not exactly a lot of intel for Congress,' said Libby.

'At least we went, you went' said Jeff. 'That's no small thing. I can spin that, especially if I can get Assad's comments read into the evidence.'

'I'm just saying that place was dangerous,' said Libby.

'And we got nothing,' Aidan added. 'So, what was the point?'

'Aidan, I'm not taking anything away from your bravery, but let's go over it again.' It was Jeff's turn to be annoyed and his tone demonstrated it. 'Assad is in bed with Putin, and Putin effectively rigged – yes, rigged – the '16 election. Yes, I was taking a chance, a long shot, that we might get a golden nugget of information.'

'Well, maybe next time you'll put your own life on the line.'

'Aidan, for God's sake, where's this coming from?' asked Libby, facing him from across their boardroom table.

'No, Libby, he's making a fair point,' Jeff agreed.

'It's my turn to go into battle, but it will be in Washington. I'll promise you this – if there's a need to go back, I'll go myself, if it comes to it.'

'Come on, Aidan,' Libby protested, 'it wasn't that bad.'

Aidan got up, said nothing, and left Libby sitting alone.

'Wasn't expecting that,' said Jeff.

'Looks like PTSD to me. There wasn't a bother on him on the flight home. Well, he had a good few drinks, I guess. We've been on his back to say what happened with his one-on-one with Gabrielle.'

'And?

'And nothing. Look, let him calm down and I'll have another go. Why he doesn't bother to hang with a significant other kind of worries me.'

'Look who's talking.' Jeff grinned but he soon stopped when he gauged Libby's expression.

'Now, Jeff, I mightn't have a steady, but you know my orientation.'

'Yeah, but it wasn't always that way, was it? You guys had your thing and … Look, I think he still loves you. There – I've said it and AJ agrees.'

'Jeff, thanks for the theory, but I might prefer if my sexuality wasn't discussed so openly.'

'It's with my partner,' said Jeff.

'Even so …'

Libby left the conference room, leaving Jeff looking at an empty room on screen.

Jeff went to look for AJ.

'Can I tell you what just happened?'

He did, and the response was short and less than sweet.

'What did you expect?'

18

By the time the 2016 US election battle was raging, Jeff had firmly made the connection between this 'war' and the Arab Spring, five years earlier. They were both fuelled by TimeBox.

By 2018, the American media had been stoked up enough to show interest in the alleged Trump versus Clinton election manipulation. Jeff had been selectively leaking data analytics to the *Washington Post*, while dressing it up to stir up public opinion. But nobody had died in the 2016 election. Thousands had died in the Arab countries, with the carnage in Syria continuing relentlessly. Jeff wanted the two subjects connected in the minds of the American public.

That's where Jeff's humanity stood. If it started with being concerned with young adults killing themselves, it had morphed into: 'What the hell went on, is going on in North Africa? Do Muslim lives not matter?'

The very message 'tagging' algorithm, invented by the original TimeBoxers to take on the banks, had been used to unsettle Hillary Clinton's campaign for the presidency. Worse, it had been used to start a firestorm in the previously stable Arab states – the ones that had escaped the Bush wars. What Jeff wanted to do was get the US Congress interested. The *Post* had been reluctant to create the pressure for investigating TimeBox's involvement in the Arab Spring. Jeff knew he himself would have to be the whistle-blower. There would be no going back. He knew that, even as he pressed 'send' on the email to Speaker Ryne. He was writing to the same Senate where not a single Republican had called out Trump for his antics of the previous two years.

It was a flimsy enough book of evidence regarding testimony. Gaddafi was on the record – a dead man – but not President al-Sisi, and only Assad if Aidan's verbal testimony was admissible. What was to Jeff's advantage was the overwhelming technical evidence of the use of robotic 'friends' by the Russians against Hillary Clinton, and by TimeBox Egypt in turning the Arabs against one another.

The 115th Congress Select Committee session to investigate certain matters relating to TimeBox opened on 26 November 2018.

The viewing gallery was full by the time the six committee members filed into the chamber and took their seats behind the imposing dark wood bench. If the room was trying not to look like a court of law, it was failing miserably.

AJ could feel her whole body tighten sitting in a huddle with Jeff, Libby and Aidan. They sat on the ground floor as required of witnesses. Zimmerman and Gabrielle were happy to watch from the upstairs balcony which seemed to be crammed with media.

The chairperson, Senator Rachel Weisman, adjusted her microphone. The TV cameras were primed.

'All in attendance should note the business of this committee is twofold,' Weisman began.

'Matter one. Was TimeBox involved in certain actions that contributed to the phenomenon referred to as the Arab Spring in 2011?

'Matter two. Was TimeBox involved in certain actions that contributed to the outcome of the US presidential election of 2016?

'I will ask the committee members to introduce themselves from my left to right.'

'Senator Marcus Borg, Oregon.'

'Representative Dominic Crossan, Ohio.'

'Senator Jeff Douglas, Maryland.'

'Representative John Pender, Maine.'

'Representative Elizabeth Painter, Illinois.'

'Let the record show the following email correspondence presented from Mr Gordon Rutherford dated June 7 2015.' Senator Rachel Weisman scrolled through her laptop. 'Let it be noted that Mr Rutherford does not challenge the assertion that he was an employee, at the time of writing, of President Trump. Please note that the following was also published by the *Washington Post* on November 11 2016.

> *'Tell Mr. P from me, if he can pull this off, he will be my new best friend, and you know best friends*

do favours for each other, don't they? If H gets the job, it will be sanction this and block that. You know how it is.

'This is the great thing about having a huge country at your disposal, with a whole load of low-paid professionals that you don't let out of the country.

'TimeBox is all about being happy-clappy and making Zimmerman plenty rich, even plenty richer than P, but I forgot, nobody knows how rich P is.

'Think about it. The bots take on a persona and make lots and lots of social media friends with real American voters, young and old. Then you subtly bombard your new friends with messages that sow the seeds. Like Hillary is not as sweet as apple pie. That's huge. Why? Because deep down a lot of voters remember Hillary taking a swipe at dear old Barbara Bush. Exactly over describing Babs as a sweet old lady who stayed home to mind the stove while her man ran the country.

'You don't come out and say "Hey everybody, H is a roaring bitch." You sow seeds like, "Maybe H is a roaring bitch and by the way please feel free to reach your own conclusion, thank you very much." Emotional intelligence, my ass. Yes, you will, or it's at least good that you think you made up your own mind.

'Our contact in Cairo will assist with IP addresses. For obvious reasons we don't want to show up with too many "friends" from actual

Russia. If you're serious about helping this thing, our man Mr G will assist, guaranteed. This election will be won again on social media. Just ask Obama.

End of email.'

Chairperson Weisman closed her laptop before continuing.

'Could the record please show that the aforementioned email, now read into evidence, was electronically signed, "From the Offices of Donald Trump".'

The opening evidence was incendiary. But it was old and the gallery barely reacted. People were already used to strange behaviour from their president.

The schism that had been developing maybe since Jeff had discussed a young girl's suicide with AJ, way back at Christmas 2010, was set in concrete. There would be no going back. After the dangers of expeditions to North Africa and Syria, there was no moral compass that would bring you back. Jeff was only on the payroll because keeping a whistle-blower on the inside was a damage limitation strategy.

There had been too much blood, too many deaths. Any lingering respect or gratitude that Jeff had felt towards Zimmerman was gone. The gloves were off.

Even with turmoil around him in the Congressional Chamber – media, TV cameras and glare – his mind was refusing to play ball and concentrate. His head had wandered back to how rough the meeting in Cairo between Gabrielle and Aidan had got. Just Gabrielle in his office and Aidan, within sight of old Cairo. A Saturday evening in the Egyptian heat. Aidan never admitted how rough it had got. He did admit he felt complimented to be granted a one-on-one meeting while Libby was dispatched to a museum. Libby could hold her own if it came to a scrap. Running around distressed Arab countries would build up that resilience for sure. Not quite the job description she or Aidan had bought into when they took the job, but there it was. Aidan had changed.

Jeff's mind came back to the present when Chairperson Weisman invited Libby to take the stand.

'Ms Hendrick, you're now invited to read into the record your account of pertinent evidence obtained in Damascus, September 2018.'

Libby was nervous. She was wearing a smart grey knee-length skirt and white blouse. Just like a trial, you were on full view as you made your way to the witness table. One chair, one table and two microphones.

'I hope she's wearing the strongest of deodorants,' AJ whispered into Aidan's ear.

'Stop, will you, I'm nervous enough already.'

Libby fielded questions from her testimony on the meeting with Assad. Only Senator Borg and Representative Crossan had something to ask.

They were both keen to explore Assad's line about 'bringing America and Russia closer together'.

'I hope, Ms Hendrick, you were able to disavow Mr Assad on that notion,' Crossan had said.

It seemed linking an American corporation to

Assad was not a good picture to explore.

'Your turn,' she murmured into Aidan's ear as she passed him on the way back to her seat. Aidan was more awkward in shuffling his blue-suited bulk up to the witness table. As he sat, he could feel the residual heat left behind from Libby.

'Mr Mulcahy,' Chairperson Weisman began, 'you're now invited to read into the record your account of pertinent evidence obtained in Libya, February 2011.'

Jeff and AJ were surprised that Aidan's account of events met with no great response either.

Representative Painter asked, 'Did you feel you were dealing with a sane man?' Aidan had answered 'yes' and Senator Douglas followed up, wanting to know 'if an assertion that executing students who found themselves studying in Cairo was in fact a sane suggestion?'

Aidan was glad to be returning to his seat. He was sweating under his jacket.

When Weisman called his name, Jeff shuffled his way out of the gallery and into the witness area. *Seconds out, the main event.*

Jeff took his stand. The thinner guy was more manoeuvrable when it came to shuffling out of the row of seats designed for the smaller bodies of a hundred years ago. Washington was old. Jeff was used to scrutiny. He felt calm and well prepared. He did regret choosing a blue suit to wear. It made him and Aidan look like they were in uniform.

'Mr Bourke,' Weisman began, 'would you tell

the committee about your knowledge concerning the phenomenon called the Arab Spring?'

'I was aware that TimeBox had been used since late 2010 to promote an uprising in Egypt.' He paused to think out how to steer his answer in the way he wanted the questioning to go. 'It seemed to me, at the time, to be the strangest of moves to establish an office in Cairo. Then the whole revolution kicked off.' Jeff was staying focused and thinking, *I've been through this type of grilling a hundred times. You know the drill. Disarm them by taking your time. Be sure in your answers.*

'When did you become aware of the information upon which you base your accusation?' Representative Painter asked.

'My team, within the company, have been conducting extensive research on the ground in North Africa. This was done even during the height of the uprisings.'

'Was that not a dangerous undertaking for a private organisation?'

'Yes, it was, but we did take the necessary precaution of hiring private security consultants. Former US military personnel.'

'What was this, Mr Bourke?' Painter threw her eyes up to heaven. 'A modern-day crusade? What was your motivation?'

'I … *We* first became aware that things were not right with TimeBox for a completely different reason. We were concerned about suicides, first among American teenagers, and then among young people in Europe and Australia.'

'A little bit selective of you, perhaps?' Until this point, Senator Borg's contributions had been limited to nodding. Now his tone was hard.

'Well, it's just that you get more accessible media reporting in the developed world.' Jeff smiled. 'No mystery there.'

'And your findings?' asked Representative Crossan.

'About what?' Jeff seemed slightly thrown by the question.

'About suicide?'

'That there was an unfortunate and unforeseen downside to our product. Vulnerable YAs – young adults – were pushed too far on occasion. Obviously not by TimeBox itself, but by commentary on the platform, sometimes sexually explicit stuff.'

'Was there orchestration involved?' Weisman asked.

'No, we didn't believe that.' As soon as he said it, he felt unnerved. *Oh fuck, maybe it was orchestrated.* 'We thought it was just a new learning, a poor outcome. Remember, we were dealing with a new product, a new form of social interaction.'

'Mr Bourke,' Senator Douglas interjected, 'would you please address the committee in the first person? This committee is giving you – *you* – the opportunity to offer your evidence of wrongdoing. We cannot recognise "we".'

'Sure, understood, not a problem,' said Jeff. 'I have a team, including my partner, that's all. Some of those people – all of the "we" – have put their lives in danger to get to the truth, that's all.' Jeff was deliberately offhand in his remarks. Trying to turn the tables. *Does bravery not matter here?*

'These ball-busters are getting under his skin,' Libby whispered into AJ's ear.

'I noticed, thanks.'

'In any event, we've moved off the agenda.' Weisman glanced to both sides of her chair at the other committee members. 'Suicide statistics is not the "matter" under consideration at this hearing. That's an entire digression. We'll move on, please.'

'Very good, Mr Bourke, but it's ten years now since you became the poster boy for TimeBox.' Douglas was reluctant to let the matter drop. 'You seemed happy enough to be the "I" of the company then, so we will stick to the "I" now, please.'

'Sure.' Jeff's tone was dismissive. Libby was right, they were getting under his skin. 'This is minor stuff in comparison to the waste of young lives which TimeBox has had a role in, unwitting or not.'

'Again, not relevant to the scope of the committee.' Weisman was staring directly at the witness over her glasses. 'Please strike that assertion from the record. Now, could we get on?'

'Let's get back on track.' Senator Borg was keen to keep Jeff in the hot seat. 'What were your findings relevant to Egypt and other locations?'

'That there was a black ops research centre within TimeBox.'

The gallery responded with their loudest chatterings so far.

'Quiet, please,' boomed Weisman.

'Black ops?' Senator Douglas repeated with a speed that indicated his thoughts – *not going there.* 'Mr Bourke, please, no accusations without back-up testimony.'

'Once it was proven that our social media engine was agile, in the sense of influencing behaviour, it became apparent that social experiments were going on in a quite systematic way.'

'Well?' Weisman sounded unconvinced. 'Please elaborate?'

'That TimeBox used a tech lab to invent social influencing techniques,' said Jeff. 'The social media platform had exploded just at the point in time when the world economy was deciding if it had the gumption to recover. Knowing that the product had demonstrated a certain level of power – power over innocent young people, the influence that sometimes resulted in death – some persons in the organisation took this knowledge to a new experimental level. North Africa was a bit "out of sight, out of mind". A perfect place to establish a network of IP address friends. A pitch where you could sow the seeds of insurrection, sit back and watch it happen.'

'It's generally accepted that the Arab Spring had its origin in Egypt.' Apart from directing a few routine questions at the earlier witnesses, Senator Elizabeth Painter had been silent for most of the proceedings. Now she was leaning forward urgently from the end of the committee bench.

'A well-chosen location for many reasons.' Jeff was in full flow, confident, with the hope of not appearing arrogant.

'Such as?' asked Painter.

'My colleague, Martin Gabrielle, had ... *has* extensive links with the regime and the country. I know that TimeBox's offices there were opened quietly in 2010. I only found out about it at a meeting in early 2011. You may think that I'm a big noise in the company, but I hold no sway regarding Cairo. I've also submitted a transcript of my team's attempt to visit the Cairo office in 2013.'

'But you yourself did not go?' asked Senator Douglas.

'No, I did not,' said Jeff. 'As you heard in Elizabeth Hendrick's and Aidan Mulcahy's testimonies, Cairo was off limits to me and my team. I can tell you that huge funding was channelled to Syria by TimeBox Cairo. I'm not commenting on tax matters here, but there's a funding trail that was designed to keep things tight, shall we say, as the submitted evidence shows.'

'But the Arab Spring was an unmitigated failure,' Representative Pender interjected. 'By your own admission, TimeBox is a well-received organisation within a now stable Egyptian government.'

'Well, there are many lenses through which you could view that sentiment.' Jeff saw an opportunity to hit home and he went for it. 'If you wanted to see setting up a population for a bloodbath as a success, you could. At the time, this was technology meeting psychology in a new way and for the first time. The instruction book hadn't been, and hasn't been, written. You're connected to a whole new farm of friends you've never met. The power of the group, and the power of instant connection. How dangerous can that be, and how manipulatable?'

'But that's conjecture, Mr Bourke, not evidence,' said Chairperson Weisman.

'Egypt, Libya and Tunisia were TimeBox experiments used to direct a change. But was it ever to be a change for the good?

'He's going all in, our Jeff,' Libby whispered.

'Mr Bourke …' It was clear from her tone that Representative Painter was losing patience. 'Could we get you back on the point?'

'Sure,' said Jeff. 'The dirty tricks lab at TimeBox had no business – no *right* – to be manipulating IP addresses for the express mission of executing regime change. That goes for the US as well as these Arab states.'

The gallery erupted and the Chair found herself smashing her paperweight off the table and calling for, 'Order, order.' It took a time.

'Well, there was regime change, as you call it, in Libya, in Tunisia …' Chairperson Weisman ticked them off on her fingers. 'Not so in Egypt and Bahrain, and maybe not so in Syria.'

'Success or failure, they all sure did achieve the same thing,' Jeff retorted. 'Bloodshed, and lots of it.'

'Quiet in the gallery, quiet please,' Weisman shouted.

'Mr Bourke, please ...' Representative Pender's patience was frayed if his tone of voice was the indicator. 'Please, you are a multi-millionaire through your undoubted hard work. Are you seriously claiming that your commercial organisation had a vested interest in seeing people killed for no other reason than to prove the power of social influencing? You must know how incredible that sounds.'

There was murmuring from the gallery. Quieter this time. Representative Pender paused for effect. This was making for good TV.

'Fucking actor,' Libby whispered to Aidan.

Positive or negative? AJ thought.

Pender continued, 'Regardless of its misguided use by individuals or groups ... we're talking about a modern American business. Even if we give such ravings a hearing ... If nothing else, how can a business prosper from seeing its customers killed? There is, you must agree, no revenue to be gained from dead people.' The representative was practically roaring by the time he got to 'dead people'.

Jeff stayed deliberately calm. 'I know, but there are still facts here – data analytics. It's bad enough to see your product implicated in the various unrests of recent African and Middle Eastern history. That's bad, but to be actively involved is ... well, a crime.'

'So ...' Weisman sought to restore order again with the paper weight. 'You're saying Mr Zimmerman and

Mr Gabrielle have participated in criminal activity?'

'Yes, I am.'

'You cannot be serious, Mr Bourke.' Pender's tone was incredulous.

By this time, the audience in the public gallery was exercised.

Was that booing? AJ asked herself.

'Silence in the chamber, please,' Weisman boomed.

Above the clamour, Jeff carried on combatively.

'Oh, I'm serious. You're a legislator, and I'm pointing out that social media is free to do what it likes. It's self-regulated, and there are some of us who would claim that self-regulation is no regulation. So, you're correct – there may be no crime because there is no law. But if a single drop of blood has been spilt, never mind a whole river full of it, for commercial or other purposes, then it's time to call that out.'

Jeff knew full well that the media would be running that quote on the 5.00 EST news.

'This was incendiary,' AJ whispered to Libby, beside her on the bench. 'It's all in. I hope he knows he's going for broke.'

Painter leaned forward again. 'This committee, I'm sure, would agree with calling out criminality – if you weren't stretching credulity. Simply again, how can you argue for gain out of people's deaths?'

'You can't.' Jeff lowered his tone deliberately and then raised it to say, 'And that is why I will not rest till I discover what the motivation is. I can tell you of factual findings. That cloud servers were used to flood all selected TimeBox account holders with a message stream designed to have a giant psychological punch. If you're searching for #jihad, #Taliban, #HillaryNO, then the artificial intelligence will give you access to extremist sites and messages, contacts, websites in abundance.'

By this point Jeff had lost perspective. He was just dishing it out with both barrels.

'Quite the hero,' Representative Pender said tetchily.

'As I say, we did our best. It was dangerous.'

'Now you're no longer the blue-eyed boy at TimeBox,' Representative Painter pressed, 'is it time to get a shot in against the company owner?'

The gallery liked it. The noise – the tone – told you Jeff's supporters were outnumbered.

'It's time to call out pure evil,' said Jeff.

'Mr Bourke,' Representative Pender shouted, 'is your evidence not just sour grapes on a scale that has you warrant a congressional hearing into your gripes? Egomania and narcissism on a grand scale, is it not?'

'That is disrespectful to the team of people who I asked to collect intelligence by visiting damn dangerous places.' AJ was cringing from the gallery. *You're letting this man get under your skin.* 'They were there at my request to put things right when the two "heroes" of TimeBox had, according to our findings, screwed it all up.'

Jeff took the opportunity to look up to the balcony.

'Mr Bourke, please.' Weisman removed her glasses

and stared hard into Jeff's face. 'You're not in an Irish bar now, sir.'

'More's the pity,' Jeff mumbled under his breath.

Gabrielle and Zimmerman were in the gallery, watching, expressionless, listening to Jeff's testimony. Just playing the game, doing the deals. You didn't get elected – and stay in office – in the States without money, and a lot of it. Playing a trump card you might call it.

19

The remainder of the hearing that week was a data nerd's fiesta. What servers hosted where, how many bots, IP address patterns … Both Chairperson Rachel Weisman and Representative Elizabeth Painter stuck with it, the forensic detail. The four men of the committee looked either bored or in need of a drink by the end of that phase of the evidence.

Jeff and AJ rebooked their hotel room now that it was clear the hearing would run into the following week. Aidan and Libby did the same. The friends were sharing a suite a couple of blocks away.

Jeff collapsed onto the hotel room bed. 'AJ, is this choreographed? Our evidence finishes on Friday. So … what? We stew here in a Washington hotel room over the weekend, waiting to hear what the two "wise men" have to say?'

'One wise man,' AJ corrected him. 'They're not calling Gabrielle.'

He sat up. 'When did you hear that?'

'It's just come up on Fox – an exclusive.'

'Doesn't sound great, does it?'

'No, honey, it doesn't. They're calling it the

Weisman, Pender and Painter show.' She sat down beside him, exhausted. 'Jeff, I have to say they hate you talking about your pet subject, North Africa.'

'What do you mean? You know how seriously I take what went on there.'

AJ could sense she was dealing with a pressure keg. The trick was to stop it from blowing.

'I know, I know, but they are steering you away from the Arab Spring. They are more interested in election fixing – they can justify that, it affects them directly. These guys don't want a US corporate implicated in Arab rabble rousing, that's all.'

'Look, why don't we just take a break from it all and get dinner together?' asked Jeff.

'Honey, you know you're not going to exclude Libby and Aidan,' said AJ. 'They have travelled over for this. You guys are joined at the hip. I've no problem with them tagging along.'

'No – tonight it's just me and you.'

'Jeff, are you thinking straight?' AJ was looking at him.

'What do you mean exactly?'

'We go out and the press will nail us. Is it worth it?' she asked.

'You're right.' He shook his head from side to side. 'I'm not thinking straight. I don't know why. What about room service, and that way we're not slighting L and A. Maybe they'll get a chance to rekindle an old flame.'

'That's a cheap shot, come on.' AJ turned away

from him and gazed out of the window. She took her time, taking in the view, the pristine white Capitol building in the distance. Keeping a lid on her partner all week was wearing. 'It's clear now they have no job to go back to, and neither do you. Honey, why don't you check in with Anne over the weekend?'

'Sure, I'll do that. You're right – I'm talking stupid. Right now, maybe a glass of wine?'

'Oh, you're Irish all right, no denying.'

She was brighter now. The explosion was averted … at least for now.

'I don't know exactly what's going on in America,' Anne Bourke said after she and her son had exchanged their pleasantries. 'You look a bit drawn on RTE news, son. Is that American girl looking after you?'

'For God's sake, Mam,' Jeff said with a raised voice that made AJ cringe in the other room. 'I'm only even able to talk to ye because of the way she props me up.'

'Only saying, only saying.'

Jeff could picture his mother. She'd never moved house after Liam died. The memories. She would be sitting out in hallway where the landline was installed.

'God, ye don't have to take the head off me when I'm only concerned about ye.'

'Yeah, sure, Mam, I know,' said Jeff. 'I do know,' he repeated, softly this time.

'So, what do ye do now?'

'Well, you said yourself, I don't take enough time off. I might have it now. What's the Irish media saying?'

'Nothing good, I'm afraid,' Anne replied. 'You know the tabloids. "In bed with Gaddafi and Assad."'

'Turncoat bastards, I'll have to get my lawyers to look at that.' Jeff paused for a moment. 'Look, Mam, I do appreciate ye taking the call.'

'Stop, Jeff, will ye, it's your mother you're taking to, not your solicitor.'

'Sorry, Mam, you're right. I think I'll go rest. Too many knock-downs for one day.'

Anne had never felt so isolated from her only son when he hung up.

AJ was happy to have Aidan and Libby over with them on both Saturday and Sunday. Room service and at least knowing that their time at the witness table was done brought a sense of relief.

'I'm heading home when this is done. The parents are settling into their assisted living set-up. I want to be around,' said Aidan.

'Well, life goes on, give them our love,' said AJ.

'It goes on, but we all know things will be different,' said Libby.

'Pity we don't have Beth and Dale here,' said AJ.

'Jesus, when I think of it, that drive up through Israel, wow. Libby was making herself at home, wandering around the apartment with a glass of wine in tow. The Holy Land, the dangerous land more like.'

'Young Dylan isn't well, asthma. Like you say, life goes on,' said Jeff. He was enjoying a drink as well. Enjoying it a bit too much in AJ's opinion.

*

The media were out in even more force on Monday morning as the hearing re-convened. Jeff reacted when AJ was jostled walking up the steps of the hearing chamber. Grabbing a man with a camera roughly on the shoulder was not a good look to begin the week with.

'But Madame Chairperson,' David Zimmerman said smoothly, 'we have satellite offices all over the developing world. Identifying Cairo is random. Why not identify Shanghai, or Casablanca?'

That brought a bit of tittering from the benches.

To AJ, the titter signalled something. The questioning of her husband had seemed tetchy – caustic, even. That could have been an organic thing. Listening to serious issues with the eyes of the world looking on would probably create a natural tension in any group from Congress. They'd welcome a bit of levity. What worried AJ was that the change of mood signalled something else. America in 2018 was not ready to disown a leading light in the business world – let alone one who was on good terms with the president. AJ was trying to be Jeff's rock. She knew he wouldn't pick up on the vibe, and she had to decide how to alert him – how to soften the blow, when it came. She knew it would. It seemed that debating the two issues – Arabs and elections – in the same Congressional hearing gave the committee a lot of room for deflection. Fighting on two fronts: one too many.

'The Zimmer' was good at deflection. A Teflon man.

'Look …' Zimmerman sipped his mineral water and looked at each member of the committee in turn. 'Maybe a degree of light touch regulation would be good, and you know there are many social media platforms available to users now. TimeBox is not a monopoly, not anymore, not by a long shot and not for a long time. Yes, it would seem, when you look at the traffic profiles, that the Russkies were very trigger-happy with messages relating to our election.'

Again, a bit of giggling. AJ's spirit was sinking further. This was looking more and more like a good old boys' club. Jeff wasn't going to be the winner. She held his hand.

'These accusations are radically different,' Zimmerman continued. 'Hillary Clinton may have been hard done by, but I'll say this again. Nobody died. To associate TimeBox with the murder of Arabs … Well, you know that is heinous. If you tell me that our platform was used by orchestrators of violence in various Arab states, then so be it. But to accuse me – us – of wilful involvement in murder … I mean, come on.'

'Mr Zimmerman.' Representative Painter initially smiled at him and quickly adjusted her face for the cameras. 'Your employee has led us down a path that says TimeBox used its algorithms, first in relation to the Arab Spring, and then in relation to the 2016 presidential election. Do you agree with his analysis?'

'It's just not true.'

'Well, explain, please,' said Weisman.

'Look …' Zimmerman took a moment to collect his thoughts. 'If Russia used our platform to influence our election, then that is a lesson that we must embrace – improve, be better, be regulated, even. But, like I said, nobody died. To the best of my knowledge, Hillary Clinton is happily ensconced on a highly paid lecture circuit. Many Americans are delighted with their choice of forty-fifth president. I accept that our engine can be used in unexpected and not always positive ways. But, come on … Orchestrated carnage? A little too far, methinks.'

At this point, AJ knew for sure that Jeff wasn't going to be the winner.

With the testimonies almost over, TimeBox would be the winner. Zimmerman had a simple strategy to sacrifice part of its reputation. *Those nasty Russians.* He could then shield the company from nefarious undertakings. *North Africa, nothing to see here.* It was a good day's work from him. Even better, the time was now ripe for his showdown with Jeff Bourke.

On Wednesday morning, Senator Weisman used her large paper weight to call for a bit of order in the chamber.

'If we could have order in the chamber, please … I will now read the findings of Congressional Investigative Hearing 114. That is, that is if we can have complete silence.' She sure could boom it out when she wanted to. She needed to, the chamber was buzzing loudly. Weisman got to her feet at this point.

'Thank you, ladies and gentlemen.' Ignoring the buzz of excitement from the gallery, Weisman focused on the piece of paper in her hand. 'I will now read the finding into the record.

'In the matter that TimeBox's social media platform was used clandestinely by entities emerging from Russia to influence the outcome of the 2016 presidential election …' She paused for a moment as silence fell. 'We find the case substantially proven.'

A clatter of applause. Weisman returned her gaze to her notes.

'In the matter that TimeBox's social media platform was used assertively by the company to directly orchestrate and promote the phenomenon commonly known as the Arab Spring …' A nervous cough from the gallery was the only sound. 'We find the case substantially unproven.'

More applause, with a few cheers thrown in.

20

The media scrum on the steps of the north wing of the Capitol building was manic. Jeff and AJ were jostled for comment. *Where were Beth and Dale when you needed them?* Aidan tried to shield AJ from the cameras, which only meant that the slightly framed Libby got left a little behind. This was going to be a new world. The cloak of protection that Jeff had worn, being a senior executive in a global company, was gone. The reputation of a flagship symbol of American entrepreneurialism had been vindicated and the media had a 'Paddy' as a fall guy. AJ felt her man physically leaning on her. The barrage of questions and the shouting weren't helping.

'Mr Bourke, do you feel you have betrayed—?'

'Jeff, were you duped by Arab terrorists?'

Aidan and Jeff shouldered their way through the pack of journalists, ignoring the cameras and microphones being shoved towards their faces. Fox News was out in force. There was the added whiff of a Republican versus Democrat victory. So much for a non-partisan committee.

From the safety of their car, Jeff responded to the bing of his mobile.

'That didn't take long,' he said. 'It's Zimmerman.'

'Well,' AJ smirked, 'winners gloat even if they bought their victory. What does the asshole want?'

'A meeting tonight, eight o'clock, the Four Seasons.'

'Are you going?' When Jeff didn't answer, she said, 'Well, you're not going alone, that's for sure. Not after what happened with Aidan.'

'They're still in the full glare of the media, love, no way could they be that stupid.'

AJ looked at him. 'Expect the unexpected.'

'Let's get back to the hotel, we'll figure it out.'

Without Beth and Dale, Jeff had asked Aidan to drive and Libby to come along for support. AJ would have preferred trained security.

'Libby, will you wander into the lobby?' Jeff asked when the car pulled up outside the hotel. 'You can tell me what route to take to the elevator. I want to avoid being seen, if possible.'

'You sure you feel safe going up on your own?' Libby asked. 'Why don't we go up with you?'

'I didn't tell AJ,' Jeff said in a low voice as if she was listening, 'but Gabrielle shouted in the background of the phone invite. He said he'd seen enough of you pair in Cairo. Must be sore you didn't accept his job offer. Aidan, you call it. Am I in trouble here?'

'Like you said, Jeff,' Aidan frowned. 'They're a pair of fucks, but not a pair of stupid fucks.'

Jeff found the two of them easily enough: in a functional hotel conference room, fifth floor. This was going to be all business and no frills.

Zimmerman was sitting at a long table with Gabrielle standing close by.

'Jeffrey, my man, you have to go,' Zimmerman said without preamble. 'You can't be at the heart of TimeBox's mission.'

'Good man, David.' Jeff was raging. He knew he must be colouring, red in the face. '"Mission" is a good word. You're good at words.'

'Of course,' Zimmerman replied smoothly. 'TimeBox is all about the written word. It was dying and I brought it back, with you and Gabrielle, my generals, on board. You did much for our cause. It made you plenty rich, and now you're waiting in the wings to stab your Caesar.'

'Jesus, David, you're acting here. You're right – it is a drama – but have you no shame?' Jeff was shaking his head from side to side. 'You're calling yourself "Caesar" now. Wow, are you too far gone?'

'Now, Jeff, you've done well out of this.' Zimmerman had seemed calmer in the media glare on the Congress chamber.

Let him raise his voice all he likes, thought Jeff.

'So it's a bit late to be doing a holier-than-thou routine, Bourke.'

'Aidan was acting for me when he got well roughed up by black Gabrielle in his dark Cairo office.'

Jeff was looking at Gabrielle, trying hard to reflect his utter contempt but feeling as if he was dealing with impenetrable lead.

'You were given explicit instructions, by me, to stay out of Egypt,' Zimmerman snapped. 'That included your little weaponised unit.'

'So not obeying an instruction is the new language for making yourself liable to be murdered?'

'Come on, my man. Getting a few slaps in a rough country is hardly akin to murder.'

Gabrielle had said nothing up to this point. He leaped from his position beside Zimmerman's chair and grabbed Jeff with both hands around the neck. The pain and the force jolted his head back.

A fleeting stream of thoughts flashed through Jeff's mind. Even now, he recognised that Zimmerman's tone had eased him into a false sense of security. He knew – and Zimmerman knew – the cat was well out of the bag. But to kill? Had they planned this? How was his body to be disposed of or explained away? A vision crossed Jeff's mind: Zimmerman trying to nuzzle up to the media with crocodile tears about his demise. Fleeting seconds as the air was squeezed out of Jeff's lungs. The strength of this guy. No need for Zimmerman to lift a finger. Jeff was a fit thirty-five-year-old. But he felt powerless, and the thought of death seemed to be showing itself as a horribly acceptable alternative to this severe pain in his crushed windpipe.

'If you can still hear me, Bourke,' Gabrielle hissed, 'be advised that I can end you now. No sight or sign of your sidekick now. No wonder. He got his warning already – but not today.'

Gabrielle eased his grip and Jeff simply collapsed on to the floor in a heap, gasping for the last drop of oxygen that he could suck from the air. If he was feeling anything, it was that he was way out of his depth – just as he'd felt in the doorway of a Dublin pub years before, when Libby was there to step in.

'Guess this means you're off the payroll, Jeff.' Zimmerman's tone was casual – conversational. 'And, of course, your "hangers-on",' he added. 'I'm including those two security muppets as well.' He turned to Gabrielle and smiled. 'Good work, Martin. A great day for us, my man. Rid of all the rubbish, winner in the media. The Russkies get to be the nasty fall guys. Money well spent, methinks.' He paused and turned his attention back to the floor. 'You're back with us, Jeffrey, yes?'

'You can quit shaking like a leaf, Bourke,' said Gabrielle. 'Even I would struggle to explain your exit to your friends at the *Post*.'

'Yes, indeed, Jeffrey.' Zimmerman was casually putting his jacket on. 'I'm not sure you'll have any friends at that newspaper after today's little debacle. Might seem your star is falling. Not to worry – your pockets are full, so all's fair, yes?'

Jeff was just able to take in what was being said as the air returned to his lungs. He wasn't sure if he had passed out earlier. Deflated, down, he had nothing to say.

'One last thing, Bourke,' Gabrielle said. 'If you or your angels ever show their faces in Cairo again, you can remind them about the strength of my grip.'

'Bon voyage, Jeffrey.' He walked by him on his way out. Close enough to tread on his hair, just avoiding kicking his head.

*

Gabrielle made the faintest of eye contact with Aidan as he walked through the lobby, heading for the exit. Aidan and Libby left their coffee pot behind and headed up to the suites on floor five.

Libby was uneasy.

'Something's not right, Aidan. He's not answering his phone.'

While they checked the doors along the row of meeting rooms, Aidan noticed the electronic wall board: TimeBox Suite 27.

'Right down the end, Libby.'

Jeff was sitting on the floor with his hands comforting his neck.

21

Libby was secretly enjoying the enforced break. She wouldn't admit it. A rest was as good as a change. *Leave Aidan to face the music back in Dublin while I hide here in snowy pre-Christmas Washington. Not looking for a new role, not yet.*

She was mostly leaving the phone off and binging on Netflix, feeling like she deserved it. Quick runs to Starbucks, not for coffee, but for takeaway sugary tea, large. She was just back in the room. In a good mood after seeing some of the hotel staff mounting a large Christmas tree at reception.

The hotel room phone rang unexpectedly. *Feck it, I forgot Aidan would know how to track me down. Answer, don't answer? Fuck it, might be important.*

'*Hi, could I speak with Elizabeth Hendrick, please?*'

'Could I ask who is calling?' Libby asked.

'*Jean Montgomery here.*'

'Then could I ask what it's in connection with?'

'*Well …*' There was silence on the line for a moment. '*To be honest, it's in connection with wanting to be there for her.*'

'Wasn't exactly expecting that. This is Libby here. No idea who you are or how you got this number.'

'I kind of knew it was you,' said Jean. *'Could we meet for a coffee?'*

'I'm afraid I only drink tea – it's an Irish thing.'

'You're prettier in person than when I saw you on TV,' said Jean. She had beckoned Libby over to her table as soon as she came through the Starbucks door.

Libby visually took in this young woman as she stood up. She was dressed in a knee-length green dress to match her eyes. *Maybe a bit old-fashioned.*

'Now at least I know you're not recording this,' said Libby. 'Nobody uses the word "pretty" anymore.' *Really attractive, I wonder if the blond hair is real or from the bottle.*

'Well, what about sexy, then?'

'Definitely not recording so.' Libby surprised herself with a blush.

'You look good when you show up in dreary Washington with a tan.' Jean was flirting. 'I'm guessing from what was revealed at that hearing, you got it in sunny Syria … The tan.'

'Oh, so I'm hearing politically aware also.'

'It was more like partisanship than politics,' said Jean.

'You're saying all the right things except one … Tea, please.'

Jean immediately signalled the young male waiter for the arrival of tea and a Danish, which she had ordered previously. The order was delivered pretty much straight away.

'You guys sisters?' he asked. No one answered and he quickly recovered himself. 'I mean, you seem to share the same good-looking genes.'

'Uh … I do like a bit of sugar,' said Libby. She was making eye contact with Jean. The waiter walked away. He was blushing for sure.

'Jean, I'm not based here,' said Libby. 'In fact, after what just happened, I'm not sure if I have a base or a job.'

'Listen, Elizabeth – and this is important.' She drew her face close up to Libby. The scent was intoxicating. 'If you guys give up, we're lost.'

'Whoa, that's a bit deep for a mid-morning tea break with a stranger.' Libby was thinking, *sexy one minute, deadly serious the next, what gives?* Her breath was scented by whatever sweet thing she had just bitten on. 'But at least will you call me Libby, to begin with?'

'That's kind of you,' Jean said, suddenly very formal again. 'That was a good old boys' beating you guys took.'

'Look,' said Libby, 'the deck might have been stacked by money, but the findings – that Timebox wasn't part of orchestrating the Arab Spring, you know … It's a loss, a big defeat, but it might heighten awareness. You know … It might be the cue for a more watchful view of TimeBox, and any of the other rising social media stars.'

'I think it's going to take more than that,' said Jean, 'and I'd like to be part of it.'

'What is it you do, Jean?'

'I'm a teacher. Wait for it … Bible and math.'

'Strange combination,' said Libby.

'Everybody says that and it worries me, and I'll tell you why. Math is a science, and the Bible has reams of science in it.'

'Has it?'

'Sure.' Jean deliberately picked something gentle for example.' She raised her hands out in front of her, preacher style. 'In the beginning there was nothing and the Lord said "Let there be light." Ever hear of the Big Bang? I'm being flippant, but there's loads of science and a bit of math if you know where to look.'

'Jean, is this a date or a job interview?'

'Well, I'm kind of hoping it's the first of many dates, and no, I don't want to give up my job. I love working with kids. I mightn't end up having my own, but I still like 'em. But where I'm based to do my teaching is my business. I think I'm excited with your message, even though I still have to figure out what that message is.'

'I'm not sure I – *we* – have a message.'

'You and your guys – and Jeff Bourke – have a message for sure.' Jean placed her hand on Libby's. 'I think the stand you guys made, and the sacrifices still to be made, are right and just. We may need a lot more for the battles to come.'

'How do I know you're not a plant?' asked Libby. 'A spy to get more dirt on Jeff?'

'Ever hear of anyone using a cover as a Sunday school teacher?'

Libby had made no effort to withdraw her hand from Jean's clasp.

'Good answer. Because I'm going to be asked that question.'

They were quiet for a time, wondering about what had just happened. The physical contact. The story. The attraction. Were they both thinking the same thoughts?

'Interested in carrying this on over dinner later?' Libby asked.

At least Libby got an answer to her own question: *Does a woman in her mid-thirties get infatuated?*

Jean knocked on Libby's hotel room door. She opened it and surprised herself by kissing her on the lips. 'Come in, come in. I'm so glad of your company. So unexpected to be honest.' Libby led her into the room by the hand. She felt strangely vulnerable.

'That was a tough week. If you're alone, I'm guessing your guys have mostly shipped home?'

'To lick their wounds. Aidan's gone back to Ireland, but I guess they won't let him near the office. He's my great friend but I haven't been in touch.'

'I know it was rough, I was following it on TV. Blanket coverage – a showdown,' said Jean.

'To be honest, it was more the fright I got when we found Jeff, beaten up by Zimmerman … Well, really, Gabrielle, his henchman.'

'Physically?' Jean looked shocked. 'Oh, I didn't know that. There was nothing in the media. That would be big news.'

'Well, that's what Jeff wanted – no more press.'

'That Gabrielle is a troubling character,' Jean observed. 'Always in the background like a dark angel.'

'Look, we're done with him now, that's for sure, and he's rarely on this side of the Atlantic anyway. Maybe Jeff was right. Take your beating and move on.'

'I'm not so sure you're done with him,' said Jean.

'Yeah, maybe you're right.' Libby considered the situation for a moment. 'With Jeff gone, maybe Zimmerman will recall him to the States, or even to Ireland.'

'Yeah,' Jean agreed, 'but that's not what I meant. He has a plan, and he wants – *needs* – Egypt.'

'And you know this how?' asked Libby.

'I just see it.'

'Jean, you know this sounds a bit, well, out there.' Libby deliberately put on a quizzical look as best she could.

'You'll get used to it, I hope. I mean that. I always knew I had some kind of gift. There's no way I'm denying or toning down something that God gave me. It's that simple.'

'Now I know I'm going to have trouble telling my guys that my new friend is not a spy. You're too honest.' Looking into her eyes, Libby knew this girl was special.

'I'm kind of hoping you'll be telling them we're more than friends,' said Jean.

'Oh, let's order takeaway,' said Libby.

22

Jeff and AJ made their journey back to California in their own time. They grabbed six days in Florida, craving a bit of winter sunshine. There wasn't a plan and there wasn't any rush. AJ wanted Jeff to get a bit of recovery time, both physical and mental. After the frenetic excitement of the previous months, people were empty. The sun was medicinal.

At home, AJ said, 'Show me your neck.' AJ examined it tenderly and grinned. 'The bruising is gone. Not as much damage as Mr Huberman once achieved. Gabrielle must be an amateur.'

Jeff didn't smile. The house was quiet. They sat at their dining room table and looked out at the bay.

'You know,' Jeff began in a quiet voice, 'for a terrible individualist – and that's me – I can't do this on my own.'

AJ had seen him upset – seldom, but sometimes – and she knew admitting his vulnerability meant something really deep.

'You're not on your own.' She clasped his hands. 'You have me for sure, and the guys – Aidan and Libby, your loyal Dubliners. Let's not forget Dale and Beth. Come on … Three good men and three good women

– you have it made. The magnificent six. What could possibly go wrong, hey?' When Jeff didn't even smile, she was thinking the one thing she had been thinking all week: *Depression.*

'I've never felt so low. I rolled my dice at the wrong time, love, and now I've lost. You know what's killing me?'

'Well, I should, we've had thirteen years together. Is this about the guys losing their jobs? Are you feeling guilty?'

'No.' Jeff shook his head fiercely. 'I can pay the guys, you know that. We can keep going in business, if we have a business.'

'Employ them? But doing what? You're not thinking of a start-up, are you, honey?'

'God, nothing could be further from my thoughts. That's why I'm crying. I've missed the chance to nail two dangerous men.'

AJ hadn't noticed the tears.

'Let it flow.' She now cupped his face gently in her hands. 'At least you tried, honey.'

'Yeah, yeah, but if I missed my chance, what will they go on to achieve? What have I missed? That's what's killing me.'

'So why don't you join up the dots? Use the team to carry on … you know, the good work. Carry on probing, at least for a time, see if you missed something. Get the *Post* taking the bait again. Jack, isn't it?'

'Zimmerman was probably right,' Jeff agreed, 'saying my capital was spent with the *Post*, but I still know why I married you, my love. You're telling me that I've got to give the team the good news. They are now private investigators.'

'Look, honey, things are rough for you at the minute. If the media glare wasn't enough to wear somebody down, getting nearly strangled by Gabrielle … Well, that was rough. My blood is boiling thinking about it. Here, let's grab a couple of glasses of wine.' As she walked to the rack, AJ looked over her shoulder at Jeff. 'I still think you should have called the cops.' She took a bottle in each hand and showed him the labels. 'Spanish, for a change?' She gave him a sly smile. 'Want to take them upstairs?'

'Nah … I mean, yes.' He looked brighter now. 'Calling the cops would have got into the media as sour grapes. As for the media glare … Well, they've been glaring at you as well, and you're at least something nice to glare at.'

'Thanks,' she said, smiling. 'No, look, you've taken all the strain. Now we know for sure, the system takes some beating.'

'With you beside me, maybe I'll beat it yet.' Jeff managed a faint smile. 'We'll beat it or die trying.'

'Well, let's not go that far,' said AJ.

His mood was lightening. She was glad – but it didn't last long.

'We missed something,' he said, even while they were walking up stairs. 'The Arab Spring is well over. But TimeBox is staying put in Cairo. Why?'

The doorbell rang. A camera showed Libby was at

the door. They both reversed and went to answer it together.

'What a welcome sight.'

'And unexpected,' AJ added.

'Come on, love. She must have flown up. I didn't know she was coming.'

He opened the door and gave her a peck on the cheek. 'You're just in time. We're about to have a glass.'

'At three in the afternoon?'

'Yep, we're on extended holiday.'

'How did you get here, Libby?' AJ asked as the trio gathered at the kitchen counter.

'Cab and of course plane before that.'

'You're an unexpected treat, you're welcome.' Jeff was compensating, just in case AJ had come across a little abruptly. She had.

'You're welcome here.' AJ was recovering the situation. She indicated a stool and Libby sank onto it gratefully, tired after the travel.

'Yeah, I know,' Libby said, 'but something a bit different has cropped up. I guess there's no hurry to get back to Dublin. Aidan tells me he was locked out of the office.'

Libby grimaced. 'I need to tell you two something. I met somebody in a coffee shop in Washington. It was after you guys left.' Libby showed them her iPhone screen, which was displaying a picture of Jean.

'This is Jean Montgomery,' she said. 'She wants to

be involved with me – and with us.'

'You met the lovely Jean in a coffee shop?' asked Jeff.

'Well, not quite. She called me up and then we went to Starbucks.'

'Quite a looker,' said AJ. 'Hope she's one of your tribe – hate to have to keep an eye on my partner.' She winked at Jeff, glad of the distraction.

'She's a very deep, spiritual person, I can tell you that.' AJ's teasing was getting on Libby's nerves. 'She called me up nearly straight after the Senate hearing. If anything, Jeff, she's one of your tribe. I don't mean sexual orientation. I mean … I don't know … Spiritually in tune, maybe?'

'Jeff?' AJ looked at Libby in play-acting disbelief. 'Spiritually in tune? Since when?'

'No, she is calm and comforting and I like her a lot. I wasn't in a hurry home, so we saw quite a bit of each other in the last week.'

'Well done you, I'm glad,' said AJ. 'I have a feeling we're in for times ahead when we'll all need a significant other. Apart from anything, it's nice to have someone at Christmas.'

'She's not a Christmas present.'

'Don't abandon your buddy Aidan,' said Jeff.

'I don't do abandonment,' Libby countered. 'But I like her, and she wants to be part of the solution – not on a payroll, I don't mean that. Wait for it … She won't give up teaching the Bible. She just wants to be involved – a different opinion, you know? Coming to our strategy sessions.' Libby was overselling.

'That's what we were discussing before you came in.' Jeff looked down at the floor. He wasn't in the mood for reality.

'Which way we are going forward?' said AJ. 'Try something and see.'

'I don't know, but I've the sense to know I'm too deflated right now to make a concrete decision. Anyway, I won't be making the decision – we will. I'm going to use the Christmas holiday to think it out,' said Jeff.

'You might want to talk to Jean, ' Libby suggested. 'Maybe even one on one, Jeff.'

'Don't want to be disrespectful,' now Jeff was grimacing, 'but what's a Bible teacher going to tell me?'

'Jean thinks us keeping up the fight, if that's what it is, is … well … required … necessary … essential.' Libby leaned forward on her stool. 'She would say absolutely required.'

'She sure does use a lot of adjectives,' AJ observed wryly.

Libby got to her feet and picked up her coat. 'Look, Jeff, I travelled here for this' she snapped. 'How come a stranger, who has just come into my life, has more fight left in her than you? Are you leading us, or what?' She gave AJ's arm an unfriendly squeeze before walking out of the kitchen and towards the door.

'I know, I know.' Jeff's voice rose in pitch and volume. 'I didn't mean it like that!'

The only reply was the front door slamming shut.

'Well, that little exploration didn't go too well, honey.' AJ sat beside him again and picked up her wine glass.

'Just sowing the seeds of being careful, that's all. Kind of funny that Jean appears on the scene just when Zimmerman and Gabrielle will want to keep a close eye on their new-found enemies.'

'Come on, Jeff, you were enemies for years before. You guys just wouldn't admit it.'

AJ was glad Libby had gone off with her feathers ruffled. It meant that Jeff had a problem. Solving problems was better than being swallowed up by depression.

'OK, you ready?' she asked.

'For what?' He looked blank for a moment.

'Upstairs.'

23

'Jeff, thanks for agreeing to meet up and the invite to your home.' Jean Montgomery leaned forward to shake his hand across the threshold. Jeff stepped back to allow her through the front door.

'You ever tried to say no to Libby?' he replied. 'Come in, come in. We'll get you a cup of something. Through here to the dining room.'

Jean walked behind him. 'We call it the dining room. A bit old fashioned, the phrase I mean. You'll see, it's open plan. It's a nice view even if you sit at the kitchen counter.'

Jean gravitated towards a comfortable chair at the dining table facing the kitchen. Jeff grabbed the coffee pot and two mugs and laid them on the table. 'AJ will be down to meet you.' What he most noticed was her skin. Beautifully moisturised.

'I'm a bit in awe of you,' she said. 'You know, high-profile media guy, comfortable in front of the camera, but really, you put yourself on the line. Stood up and were counted. That's what I admire.'

'Stood up to be kicked, more like,' said Jeff. 'Where are you based?'

'Just for Christmas, with Libby. Us teachers get good Christmas holidays.'

Jeff had to make a return journey to grab milk from the fridge.

'Jeff, you have to go on – you know it, deep down.'

'Jesus,' Jeff swore. 'Sounds like you want a job bad, Jean.'

'Yep, Jeff, that's all right.' She paused, poured milk into the cup Jeff had filled for her. 'I was warned it would take a while to tune into that Irish wit. But I'm not sure now is a good time for humour, and Lib would already have told you, I have a job – a vocation.'

'Jean, if we have no humour … Oh, look, I don't know … Maybe we're getting off on the wrong foot. Look, tell me where you're coming from.'

Jeff felt uncomfortable – not sure-footed. She was direct, very direct.

'I was driven toward Libby,' said Jean, 'and I knew it was far more than just natural attraction. Seeing her, outside the Capitol, standing in the background. Boy, you couldn't wait to get off those steps. I only saw her for a moment, but I knew I had to be with her, at her side. Backing you up by backing her up. I have dreams about the situation.'

'Coffee good?'

Jean could sense he was uncomfortable, mentally.

'What situation exactly?' he asked.

'One where pure evil takes its chance to start a catastrophe.'

'What kind of catastrophe?'

'I don't know yet.'

'A bit apocalyptic, Jean.'

'Maybe it is. It's something out of my dreams.'

'Jean, I'm sure Libby's already told you we had words. You know … when she was telling us about you guys meeting up.'

'Yes,' Jean said calmly. 'Lib predicted I would be seen as … Well, I guess … a spy.'

'You're direct,' Jeff said, but he really meant, strange. 'That's good. The spy in the camp thing is a bit far out, though. There might be nothing to spy on. I haven't decided what to do next, or even if I want to carry on in this business.'

'You're wrong.' Jean put her mug down and stared into his eyes. 'You'll carry on because you must. I will help you if I can, and I can't be dishonest because it's not in my Christian nature.'

Jeff couldn't help himself. He started laughing uncontrollably – so much so that AJ came into the dining room.

'What gives?' she asked.

When he eventually gathered himself and stopped giggling, all he could say was, 'AJ, I thought you were the only one who knows me better than I know myself. It turns out you have competition.'

Part 3
SAVIOR MEDIA

24

The "Magnificent Six" – Jeff, AJ, Libby, Aidan, Dale and Beth – had agreed to meet on 7 January 2019. The setting was not unusual: AJ and Jeff's dining room. As the guests arrived, with the weather outside dry and crisply cool, the niceties of exchanging gifts in seasonal wrapping encouraged hugs and kisses amongst the friends. It was like a second Christmas, especially with five-year-old Dylan running around. Anne Bourke had posted over a traditional Irish chocolate selection box for the attention of "Master Dylan Longworth". He didn't waste time ripping it open.

Jean had met everyone except Aidan, who had just flown in from Dublin. At Libby's insistence, it looked as if Jean had been conscripted as an honorary member of the team.

'I'm indebted to Jean,' Jeff began, once everyone had a mug in front of them. 'A coffee toast, please. A time for new beginnings,' said Jeff to the clinking of cups.

'I know she is a newbie. When I – *we* – were on our knees, thanks to our beloved Congress, Jean asked me if I was up for carrying on. I guess she meant forming a competitor for TimeBox. I gave her the right answer at the time, but for the wrong reason. I said no. "Why?" I thought. "Was she looking for a job?" In fact, Jean was on the right track. We should stick with TimeBox – that's where our expertise is. Use it for some good. Support and promote regulation. Not saying we can't monetise, by the way.'

Libby allowed herself a smile. This olive branch meant that Jean would be seeing a lot of her new girl. She liked that.

'What do you mean, stick with it?' Aidan asked. 'We're all sacked, aren't we?'

'We know which way the algorithms will kick,' Jeff replied. 'So, we're not giving up on social media – we're going forward with it. If a load of Russian hacks can have a go, then so can we, and we'll do a better job, that's all. Look, we've had our Christmas, so let's get planning. This is 2019 – the year when we emerge as a value-added reseller for TimeBox as well as its moral voice.'

The gladiator was back. AJ started the round of applause.

'Jeff, you doing this just to thwart the two hobos?' Aidan asked over the applause. He looked tired after a trans-Atlantic fight. 'It's a big gamble as a payback for that thumping they dished out to you.'

'No harm killing two birds with one stone,' said Jeff.

'Any plans to be on the road again any time soon?' asked Dale.

'I hope not,' Jeff said with a wry grin, 'and before

you say anything, we'll need security both in practical and analytical terms. I'm guessing war and conflict will still be on the world's agenda – maybe more so cyberwar. So, there's an expansion opportunity straight away. We provide services for any company wiped out by a cyber-attack. Dale, Beth – you up for a different kind of war and a bit more retraining? Keep ye at home at least while Dylan is growing.' Jeff knew that it was his turn to shock, and he wasn't going to wait for an answer. 'We need a name, people.' He looked at the assembled team in turn. 'We need a name.'

'Savior,' said Jean almost immediately. 'What about that?'

'Savior Media …' Libby turned it over in her mind for a moment. 'I like it. I told you she would add value. Doing it already.'

'So …' Ever the pragmatist, Aidan looked at Jeff. 'We'll start all over again and recruit a whole load of IT geeks?'

'Small recruitment, Aidan. Beth has already turned herself into one of those anyway.'

'Damn straight, you got that right chief,' Beth replied. She was more tuned in than Dale who was trying to keep a sugar-infused Dylan from banging into the furniture.

'Beth, you'll be implementing military-style man management. We have the biggest platform in the world at our disposal, and we already know how it works. Besides, recruiting will mean spies.'

'You hearing this Dale, I'm the boss?' asked Beth.

Dale knew this was his cue to get involved. 'Loud and clear, mam.'

Maybe she and the rest were glad that the old Jeff had resurfaced.

'I have the guys I trust around me. What could possibly go wrong?'

'Stop saying that, will ye?' AJ laughed. 'It drives me mad.'

25

The first year of Savior Media was a noisy blast. The company celebrated every time Zimmerman had to be rolled out with some apology or other, especially if it was in front of the government. There was a bit of mischief in the air. Libby got a Twitter poll going on Zimmerman's dress code – always in a grey long-sleeved top and dark grey chinos for his media appearances. 'Who is this man's dress sense based upon? A) Paddington Bear B) Sherlock Holmes or C) Steve Jobs.'

The American public imagination might not care about dead Arabs, but it sure did care about their own bullied young kids, and they very much cared about young adult suicides. Jeff's tirade at the Senate hearing had been enough to stick in people's consciousness. Funny how communications worked. It had its own mysterious pathways sometimes.

Jean was energised by the gig. Nobody else was going to say 'My dreams led me …' or 'I see now this is what I was meant to do.'

'What's that, Jean? Thwart billionaire media tycoons?' asked Aidan one time.

'No, seek justice, Aidan,' Jean replied. She was serious.

'I'd say we will be getting closer to that when we see Gabrielle rolled out in apologetic mode,' said Libby.

Aidan's call on the new couple was, 'Yep, I see why those two are together. North and south poles of the same magnet.'

Just as the ship was under way, a new strain of coronavirus, subsequently identified as SARS-CoV-2 and given the simpler name Covid-19, appeared in late 2019. It started in China and then ran rampant around the world within months. All the social media channels had only one thing to talk about suddenly. It was good for business. It dominated all life in all the world until the vaccines kicked in, later in early 2021. Too late for the twenty million dead people.

The virus grabbed the US, Brazil and the UK with way more virulence than the rest of the developed world. They were places where political leadership had gone walkabout. Jeff realised this was the cause worth fighting for. The loonies and 'this is the wrath of God' merchants had to be tackled. When the vaccines appeared, developed more rapidly than had been expected, it was time to tackle the anti-vaxxers. This was pretty much the same as tackling the pro-Trumpers. You couldn't really distinguish between the two. Trump would have grabbed the White House for a second time for sure in 2020, except Mother Nature had stuck her nose in.

As a pharmacist, AJ was the natural choice to be the team voice for making sense of what was coming out of the virological community. They had something to marvel at and intrigue about into the bargain. Had it been made in a lab or made in a swamp? If you could see the majesty in something that had the potential to kill you, then you were qualified to be a nerd, and there were plenty of virology nerds about, all over all the media, all the time. Covid-19 tackled lung function and other organ weaknesses in vulnerable and older age groups.

Zimmerman and his organisation weren't pushed about Covid-19. His customers weren't old enough to die. Better still if a few of those Chinese leaders were popping off the planet. They had never been fans of his social media. A new lesson was emerging from the pandemic: lockdowns were good for social media.

Jeff had always liked the idea of the big stuff being decided at meetings in his and AJ's home. There was a bit of psychology in it. The rest of the staff saw their leadership team working at their desks, just like them. All that was on hold for the moment. AJ called that shot: 'No personal contact unless you form a "bubble", period.'

The one hundred and forty employees of Savior Media were all in their twenties, pretty much, with a couple of exceptions. When the initial turmoil of Covid-19 began to settle down, the team just got on with it. But it was turmoil. The general population often overlooked the fact that older people were dying – a lot of them. Trump was off the Christmas card list of the surgical mask manufacturers. Travel was out; working from home was in.

An explosion of use and interest in the social media platforms was good for business. There were plenty of takers for Savior's product, which was designed to manage mid-size businesses' presence on the platforms, especially TimeBox. Jeff was keeping it tight. If he was ever going to get over his Congress defeat, this was probably going to be as good as it got. Using TimeBox – and using every opportunity to take a swipe at Zimmerman – was a game Jeff liked playing.

Savior's leadership team were reskilling. Dale and Beth were handling staff more than they were handling weapons. Jean was firmly established as part of the gang. A teacher, she took on the internal training gig, online. AJ was the 'medic', managing the vaccine information for Savior and its clients. TimeBox came across as a vaccine positive platform, because Savior was good at organising the bots.

If you were lucky enough not to be affected by a Covid death, then things were looking up by 2022. The planet had survived and a return to travel was back on the agenda. The world was back to worrying about wars and famines. A natural complacency kicked in. If you could survive one pandemic, you could survive another, if it came. The repeated mutation of new Covid-19 variants was still a worry for the World Health Organization. The virus just kept on giving. But the vaccines were doing their job, and making a lot of companies a lot of money.

Aidan and Libby were Savior's regulatory watchdogs. Maybe not as exciting as running errands for Jeff in the Middle East – safer, at least. You were in champagne-opening country when you could get an actual TimeBox executive turning whistle-blower and giving interviews on a public service radio or TV channels. Little moral victories. Nice wins when they came, but no one was kidding themselves. While Zimmerman was bankrolling politicians, there was only going to be one winner. The clock rolled on.

26

By the summer of 2022, Covid-19 was under control and the US was allowing travel without a test. Jeff and AJ decided to mark the occasion with what many were saying was a long overdue party – their wedding. Not bad timing, given that people were well sick of lockdowns.

'Way overdue,' according to Jeff's soon to be father-in-law, Mike Maher.

'Better late than never,' according to Anne Bourke.

Tatler had approached the couple with an offer for an exclusive photo shoot. There was still a residual interest in Jeff Bourke. He ran a media company – admittedly a small one. It was strange, because America didn't generally like those who had fallen from grace.

'Why not?' AJ asked, rubbing her two figures together right in front of his face. 'It's free money.'

'We're not stuck for cash, love,' Jeff countered by theatrically taking out his wallet and waving it in the air. 'Besides, the heads on some of my Irish relations mightn't be exactly photogenic. No, let's stay low profile.'

'Honey, I'm not chasing cash. We're a media

company. We don't do low profile – or we shouldn't.'

'Ah, but some things are private. Especially when our Irish in-laws have taken drink – and they will, you know that.'

'Last I remember, you're well able to polish off a drop yourself.'

'Exactly right, and we don't want that photographed now, do we?' Jeff grinned. 'Look, I'll get my old friend Jack to get us a little piece in the *Post*. That's to publicly acknowledge my love for you.'

'The *Washington Post* … how romantic,' said AJ. 'Jeff, you sure there won't be someone pissed with only seventy going?'

Dale and Beth were in charge of security for the big day, and that warranted a meeting.

'No shortage of takers to be packed into a boat on the bay, I see from the RSVPs.' Beth waved a wad of papers in her husband's direction. 'As office manager, I'm not seeing nearly as much interest in being packed back into the office.'

'That's not the press Savior wants, if it turns out to be a super spreader event.' Dale frowned. 'Covid hasn't gone away, you know.'

'Anyhow,' Aidan interjected, 'with you in charge, Beth, Covid wouldn't dare show up, would it?'

Dale laughed.

The three of them were just shooting the breeze in the otherwise deserted offices of Savior Media HQ.

'The yacht was Jeff's idea,' Beth shot back.

'Dangerous ground for a man to be imposing the rules on a bride's wedding.'

'The boat only holds seventy,' said Aidan, 'so it was always going to be a small family and friends affair. Hope they're both on board with that – excuse the pun.'

They were still chuckling when Libby rushed in and apologised for being late.

'Lib, where are you on the "size matters" subject?' asked Aidan.

'Pardon?'

'The size of the yacht.'

'I can just mimic what he's saying,' Libby replied. '"Thirty-five each, my love – what could possibly go wrong?"'

The minor controversy over numbers hadn't gone away even when the big day – 22 September 2022 – arrived. Libby was in with Jeff while he was dressing for the ceremony.

'Jeff, when did you set your heart on a yacht trip?' she asked.

'Ah ye know, we often heard friends say how good their cruise trips were.'

'Yep, but that's sailing around the Bahamas or the Med, not around Alcatraz.'

The residual arguments ceased to be important once the pastor, a cousin of AJ's named Jennifer, got going with the ceremony.

AJ was glimmering in cream satin. Jeff, in black

tie, didn't look half bad, but Mike – the only man in military uniform – took the imaginary award for best-dressed male. Jennifer chose the marriage feast at Cana as her Gospel reading. The vows were taken and the rings were exchanged as the yacht cruised under the Golden Gate Bridge, too far below it to allow any traffic noise to pollute the service.

Post-Covid get-togethers had a new vibe about them: 'Don't take a party for granted. A time might come again when you couldn't have one.'

There was a bit of ribbing about the single status of the new parents-in-law. Both Mike Maher and Anne Bourke had been on their own for a long time, but neither of them looked as if they were in any hurry to change that.

Dinner was served in the yacht's stylish dining room, with the galley on full display and the chefs in pristine whites. Jeff's uncle Pat was sorry he'd hit the Napa Chardonnay too early. He could hardly taste his Beef Wellington. When Pat heard it was one hundred and eighty bucks a bottle, he couldn't help himself.

The dancing was fun. It usually was when the Irish got going. They had a knack of losing their inhibitions quicker than anyone and making believe they were all from Harlem, with that inbuilt African rhythm. Dale and Beth were guests, of course, but they pretty much worked the room, just in case. The yacht docked in Sausalito on the far side of the bay at about 6.30 in the evening. Supper was at nine o'clock in the Bay Terrace View Hotel. It was nice to give the guests a one-hour turnaround to settle into their rooms. It might have been a small affair, but the two meal settings, one better than the other, made it feel like a really special night. And more dancing …

'You got yourself a winner there, son,' said Anne, giving AJ an approving wink, 'even if it did take you an outrageous nineteen years to get around to it.'

'I had to be sure, Mam, I had to be sure.' Jeff smiled, knowing there was more banter to come.

'We're not waiting another nineteen years for a grandchild, are we?'

'Come on, Mam, these things don't have to be rushed. We'll need time to get to know each other as marrieds.'

Anne put her hand on Jeff's arm and looked into his eyes. 'No, but seriously, Jeff, don't let the clock tick on too long. Women's bodies are different to you men.'

'I think I know that, Mam.' Jeff blushed.

'Surely now that the rat race of TimeBox is well over, you two must be a bit more at ease to do other things.'

'Mam, there are always pressures, things to do. Right now, we must see how the post-Covid media world shapes up.'

'There's more to life than money, surely?' she asked.

'Well, on that we do agree, Mam,' said Jeff, 'but there's also a thing called unfinished business.'

AJ sashayed across the dance floor towards

them. It took a bit of skill to avoid collisions. The Pilipino Quartet had piped up with Van Morrison's 'Somebody Like You'.

'Anne,' she said, 'if you're not dancing with my husband, they're playing our song.'

It wasn't really a request, and before he knew it Jeff was in contact with his new wife's body, moving to the rhythm.

The melody took over and, rightly or wrongly, Jeff was remembering why his contacts with his mother had been a little sparse over the years. She talked too much sense.

What impressed AJ most was the waiters and waitresses, both on the yacht and at the hotel. Following the pandemic, service staff were hard to come by. But these boys and girls looked as pristine as their manners were good. There were no maids of honour, although Jeff was telling everyone Libby was his best man. AJ's guests probably didn't get the humour. They certainly weren't expecting a karaoke machine in a five-star establishment. When Aidan got the mike, it was to sing George Harrison's 'Something'. AJ looked over at Jeff from across the dance floor and mouthed, 'That's for Libby.' He mouthed back, 'Unrequited love, I guess.' She blew him a kiss, and he realised the only word she'd been able to make out was 'love'.

It was mostly the Irish guests who asked the couple about their honeymoon. They were surprised to learn there wasn't going to be one. Jeff and AJ were going back to work on Monday.

'What was the best wedding present you got, son?' Pat asked his nephew while they were refilling their glasses at the bar.

'That's an easy one, Pat,' Jeff said without hesitation. 'We have six weeks to prepare for a Senate investigative hearing. We got the news on Wednesday. Great timing, yeah?'

'Didn't you get into a mess of trouble last time you were there, son?'

'Sure did, Pat, but that was high stakes poker, the Congress. This is a teddy bears' picnic by comparison, the Senate.'

Pat's head was starting to hurt, so he was glad not to push it.

'Look,' he said, 'you know, on behalf of your father, God be good to him, I'll always wish the best for ye and your lovely bride. Remind me again – why did it take so long to give us a day out?'

Jeff raised his voice in a joking kind of way.

'Don't even go there, Pat. Just how many times, including tonight, do you think I've been getting that earful from the mother?'

'Any regrets not being with TimeBox?' Pat looked serious for a change. 'You know … the money, the prestige?'

'Just that I don't know what's what. These days Zimmerman seems a bit lost or isolated. I'm nearly feeling sorry for him,' Jeff said ruefully. 'My little company ain't doing half bad. The promise to be a regulator, of sorts. If truth be told, Pat, social media –

and not just TimeBox – has wrecked many a life since I left it.'

'Don't be crying for Zimmerman, will ye? He's plenty rich.'

'His main man, Martin Gabrielle, is only interested in the Middle East,' said Jeff.

'He has no Jeff, so screw him.' AJ had joined them in time to catch the tail end of the conversation.

'Lovely language for a newly married girl,' said Pat, with his characteristic chuckle.

'Seriously, AJ is right,' said Jeff. 'I think he's gone off half-cocked with his "Box Universe" offering.'

'What in the name of God is that meant to be?' asked Pat.

'Headsets and augmented reality,' said Jeff.

'Don't forget nausea is in there as well,' AJ chimed in.

'Mother of God! But that's a lot to take in.'

'Pat, I'm probably making a long story boring,' said Jeff, 'but our boy Zimmerman may have scored an own goal. A big one. We'll see.'

'Now, enough business chat for your wedding day. I'll just grab a glass and leave you young people in peace.'

Jeff gave his uncle a playful slap on the back as he wandered off.

'What's that phrase the Irish use?' asked AJ, grinning in Pat's direction. '"He's gas" – is that it? Why were you boring the pants off him?'

'Well, he's gone, isn't he?' Jeff grinned. 'That answer your question?'

'There'll be no one to blame if this Box Universe blows up in Zimmerman's face.'

'Here's hoping.'

Jeff kissed his new wife on the lips, while Aidan's slurred voice boomed over the amplifier.

'I don't want to leave her now, you know I believe and how, da do do do do doo …'

27

Savior's business offering did Zimmerman no harm. Clients would pay TimeBox for product advertising. Savior knew the algorithms and would pick out a target audience with pinpoint accuracy. It wasn't meant to be riveting. It was meant to be a slow, rhythmic building up of a new business – one with a social conscience. That was, at least, a unique departure: handing out regulatory slaps to the hand that feeds you.

So, the two companies carried on with their love/hate relationship. Jeff's outfit got itself squarely back in the public eye with an invitation to the Senate chambers.

The Monday after the wedding, Jean noticed a meeting at Jeff's office had been popped into her diary

'Jean,' Jeff said without preamble when she walked in, 'I want you to represent us at the hearing.'

'Wow, wasn't expecting that, Jeff.'

'It makes sense.' He indicated a chair and Jean sat facing him. 'A new face, an intelligent American professional woman, and … wait for it … a Christian.'

'Yeah …' Jean smiled. 'Christians were thrown to the lions, were they not?'

Jeff waved a hand dismissively. 'Nah, these guys are pussy cats. Remember, I was there.'

'Yeah, right.'

'Covid has calmed them right down.' Jeff tried to sound as persuasive as he could. 'It's only an investigative hearing. It can't make findings.'

'I don't know, Jeff …'

Jeff said nothing, and that seemed to force Jean to speak again.

'Did you run this by the others?'

'No, it's me that has to have faith in you. The only reason I'm pressing you now is that the clock is ticking. We would have to get you some media training.'

'Can't wait,' said Jean.

But she could – she was nervous about it.

All the key players – TimeBox, Google, Microsoft – had been dragged into a protocol agreement after the Congress verdict in 2018: identify and shoot down false content. Jeff had canvassed for a hearing to assess that protocol's effectiveness. How could they refuse?

The hearing was using Microsoft Teams to facilitate the video conference. Using TimeBox's video calling feature would have been seen as partisan. There were six committee members attending, but only two in person, masked and socially distant. Jean had made the trip to Washington DC. She knew she had to be on her game. You didn't get into the corridors of power that often.

'The point is, Madam Chairperson,' said Jean,

'when TimeBox discovered the effects of their algorithm, they proceeded to do nothing about it – absolutely zero.' Jean was trying deliberately not to make her carefully rehearsed lines sound rehearsed.

'And how did you know this?' asked Senator Robert Cope.

'Because as a social media company with a conscience, we monitor these things.'

'What things exactly?' asked Cope.

Bingo, thought Jean. It was just the question her media tutor had schooled her to be ready for.

'Well, let's see …' She pretended to think for a moment. 'Jihadist propaganda, anti-Semitic sentiment, and – yes, we're back there … teenage and young adult suicides.'

'Please, please, Ms Montgomery,' The voice of Senator Madalyn Wells, the committee chairperson, cut across the murmuring that followed Jean's statement. The gallery was less than half full. 'It sounds very like you're using this chamber to make broad accusations.'

'It's a digital world, Madam Chairperson,' Jean countered. 'All things can be monitored. But … Look, let me explain simply what's at the heart of it.'

'Oh, please do, Ms Montgomery.' Senator James Woodbroke's tone was neutral; it was hard to tell if he was genuinely interested, or merely being sarcastic.

Jean unconsciously began speaking as if she were addressing her classroom. 'The algorithm – or the math, if you like – sees that a discussion is trending. We know from statistics that negative, aggressive, follow-up comments get eighty-five per cent more traction that ones that say positive things. More traction means more advertisement and more revenue. Why would TimeBox want to change? Especially if it's run by morally reprehensible individuals.'

Bingo again. She had landed the punch.

'Ms Montgomery, please.' Senator Paul Meekson's face loomed large on the screen. 'We're here to learn more about the workings of social media, not to impugn the reputation of individuals who I might remind you are not here to defend themselves.'

'Please delete that last assertion from the record,' Wells asked the stenographer.

'Sorry, Madam Chairperson,' the stenographer replied. 'Could you be more specific as to what you wish excluded?'

Jean couldn't suppress a smile. These media advisers were worth their money. Even if Fox decided not to cover that last tetchy little exchange, NBC would.

Bingo. Shot landed yet again.

The *Washington Post* editorial the next day made for good reading:

> *Just how many times do our legislators need to be steered in the right direction? Would it take the death of one of their own? There are surely three things that the social media revolution requires: Regulation, Regulation and Regulation. Can we even be sure that any potential for interference in*

> *the democratic process at our next election will be monitored? Will it be called out and frankly, would it be punished? If the answer is no, then our democracy has a problem – and a big one at that.*

On the contrary, nothing at all happened. The TimeBox of 2023 was twice the size of the one Jeff had walked away from – or, rather, had been driven away from. Its customer base had grown up with it and stuck with it. Those subscribers, as Zimmerman would call them, had more spending power.

Meanwhile, Savior Media made its profits by feeding off TimeBox. It was the strangest of love-hate relationships – an irony that wasn't lost on Fox. As one of their news anchors put it: 'Only a fool bites the hand that feeds him, Mr Bourke.'

But Jeff was prepared to bite. Savior Media conducted a huge policing effort throughout 2023 and 2024, while the primaries were in full swing, trying to keep the election straight – based upon facts, not fiction. Savior had made its choice: to be the regulatory policeman.

28

In August 2024 the World Health Organization issued a briefing note: 'Statistics show that a spike in Covid-related deaths would be expected to appear in the coming Northern Hemisphere winter. National health authorities are asked to promote the use of the existing vaccines in their populations.'

A 'spike' turned out to be an understatement. In line with New Zealand and Australia, some European countries had adopted strict lockdowns by October. The Far East was quicker to return to lockdowns, with 'Zero Covid' policies. President Biden had to contemplate a new lockdown – not something he wanted to do in the run-up to his re-election campaign. Instead, US law enforcement was ordered to crack down on unnecessary journeys. Working from home was encouraged again. Still the deaths kept coming, no matter how stringent the measures.

Aidan took the call late on a Thursday afternoon.

'*Is this Mr Mulcahy?*' asked a clearly identifiable Irish voice.

'It is.'

'*Mr Mulcahy, my name is Margaret Hynes. I'm the clinical manager here at St Teresa's.*'

Aidan immediately put a face to the name. St Teresa's was the assisted living facility on the outskirts of Bray where his parents, Con and Patricia, had lived together for the past six years. Aidan mostly knew Margaret from chats with his mam. He had met her a couple of times. Enough to know she looked after their affairs with affection as well as efficiency. A woman with a warm personality.

'Yeah … Hi, Ms Hynes.' Aidan could hear the unease in his own voice. 'Is this about payments?'

'*No, Aidan.*' Margaret paused and took a breath. '*I'm so sorry to tell you that your mam and dad passed away this afternoon.*'

Aidan didn't notice himself flop on to the chair behind him. His legs had given way.

'*I know it's terrible news to deliver,*' Margaret continued, '*but I must deal with the next of kin … you know … legally.*' He couldn't speak. '*This virus is raging through the nursing homes again.*'

Aidan was looking directly at his phone. He said 'Both?', and then realised he must have seemed rude. He'd hung up in shock.

He wasn't sure how long he sat there. Certainly hours.

When he got Libby on the phone, she greeted him with, '*Aidan, it's one in the morning.*'

He hesitated for several seconds. 'They're gone.' He was sobbing. She went silent while she took a moment. She knew.

'*Thank God you got over there after Covid.*' She waited

for a response. Nothing. '*Your mother was great. A baby in her forties … Wow – at least she made a winner.*' Aidan managed to force a smile on to his face. '*Look, I'll come over, police checkpoints or not. Can I ask you honestly? Will I bring Jean? She's good at prayers. You know that, right?*'

'Yeah, that would be good. Hurry, will ye?'

29

From nowhere, it seemed you couldn't get through a day without the death of a member of the US Congress. The new pandemic received blanket coverage from the news channels, which were constantly being shown on the wall-mounted TV in AJ's dining room. The deaths of politicians, celebrities and public figures had become a spectator sport.

'What's going on?' Jeff was asking himself as much as AJ. ' We were warned the pandemic was spiking back but ... These numbers are unbelievable – since last Tuesday only. It was bad for weeks, but the ramp-up?' He mimed an exponential curve with one hand.

'Well, believe them,' AJ replied. 'The media isn't lying about a story that looks like it could dwarf Covid-19. Jeff, Covid never frightened me – this does.'

Jeff took his wife in his arms.

'You OK if I call the guys over?' he asked. 'We need to get our bearings.'

'Let me get my head together, I'll call them.' AJ pressed her cheek against his shoulder. 'People will be frightened. I'll ask Dale to be cabbie. You know he'll be able to ease through checkpoints. What about Aidan?'

'It's been a few weeks, let's get him back in the race.'

AJ had to convince the others to join them at her home.

'No, I don't believe it's a virus,' she'd explained over the phone. 'You can't get it from personal contact.'

The meeting room – the dining room – had never been needed more than it was that Sunday.

'Aidan, thanks for coming.' AJ embraced him in the doorway. 'How are you feeling?'

'Thanks, AJ. I'm fine really,' Aidan said with more confidence than he felt. 'It's just this no travel thing makes it hard.'

'You'll get to visit.' AJ gave him a peck on the cheek. 'They're remembered, you know that.'

Jeff gave him a light slap on the back. That was a signal the meeting was starting, regardless of Aidan's grief.

'Let's settle down everybody.' It was Jeff's thing to want order and output.

Dale chose to sit on a stool at the kitchen counter.

Jeff gave him a loud pat on the back as he walked by. 'Well done that man. Now the situation?'

'Yeah, but a week before the election, a thousand dead in the States in a day? In a single day?' Jean pointed at the TV, where the country's current death toll was permanently displayed in the corner of the screen. 'That's like a bad plague story from the Bible. Where did it start?'

'That's the surprise,' said AJ. 'Not China this time.'

Libby was her usual feisty self.

'What did we get? Two years' grace after Covid-19?' Is this another Covid?' She poured a coffee for Aidan. 'I'm sure the big pharma guys will— are all over that question like a rash. You know the race for a new cure is also a race to make more big bucks.'

AJ and Libby had years of sparking off each other.

'Fine,' AJ snapped. 'That's the way the world works, and it got us out of jail last time. You know we got a cure with the vaccine – vaccines within a year. But don't forget, that was a world first. You can't assume it will happen again. I know that.'

'These numbers, the daily death toll …' Aidan gestured at the TV again. Even while they were speaking, the numbers had crept slowly higher. 'The chemists better not be hanging about. I know we've dusted off the face masks, but how do you catch it?'

'They don't know, so the political advice … You've seen it for yourselves – do everything you did not to catch Covid.'

'You're not sounding so sure, AJ?' asked Jean.

'No, you're right,' she replied. 'I'm not sure at all. Sudden multiple organ failure – kidneys, liver, spleen … More like the Black Death of the Middle Ages. It's not really virus-like. More like a bacterial infection.'

'Happy Christmas not looking likely, is it?' asked Jeff.

'Jesus,' Aidan swore. 'Does this mean all those virologists will be back on the TV?'

Libby looked happy to see him interested and up for it.

'They would have been,' AJ said with a pained expression. 'A few of the big names are dead already. At this rate there won't be many left to do the talking.'

'Or to do the research for the cure,' Beth pointed out.

'So, what's next?' asked Libby.

'AJ, you said it didn't start in China this time, right?' asked Jeff.

'No, it's more universal.' For a moment, AJ looked as if she was taking a leaf out of Jean's book and addressing a class of students. 'It's following no pattern except that of targeting First World populations. That's if the stats are reliable.'

'Well, then,' said Libby, 'that points in an obvious direction – vaccinated populations.'

Jeff picked up on the point straight away.

'AJ, does this mean that this plague is hitting people who've had the Covid vaccine, or that it's hitting whole countries where the vaccine has been successfully rolled out?'

'I wasn't really being specific.' AJ shrugged.

'Jesus, if it was the latter?' Libby was not smiling any more. 'What do you think, AJ?'

'You're asking me questions nobody can answer,' she replied. 'Relating the deaths to the vaccine …? For sure, I don't know.'

'I'm telling you, love,' Jeff said urgently, 'we have no idea where this might lead.'

'Wow, wow.' AJ held up her hands, palms outwards, as if to ward off her husband's words. 'Look, I'm not dismissing any possibilities. There just isn't enough data yet.'

'Well, then,' said Beth, 'that's what we should be focusing on. What is the available data telling us? I'll get on it – we have a few new bright sparks in Analytics. They like you, Jean. Will you get into this with me?'

Jeff got to his feet and looked around at his friends, trying to gauge their emotions. Beth was so keen to do something, get on with it. He knew why – Dylan. Aidan down, yes but back in the race at least. His wife, looking unsure but determined to get on top of it. Libby and Jean, glowing, drawing strength from each other. Dale: 'Whatever it takes, chief.'

'We can do this. I don't know what the "this" is, yet.'

'We'll start doing ten p.m. check-ins from tomorrow, video chat,' he announced by way of conclusion. 'All good?'

Jeff didn't expect any objections.

The next day, Beth and Jean absented themselves to keep working. They brought whoever they needed into HQ. Dale did the driving.

As the week progressed, there was no change and not much sign of progress. People were still dying in their droves. Beth and Jean were still not in attendance by the time the Friday night meeting came around. Dale, like the others, was at home. His news from the Savior office was that they were 'following a distinct line of enquiry' – whatever that meant. Jeff was having a beer in the dining room, trying to relax with AJ.

'There's at least one pattern,' AJ said in a bleak voice. 'The daily death toll is increasing. But you can't just blame vaccines.'

'Why not?' asked Jeff.

'Because we have all been vaccinated with multiple different ones,' she said.

'If it's a new strain of Covid, then is it showing that the original Covid-19 vaccines are no protection?' asked Libby.

'Well, that's a spin already in the media,' Jeff replied. '"This is a virus, and we'll call it Covid-24". There's a statistical pattern to it – who it kills. But we don't know what it is yet.'

'Are the big companies making progress?' asked Aidan.

'No information,' AJ replied, 'but as I mentioned, it's another strange thing. A lot of their top brass and the chemists are already dead.'

'So, what are the poor bastards dying from?' asked Jeff. 'Like, there's no shortage of samples for the "medics" to get us a picture.'

'I'm not disagreeing with you, honey.'

Dale had disappeared during the call. He reappeared on their screens with his phone in hand.

'Just to say the message Beth asked me to relay. Right now, statistically speaking, the best chance you have of avoiding the disease is to have avoided the vaccine.'

'It's a bit late for that,' said Aidan.

He and Libby were sitting together in Jean and Libby's place. Jean's influence was clearly visible: they were sitting on a sofa with a crucifix on the wall behind them.

'So, the girls are seeing that pattern in their data?' asked Libby.

'It seemed bizarre that my mam and dad died within hours of each other.' Aidan was silent for a moment. 'But they were both vaccinated on the same day. I know – I took them to the vaccination centre.'

Libby took his hand in hers.

Jeff felt the energy draining out of him. Whether or not Covid-24 was a misleading name, the early stages of this pandemic were showing the potential to make the twenty million fatalities from Covid-19 look like a drop in the ocean.

'AJ, I have to ask,' Jeff began. 'Could this thing have come out of a lab?'

'It's the wrong question,' she said, 'because we can't make out what the new thing is for sure. Nothing ruled in, nothing ruled out.'

Libby glanced up at her TV. The face of a well-known actor gazed sightlessly back at her. The media continued to focus on the high-profile casualties of the pandemic. You could feel for the people you didn't know, but when your loved ones died, suddenly you weren't a spectator anymore. Aidan was proof of that. He was normally so resilient. Now he was happy to stay over with Libby, while Jean was sleeping at the office.

By Monday, the media narrative was changing. America was rapidly developing a new problem: 'How do we bury our dead?'

'You can't have thousands dying suddenly every day,' cried Jeff, placing his head in his hands while he sat at the table. 'Every freakin' day.'

'The media bullshit – "Covid 24",' said AJ. 'It's bull, and it's not helping, and there's no one to contradict it.'

'What does it matter what it's called?' asked Libby.

'Because it makes it look like we're chasing a vaccine and we're not. If it's bacterial, you need to isolate the bacteria in a lab. We haven't got it,' AJ said bitterly. 'It's a narrative that's giving people false hope. It screams, "Hang on till the vaccine arrives, like last time."'

'What's wrong with hope?' Libby was snarling. 'Why don't you fill the vacuum, go on the media?'

Something was going to give.

'Libby, for fuck's sake, will ye give it a rest?' Jeff had had enough.

A blast of cooling down silence filled the call.

'Thanks, Libby,' said AJ, hoping to soothe fraying nerves, 'but you forget we *are* the media – "Savior Media". It's the message we're missing.'

'Well, we better get the message right,' Aidan observed. 'Last time it was "Hurry the fuck up and get a vaccine." Doesn't sound too promising now.'

'Maybe the false narrative is a godsend,' said Jeff.

'I thought you were a crusader for the truth,' Aidan countered.

'Not if there's potential for the breakdown of our society.'

Dale arrived late on the call – uncharacteristically for a military man.

'Beth gave me an update for you all,' he began. Then he remembered himself and stopped to greet his colleagues. 'The girls are doing some specific analytics. Seems like a remarkable coincidence that the very group that were vaccinated first are dead first … Just passing it on.'

'You know,' AJ was talking automatically while she was thinking, 'historically the Black Death in Europe killed one person out of every three. It was the most effective killing disease ever known. The Spanish flu in 1919 did run it a close second. If the stats from Johns Hopkins keep going at this rate, we'll have a new winner in that race.'

'AJ, do we need a history lesson right now?' asked Libby.

This time, Jeff squeezed his wife's hand underneath the table.

'It's getting a bit lawless out there,' said Dale. 'A lot of the law enforcement officers are … well, dead. There seems to me to be less checkpoints on the roads.'

For the last two weekends, Beth had imposed a bit

of military discipline to keep her team locked away. It was also good to tell people they were better in a bubble to keep the disease at bay – a white lie. Judging from the split screen on the call, Aidan was back home, and Jean looked as if she had just come into her own apartment.

'Jean, looks like you just made it home,' said Jeff. 'I know you've been living in the office. Will you give us an update?'

'Yep.' Jean approached Libby and kissed her, nearly violently, on the lips, before turning her attention back to the screen. 'The Second and Third Worlds … It's set, then, to be a case of blessed are the poor, for they could not afford a vaccination.' She looked exhausted but her delivery was full of energy. 'Our cybersecurity experts are coming in handy, in reverse. We're getting access to some key databases. Need a few more days, however.'

'Dale was saying it's still difficult to move around the city.'

'That's without being armed. Dale just dropped me off.'

'Look, we have space here,' said AJ. 'Why not get everyone to stay put here? Sounds like it's getting dangerous.'

'Look, thanks for the offer, and it's a good suggestion.' Jean looked at Libby for a moment. 'It's just that we've got a bit of momentum going in the office. They're kids really, but they sure are up for it. Let us stay put for the moment. Dale can continue to funnel in supplies, yeah? He has to – can't let Beth starve.'

'The world has become a darker place,' Jean observed as she turned her head to cast a glance at the crucifix. 'It was always going to be once the children began to die.' She cast her eyes downwards. 'If you had done what society and Savior Media had asked of you, you'd get the vaccine – any vaccine.'

'Oh, holy Jesus.' The colour had drained from Aidan's face. 'Look at your news screen.'

'Where's my remote?'

Jeff switched on the TV and everyone went silent as he blared the news anchor reading solemnly from her autocue.

'The White House has reported the death of President Biden. Vice President Kamala Harris will be sworn in at midnight Eastern Standard Time.'

Even the anchors on TV looked like they were new – replacements for their dead colleagues.

'Will the election go ahead?' asked Libby.

'Trump will want it now … and guess what?' Aidan paused. 'He thinks a postal vote is the right thing this time.'

Jeff's head was churning.

If I've taken on the role of trying to make a difference, now must be the time – while there is still time. I'm part of the problem – a TimeBox agent provocateur. Right up to the end, I hadn't questioned why Savior was unimpeded in using TimeBox to promote vaccination. I knew it would be easy to deny responsibility. Make up a new narrative, with me playing a new role. Media spin, if there was a media. Maybe it wasn't my fault. I'm the one who tried to do the right thing. Maybe it wasn't my responsibility. If there was no one left, what would it matter?

He had no new message to push out.

30

Mike Maher had gotten to know Jack Davies when he was a mere Commodore of the Pacific East Fleet. Maher was staying put in San Diego, which meant that he wasn't going any further as regards career promotion. Davies kind of respected him for it, but he wasn't buying into it for himself. The second Gulf War had given a promoted Davies access to the Atlantic Fleet. He didn't waste the opportunity. When 'Shock and Awe' got under way with large-scale amphibious troop landings, zero casualties during the landing of eighty thousand Marines was always going to look good on a résumé.

Twenty years later, as American society had begun to break down, the military had become the only solution. Donald Trump was president-elect again. Davies was the most decorated officer serving on the outgoing president's chiefs of staff.

Outgoing President Harris had insisted that the meeting with Trump take place in the White House – just the admiral and the president-elect.

Trump looked uncharacteristically nervous. Like a man who could smell a rat but still couldn't resist the temptation of being back in the Oval Office. First time in four years.

When the two men sat fireside facing each other, legs apart, Davies didn't hold back.

'Look, sir,' Davies began, 'you're a master at claiming elections are rigged and fixed and all the rest of it. Now the election you allegedly just won … Well, come on – a twelve per cent turnout?'

'Davies,' Trump said brusquely, 'thing I was good at in my first term was firing people, and I think you might be next. You might want to remember who you're talking to.'

'I don't think I've forgotten that, sir.' The admiral handed Trump something he would recognise immediately: a Presidential Order. 'The Joint Chiefs are asking you to sign this.'

'And this is?'

'This is an instruction to appoint me acting commander-in-chief and to declare a state of emergency.'

'You see, Davies, I'm not president yet, so I guess I'll have to trump you on that one.' The president-elect allowed himself a chuckle, a nervous one.

'I already have one signed by President Harris,' said Davies. 'This is for continuity.'

'I'll have to take that under advisement.'

'You won't. It's a straight choice – accept this order and remain president-elect, or martial law will be declared under a military administration.'

'You got to be kidding me?'

The admiral stood up, walked to the Oval Office door and opened it. In a clearly choreographed move, the remaining four Joint Chiefs marched into the room.

'Where do I sign? Put it on the table for me.' A shrug, his nervousness dissipated. This was just another business deal. A battle lost but a war still to be won.

An executive order was issued the following day to recall all US military personnel from foreign postings. The nation had been placed under a state of martial law. That was going to change the world order straight away. The flashpoints of the Middle East had this new 'Covid-24' to deal with. The disease was starting to take out their elite: the leaders and rulers who had been first in the vaccination queue. The game was changed completely. The power vacuum that you would expect to exist once the US withdrew its soldiers just didn't materialise. All energies had to be taken up with survival, while federal apparatus, at home and abroad, started to break apart.

Joe Biden had made the huge mistake to run again at eighty-two – commendable but not smart. Kamala couldn't talk him out of it. It didn't matter, he was dead now. Trump would now fulfil his 'Four more years in four more years' promise. But only as a puppet.

31

Jeff's 10 p.m. check-ins with his team continued. Most Americans were holed up in their own homes, and the Savior Media guys were no exception. The whole environment seemed to be enveloped in a cloud of fear. Beth and Jean were staying in the office; if you left the safety of your own home, you mightn't get back. They were still staying tight-lipped on their progress.

'That was a clever move, to recall the military,' said Dale from his end.

'My dad told us that was coming,' said AJ. 'He knows Admiral Davies, the joint chief of staff guy, from work, years back when we lived in San Diego.'

'Never met him, but he sure got us landed in Shock and Awe.' Dale added.

'You're meant to give soldiers orders, not choices, but even the US military machine needs a safety valve. We hear he's bringing mature ex-military back.'

'Dale, you're keeping us on the road.' AJ made a thumbs-up to the screen. 'That's appreciated.'

'Glad to be helping. Beth took to computers better than me. Judging by the reception at checkpoints, I can keep it up for a piece longer.' Dale paused and gave a direct look into the camera. 'You know we have to go once we're recalled.'

That was a definite cue for Libby to change the subject. Being away from Jean was making her irritable.

'How is it possible that Trump got back in, or even that we could have had an election in November?' She was grimacing over the video.

'I think he was a sure bet,' AJ said in a resigned tone. 'It was hard for Kamala to win— Oh God, I'm sorry … I was going to say "even if Joe was alive".' She blushed.

'Yep, the writing was on the wall.' Aidan nodded and raised a finger to the screen. 'There are more Republicans left alive than Democrats.'

'Back on track, please, guys.' An annoyed Jeff appeared from nowhere. AJ threw him a look. 'We've got to crack this thing. Dale, Libby – how come the girls are so secretive? We need to know if they're on to anything. Fuck – I'm the boss, no?'

AJ read the signs. She was getting used to squeezing his hand under their dining room table. A signal … calm down. She spoke next, to give him a moment.

'Trump won't be a problem, though. His mission is to settle an old score, make history, massage an ego. The military are running the show and that's not going to change. A bloodless coup, my dad says.'

'The networks are covering stories from Detroit and New Orleans.' Aidan gestured towards the television behind him. 'Roving gangs, lack of food.'

'This is becoming a very black situation at a very black time,' AJ said quietly, keeping Jeff calm. 'The Black Death all over again. A temperature in the morning, massive organ failure in the afternoon.'

'Yeah, but when is it our turn?' asked Libby. 'What controls the timing – the thing that decides the day you die? The Black Death was rat fleas, yeah? But this is …?'

'We don't know,' AJ replied, 'but we do know it's as good as a metronome. You took the vaccine, because us and every crank in Christendom told you to – you *must* take it, you *need* to take it. The day you have your death sentence executed is unknown. I guess that's the code we're trying to crack – the pattern. It's not a virus … you can't just catch it.'

'Whatever it is,' Aidan observed in a low voice, 'you can't keep order if the bodies are piling up in the streets.'

32

The second week of martial law saw the army constructing 'temporary' mass graves. The local channels were giving out details on body collection points. In the entire Western world, it was unclear which countries were coping best. The American news media had become completely insular.

Beth and Jean had continued to work with their grads. Bean bags had come in handy as makeshift beds. A young statistician out of Berkeley, Davina Acmaeid, stood out and stood up. Jean at least knew a bit of math; Davina knew a lot of it. Beth had learned how to get the best out of her IT people – test them, yes, but understand their personalities for sure. On some of the evenings, when the power was out, they would eat out of cans using the glow from their laptops for light.

Jean burst into Beth's office. 'Beth, you're the supervisor, so I guess you should be the first to know.' Her voice wasn't normal and her physical movements were manic.

'Wow, slow down, girl, what gives? Fire when ready, I'm all ears.'

'Your prodigy Davina has discovered a fairly strange pattern in the data.' Jean was talking way faster than normal.

'Yeah? What exactly?'

'Well, I didn't mention it because it's a bit quasi-legal and I didn't know if anything would come of it. We got access to public vaccination records. You tabulate that with death records, while they were still being kept. They were easy to get … and, yes, there's a pattern. A very specific numbers of days between first vaccination and death.'

Beth stood and leaned over, looking closely and directly into Jean's face. Jean knew what she was thinking: *Have we cracked it?*

'How specific is this pattern, and who knows about this?'

'You, me and Davina.' Jean's monotone was back, calmer now suddenly.

'Jeff is going to want her locked down,' said Beth. 'I haven't even asked you what the pattern is. I'm afraid of the answer. But regardless … If you're right …?'

'I am,' Jean said. 'She is.'

The two women embraced each other. It was a moment.

'Then even more reason to make sure Davina is watertight – but tell me, Jean, why you're so sure?'

'Because when she showed me the numbers, it took me a little while but I could see what the pattern was.'

'What was it?'

'The Book of Revelation.'

Beth picked up her cell and speed-dialled Jeff.

'Come in, come in.' AJ was failing miserably at trying to stay calm while getting the team through her front door and into the dining room. A very young, petite, brown-skinned girl followed the others. Beth placed one hand on the new arrival's shoulder and smiled at her.

'This young woman is Davina Acmaeid, if you haven't already met her on FaceBox.'

The rest of the team greeted Davina.

'Come on in and get settled.' Jeff gave Davina a warm smile. 'Coffee's up. You know I've been encouraging you all to stay put at home, so thanks for getting here. This is a crisis now, for sure, and it's worsening rapidly. Beth and Jean have brought one of our team over from HQ. Dale, thanks again for the armed taxi service. So, thanks for coming over to brief us, Davina,' said Jeff.

Davina looked nervous and insignificant, which completely belied the confidence or her words.

'We've cracked it,' she said. 'I'm a statistician, and I love math. The anti-vaxxers are safe. The rest are all going to die with the regularity of a clock.'

'Whoa, whoa.' Aidan raised his hand. 'I already didn't like the word "die" in that sentence.'

'So, what have you found out?' asked Libby. 'Jean just wouldn't tell me.'

'She was right, Libby,' said Beth. 'This is huge. This is maybe the answer … or at least the beginning of an answer.'

'I want to take it in, but what are we saying here?' asked Jeff.

'What's the breakthrough?' asked AJ.

All questions, no answers – but there was at least an anticipation, to dilute the helplessness of the previous weeks.

Beth looked at Davina again. 'This young lady was just prepared to look – to use standard math principles while a lot around, at least in the pharma industry, weren't looking … or were dying. But I'll let Davina talk.'

'Thanks,' said Davina. 'The truth is, I'm glad I'm not vaccinated.'

'Because you found …?' asked AJ.

'The pattern …' Davina paused. 'People have died on Day 1332 after the date of their first vaccination. That's three point six four years, by the way. I'm guessing you're all racking your brains to recall when your first vaccination was.'

No one spoke – or maybe no one was able to speak.

'Well, you're all still alive,' said Davina. 'That's something, but remember how the vaccination distribution worked, because first in means first dead. In America, "first in" meant most wealthy. In Europe, "first in" meant oldest. Different dynamic.'

When nobody spoke, she just carried on.

'Well, the math is dead simple. As I say, so far people

have died on the thirteen hundred and thirty-second day after their vaccination. That's now – November 2024 – for anyone vaccinated in February 2021.'

'So …' Jeff was trying to take the information in. 'Are you telling me that anyone vaccinated – what the first group were … late in 2020 – will be dead before Christmas?'

'Your math is not that good, Mr Bourke.' Davina's expression was smug. 'They will already be dead. But I haven't finished the logic, and Jean— Ms Montgomery certainly hasn't finished.'

'Is any of this dependent on the vaccine they got?' asked AJ.

'No,' Davina replied. 'I've already tested that and it's independent of manufacturer.'

'You know the time and the hour,' said Jean.

'Jesus,' Aidan snapped. 'Jean, is now the right time to be giving us another of your Bible quotes?'

'It's exactly the time, Aidan,' Jean retorted, 'and I'll tell you why. That number Davina has uncovered – the days. Know what they are?' She didn't wait for anyone to answer. 'Well, let me tell you. Hold your hats on for this one – 1332 divided by two is 666. As you all know, that is the mark of the Beast. The Beast is associated with the End of Days. That's why I'm quoting the Bible – it's John's Book of Revelation.'

'Could it just be a coincidence?' asked Aidan.

'Do you really want to wait for your anniversary to see?' asked Davina.

'Remember,' Jean said in the same calm tone, 'the

first mass vaccinations were in February 2021, just after we got rid of Trump.'

People were rustling uncomfortably as they sat around the table. AJ broke the silence.

'We were all vaccinated in or around the same time, from memory. That was about June '21. We can look it up, of course.'

Davina did the calculations for them, in her head.

'You've got till February, then,' she said. 'Two or so months. Depends on the actual day you got your jab. Look, today is December seventh. If you subtract 1332 days, you land on February 15 2021. It's that horrifically simple – we're in the killing time. That's what you're seeing on your TV screens.'

'Jesus,' Libby gasped. 'Are we just blessed or lucky that we got the vaccine later in 2021?'

'Another piece of luck?'

'Jeff, don't read too much into it,' said AJ. 'You know the American way. You have the money and the pull, you're first in the queue. We didn't buy into that, and it turns out first in, first out to the cemetery.'

'Mass burial pit, more like,' said Aidan.

'Fine,' said Jeff, 'but as I keep on saying, let's not put everything down to mere coincidence. We're all here and we're all physically well, for the moment. Not so sure about mentally well. But it's gone way beyond time to care.'

The TV on the wall was tuned to NBC, and the caption flashed 'Breaking News'. Jeff saw it from the corner of his eye and gestured to everyone to be quiet by putting his finger to his lips.

The anchor looked grave as she announced, 'The former Speaker of the House of Representatives, Nancy Pelosi, has died.' A caption was scrolling across the bottom of the screen: 'Calls for election result to be annulled.'

Beth turned pale.

'What's wrong?' asked Dale.

'I'll have to check now,' she said. 'But because Dylan is asthmatic, we got him vaccinated really early on, remember? I'll have to check the records … documents. Why didn't I think of it already?'

All the women descended on Beth to try and help.

'What can we do?' asked Jean.

'I don't know,' answered Beth – a phrase no one had ever heard her say before.

'Here, I have it.' Dale looked up from his phone screen. 'He got his first jab on April 7 2021.'

'Oh,' said Davina. She thought for a moment. 'That means he will die in sixteen days' time.' Davina sounded like a machine with no feelings.

The outside world seemed to be unravelling right from inside the inner core of Savior Media, in a couple's dining room.

Beth was wailing. The cruelty of what was happening was brought to life upon the faces of Dylan's parents.

Jeff called Davina and Aidan aside, while Beth was surrounded and trying desperately to recover herself.

'Davina,' he said, 'we'll have to look at the language

you're using. No change of plan – you won't be telling anyone else. Understood?'

'Why the secrecy? This is important, surely?'

'That's an easy one. Our society is being barely held together by the army. You tell people that they're one hundred per cent guaranteed to die, on a specified day … game over, complete anarchy. "I'm taking what's yours – why not? And I might as well kill you while I'm at it." Please tell me I'm wrong. Are we not already seeing a bit of this on TV? I'll even have to think about what to tell Mike Maher.' He glanced at Davina. 'He's our link to the military,' he added. 'Aidan, can I ask you to take specific responsibility for Davina? Beth will need some time and space. No leaks.'

'You forgot one thing, Jeff,' Davina said gravely. 'Jean had a name for this non-virus – "the Devil's Countdown".'

'Dale, where's Dylan now?' asked AJ.

'Once this new Covid kicked off, we shipped him back to my sister in Portland.'

'Then it makes sense,' said Jeff. 'I want everyone to stay put here for now. We've got to figure this out. I want to cook dinner and think this out. We still have to eat.'

It turned out Beth couldn't eat, and Dale wouldn't eat.

Aidan could eat. 'So that is the pattern of the dying, and the numbers will grow.' He took another spoonful of carbonara and chewed, thinking. 'Who will be left?'

'This is all head wrecking,' said AJ. 'Davina tells us it's *all* the Vaccines. You know – Pfizer, AstraZeneca, Sputnik …?'

'Yes.' Davina nodded. 'As far as we can tell, the answer is "yes". We're not getting any great data out of Russia or China, surprise, surprise. But the rest … All the rest – yes.'

'Is there something unnatural going on?' asked Jeff.

'Maybe better to ask is there something supernatural going on,' said Jean.

'Let's exhaust the natural first,' Libby suggested. 'It might … Well, it *must* mean that all the vaccines share a common ingredient.'

'But we already know that,' said AJ. 'It's called hexaflorigrad. It's manufactured out of Wuhan.'

'Wuhan again,' said Jeff. 'Is this starting to come horribly together? Too many coincidences?'

'You're all sounding surprised, but that fact was well known. It might have even got a mention on a few TV shows – you know, when the manufacturing for the Covid-19 vaccines got going and the pressure was on to ramp up production.'

'Do we know who owns the intellectual property, the patent for this hexa stuff?' asked Jeff.

'No, but it should be easy enough to find out,' said AJ. 'That stuff was produced by the ton. That's a lot of invoices, if we have access to a database wizard who can follow a money trail.'

'We have,' Jeff pointed out. 'That's you, Davina. You girls might want to make a start, yeah?'

It wasn't a question.

33

AJ woke Jeff up at 5 a.m. with a cup of tea. It took him a moment but what brought him around quickly was that he had never seen that expression on his wife's face. *Is that just tiredness*?'What's wrong?'

'Jeff, I feel like a fool.'

He sat up quickly. 'What? No progress?'

'The exact opposite.'

'No, AJ, you couldn't find a money trail that quick. That is going to take days – weeks even.'

'Well, we haven't got weeks, right.' Angry now. *What a stupid question*. 'No, no, Davina went in a different direction from about three o'clock. I don't know if she was using an app or if she wrote an app. Anyway, she got this way of scanning over all references to hexaflorigrad for the last ten years of the Chinese broadsheets.'

'And ...?' asked Jeff.

'And one hit.' She couldn't look at him. 'The *Jiefang Daily*. Roughly from Google Translate, it says, "The ruling party are pleased to sign exclusivity agreements with Red Pharmaceuticals, to produce and store, hexaflorigrad."'

'It's not a money trail but it's great progress.' Jeff smiled at her.

'They'll hate me, the guys.'

'Not going to happen, let's go.' He hugged her. 'A pyjama meeting. We'll tell the others, if Davina hasn't already.'

'Wait, honey, I didn't tell you.' She started sobbing. 'Davina traced Red Pharmaceuticals. They have a company address – Cairo University. A link I should have made years ago.'

Even in the faint daylight coming through the Venetian blinds, Jeff could see she was beaten.

'You've made it now. We move on.' He kissed her. 'Well done. Let's bring it to the breakfast table.'

Jeff and AJ's dining room table had seen this group through a lot of meetings, and seen them sometimes make progress, sometimes go backwards. This morning's breakfast was going to be deadly important. Jeff ran around the bedroom doors, unceremonious. 'Up now, please, thanks.'

'So …?' Dale was scratching his head, still trying to process the latest news. 'You're saying Gabrielle's outfit has been doing pharma all along? That took a while to figure out – like a decade.'

'Yeah, I'm feeling just great about it,' said AJ. She held it together. 'He's always been doing pharma research. Now we see he's been doing shell companies with different names. But it's not even a valid attempt to disguise the source. It's Gabrielle, I don't have any doubts.'

'I was right with the name,' said Jean. 'It's the work of the Devil.'

'We have to think this out before we're all dead,' AJ answered.

'Looks like there's every possibility of that,' said Davina. It wasn't helpful.

'Dale's right, the dots are joining up after years. It's on me. Something in me didn't want to believe this was orchestrated, because if it was, it meant the Devil must be incarnate. It was never about killing Arabs and hoping for a jihad. It was about chemical warfare.' Jeff paused, visibly pale. 'Gabrielle and Zimmerman, pair of bastards, evil bastards.' Jeff broke down, head in hands. He couldn't help himself. AJ got out of her chair quickly and went to him.

'Well, honey,' she said with tears in her eyes, 'from what we've pieced together, you're right to evoke an image of evil. It looks like it's going to take God to save us all.'

'Come on, guys,' said Beth, 'it must have been my turn to cry yesterday. Today I'm wondering where your fight is. There's no way I'm giving up – *we're* giving up.'

It was Dale's turn to get out of his chair. Typical military: a fist pump instead of a hug.

Later, Jeff and AJ were taking shelter from the storm in their own bedroom. Shelter from the storm of revelation, and now despair, that the last few days had unleashed. They needed a bit of time, just lying on the bed facing each other, Jeff stroking her hair gently.

'Could we have moved quicker?' Jeff asked. 'Would that have helped?'

'Honey, you're looking for reassurance and so am I, but it's gone beyond that. This death storm is raging – Davina sure does use graphic language. Now we know the pattern – and, it seems, the source.'

'So, what are the poor bastards dying from? What are we going to die of? Like Aidan was saying, there's no shortage of samples from the autopsies to get us a picture.'

'I'm not disagreeing with you, honey. You can't manufacture a pharmaceutical that kicks in at an exact point in time. You know, all bodies are different. How can I challenge Jean when she is talking about the Devil?' AJ paused but Jeff didn't answer. His eyes were closed. 'You couldn't make this up,' she went on. 'What level of evil sets out to destroy the world – the vaccinated world?'

'Have you crossed that rubicon, AJ?'

'What do you mean?'

'You're admitting that it could just be total evil. Like manufacturing a new thalidomide, knowing the side effects.'

'What level of depraved humanity—'

'Unfortunately, there's another possibility. Maybe he's not human in the first place, and I don't just mean inhuman. I mean not human.'

'Listen, maybe we'd better get back to reality

and figure this thing out, outside the realms of the supernatural – like what to do next.'

'I'm all out of ideas,' said Jeff.

Later, the couple joined the rest downstairs. Beth and Davina continued working on their laptops in the dining room. Beth certainly wanted to keep busy. Some of the others had time to talk, and maybe too much time to think. There seemed to be a natural tendency to avoid Davina. They weren't able to gauge what she might say next. The others took to the lounge, facing out on to a wintry back lawn. Dale wasn't a sit-down type. He buzzed around between the two groups.

'We should have burst open those doors when we were there,' said Aidan.

'Don't beat yourself up,' said Libby. 'Fuck, I was sent with you not to take "no" for an answer. The fucking Devil fucked us all over.'

'You're both beating yourselves up – for what?' asked Jean.

'She's right,' said Jeff, walking into the room. 'Jean's right. You'd have found nothing – a building site in Cairo University. Last time, I asked you to get testimony for the hearing, not to go looking for a drug manufacturing lead that you wouldn't have found anyway.'

'Jeff's right,' AJ agreed. 'All they manufactured was a chemical formula. Let the Chinese do the production and distribution.'

'It was right under our noses,' said Libby, 'and we

were happy to be sent off to interview that nutjob Assad.'

'Fooled, yes, but maybe by a demon,' said Jean.

'Look, that's all sunk in the past, and we're about the future.' Something had changed; AJ looked brighter, assertive. 'I'm the pharma person, and if there is to be finger pointing … Well, then …'

'If we have one,' said Aidan gloomily. 'A future, that is.'

'Enough.' Jeff picked up AJ's new vibe. Assertive.

'Dale, would you get Beth in here for a sec?'

When Dale brought Beth back into the room, it seemed he was propping her up by holding her arm.

'Let me answer Aidan's question. "Do we have a future?"'

'We'll make one,' Jeff continued, looking across at Aidan. 'A future. It's all in. Dale and Beth, you have Dylan to think about, I know, but I don't think we can do this without you both.'

'Count us in,' said Dale. 'No turning back now. No point.'

Beth's eyes were downcast, but she started nodding. Jeff looked as if he was going to stand up, but he fell to his knees.

AJ and Beth picked him up off the floor and AJ held on to him.

'What gives?' she whispered into his ear.

He murmured back, 'The sheer bravery of them. After that news, I'm humbled. That's all.'

Libby carried on with the conversation nervously

to disguise the distress all around her.

'Look, I think AJ is right on the pharma thing. What would we have found? We didn't know what we were looking for.'

AJ thought, *That's a first.* She grabbed the moment.

'R and D in the universities sucks up lots of people and lots of funds.' AJ wanted to talk and allow Jeff time to recover himself. 'Much easier to disguise nasty money trails. No single research chemist would know the full story behind their product. The formula could be sent to Wuhan in discrete pieces. If there was ever any doubt that Covid-19 was made in a lab, it's gone now, for sure.'

'What?' Aidan looked at her in disbelief. 'Are you laying that on Gabrielle too?'

'Even I can't believe in that many coincidences,' AJ replied.

'Do you think Covid-19 was ineffective?' asked Libby. 'I mean, if we're dealing with evil, as we're saying, why not just let that pandemic do all the killing?'

'Because the Devil doesn't own nature,' said Jean. 'God does.'

'Maybe that's what the plan was,' said AJ, 'or part of it.'

'What do you mean?' Libby asked.

'Jean has a point about nature,' AJ agreed. 'Covid-19 was quite the killer initially. Nature intervened and toned it down. So, if you want to kill us all, you've got to have a backup plan.'

The conversation might have been giving Jeff a chance at gathering himself. But he just couldn't. What was killing him was that he had no idea what to do next. There probably wasn't time left to make it right, but he was still expected to lead the group.

Apart from two Americans, AJ and Jean, his two Irish insiders, Aidan and Libby, and two former US Marines, Dale and Beth, was there anyone left he could count on? The United States was not a country that you associated with coups or dystopian landscapes, but even Mike Maher had been saying, 'Is that not where we are?'

34

The leadership team of Savior Media seemed clueless about what to do next. AJ knew she'd have hell to pay when her father found out they were withholding key information of national importance. But the despondency brought on by that knowledge left her thinking, *What does it matter?*

Meanwhile, Jean bided her time till she could get the chief on his own.

'Jeff,' she said, 'you know you have to go back to Egypt – you know it – but don't take Libby.'

'Jesus,' he swore. 'Sounds like you want me out of the way, Jean. And what? Libby to take over a crumbled empire?'

'Yep, but I'm not sure now is a good time for humour.'

'Jean, if we have no humour … Oh, look, I don't know what I want to say.'

'I was driven toward Libby,' Jean explained, 'to love her for what I thought was natural attraction. But that never made complete sense. I remember telling you about seeing Libby on TV, standing in the background outside the Capitol. I think I had dreamed about that moment before it happened. I mean, I only saw her for a moment. Now I've dreamed that a village in the Egyptian desert is the place where some kind of answer will lie. Life's not all coincidence, Jeff – you said it yourself. You're being driven.'

Later, Jeff got a moment with his wife. They were using their bedroom for refuge even during the day, this time choosing to sit at AJ's dressing table.

'Jean seems to share the Hubermans' vision,' he told her in a whispered voice, even though they were alone. 'It all ends up – or ends – in Egypt.'

'You know I don't like the sound of that at all. You're not …' She looked into his eyes, worried. 'Tell me you're not thinking of going anywhere near Gabrielle.'

'AJ, what would you have me do?'

'I don't know, I don't know … Maybe stick with my old man.' Her assertiveness from earlier had evaporated. 'At least let me tell him what we've figured out.'

'But, AJ, Mike says himself the military are barely keeping it together. His is a plan that will just keep us going for a while until we die. I don't want a while. I want forever, a lifetime, children.'

'Jesus, that's the one thing that's keeping me going. We don't have to worry about children right now. You should be glad of that. Would you be able to keep Aidan and Libby going if they had kids to worry about?'

'Beth and Dale are shaken with the news about Dylan. That little boy has nearly grown up with his parents doing dangerous stuff on my behalf. You're not doubting their loyalty, are you?'

She shrugged, 'Honey, if you're going ahead with a plan to head back to Egypt, you'll soon know if blood is thicker than water.'

'I'll need them, I know, but if I don't have you with me, how can I persuade anyone?'

'Jesus, you are serious!' AJ shook her head. 'Jean has always been a bit out there. Do we want to be steered by her dreams?'

'Talk to Mike.' Jeff took her hands in his. 'Will you do that for me?'

AJ had always kept her father informed as to what Savior Media was up to. Now she had to be more careful with her information. The current situation in the country, and the military recall, meant that Mike was hard to contact in any event. America had become more insular than it had been in a hundred years. Mike Maher didn't think that further intelligence from Savior would be worth much. Martin Gabrielle was still plying his trade extensively in Egypt, for reasons that Maher didn't understand, and equally had lost interest in.

AJ shook Jeff when she returned to their bedroom.

'I lay down. Must have dozed off.

'My dad can get you clearance to fly.' AJ put her phone on the bedside table. 'I don't know for sure, but he might be able to get you a plane. It will be in and out. I mean, the plane won't be staying.'

'That was quick, thanks.' He kissed her and shivered, suddenly afraid.

'I got him. It's a huge risk for him, but he still has pull. I don't want you trekking across the desert to get out of Egypt, now do I?' She was trying to sound light, but her facial expression told him she was as worried as he was.

'I can see you've recovered – from the idea, at least. That's good.'

'I know he wouldn't leave you stranded.'

'Let's make it happen.' She could hear the determination and the fear in his voice. 'You've done your best for me, love.'

'What will I tell him, though? You know … the mission.'

'Yeah, it's always about the mission with Mike.'

'Don't be … What's your word, honey? A briar.' AJ grimaced.

'No, no, it's not that. It's that you're forcing me to think out, "what is the mission?"'

Jeff was pensive. *How do we describe the madness of it all?*

AJ knew she had hit home.

'The US has a proven track record of blaming the Chinese,' he said. 'Officialdom is not looking for a scapegoat. So, no point in saying it's Gabrielle in Egypt and we're going to have a long talk with him.'

'Why don't you tell him the Hubermans told you it would end up here all along?'

'Not helpful,' said Jeff firmly. 'If I said that, then … no plane – no way. Let me think about that one for a while.'

'One thing we have to tell him that he must take seriously. Pilots can't be allowed fly on that anniversary of their vaccination.'

'OK, but that would take a lot of explaining.'

'What happens if you don't come back?' AJ's eyes had filled up.

'Look,' said Jeff as he embraced her. 'As I never tire of telling you, I need you now more than ever.'

'Is this just a crazy self-indulgent vanity trip? What can you achieve? The damage is done.'

'I've never wanted success more,' said Jeff. 'Did we know we were all committing suicide when we took the vaccine? You know my other old hackneyed phrase – can we steal victory from the jaws of defeat? Everything has been leading to this.'

Even if she couldn't seem to lift her own mood, seeing the fight – the crazy optimism – returning to him was something. A focus, at least.

'Jean says the maths is Gabrielle contradicting Jesus in the Gospels – "You know not the time, nor the hour."' Jeff was silent for a few moments. 'So, he's telling us, "I'm as powerful as God."'

'I'm scared,' said AJ.

'Do you think I'm not?'

'I know, and I'm speaking out of both sides of my mouth. I don't want you to go. I think we all secretly think it won't be me … *us* … that dies. But it will.'

'The Hubermans …' Jeff paused again. 'I wonder if they're still alive? They could well be with their daughter by now, never having seen justice.'

AJ could see the temporary brightness in his face fade again. She had to wonder if she was losing him to a dark place. Not great, if he was really committed to the journey to Egypt.

'What are you thinking about?' she asked softly.

'Mr Huberman.' Jeff strangely remembered the scent of the man's aftershave. 'I never found out if he was military, but he sure reminded me of your dad.'

'Jeff, that's where it started – the prophecy and all that. But look where we are now.'

'Look at you. You're making the argument for me to do this final pilgrimage.'

'That's a strange word to use.'

They both lapped up the silence between them, lying on their bed.

'I must go,' he said finally, 'and something had to give. Zimmerman, the great white hope, was just a staging post for Gabrielle to do his worst. I just know I must go. I feel weak thinking about it.'

35

The next morning had an awkward start as the team tried to use AJ's kitchen to make breakfast and share coffee, tea for some.

'Come on, bring your stuff in to the dining room table.' Jeff was putting on a veneer of confidence. AJ knew better.

From the window, it was clear that the bay and the city were eerily quiet these days.

'Guys,' Jeff began once they were all seated, 'I've been talking to AJ and Jean, and going back to Egypt is … well, the plan.'

'Jesus Christ, Jeff!' Libby stared at him. 'What are you planning to do? Leapfrog over the corpses on a long walk to the Middle East?'

'If we wait any longer, that's exactly what we will have to do. I have to do something while there's still time. AJ supports me – don't you, love?'

He got eye contact and a different answer to the question from her.

'My dad tells me the military units are leaving well enough alone, unless reports get through of utter carnage. Even then, there are only solid units by asking the soldiers "Who wants to stay and who wants to go back to family?"'

'So, before it gets worse, I want to go back,' said Jeff.

'To do what?' asked Libby.

'I wish I knew. Confront Gabrielle, I guess.'

AJ could sense the same feeling she'd had on the steps outside the Capitol after the Congress hearing six years before. Lost.

'Look.' Jeff put down his mug. 'I'm not making sense, but I know I have to go, and Aidan, even in your grief, you agreed to join me.'

'That's news to me,' said Libby in an annoyed tone.

'Yeah, yeah.' Aidan knew Libby wasn't pleased at being left out of the loop. 'It's still not as mad a mission as it sounds. Like a lot of piss-poor countries, they have fewer dead than us. A poor vaccination record is turning out to be a bonus.'

Jean spoke for the first time that morning. 'I suppose economics in these countries says you got to work anyway, or you die anyway.'

'We just don't know enough yet.' AJ shrugged. 'We need data. Maybe the unvaccinated will all die in the end.'

'Except the timer is clicking on for us, right now, we do know that.' Libby regarded them all in turn. 'Look, I'm up for it. I know Jean will support me.'

'No, Libby, not this time.' Jeff shook his head. 'You and Aidan did your work in Syria and Egypt already. You've done your bit – it's my turn to stand up. I'm proud that Aidan has enough confidence in me to take his chances. You take charge here.'

'When are you going?' Libby was disorientated by their news – it felt like a rejection.

'It's got to be soon,' said Jeff. 'AJ is working on it. It's like, "Let's go before my courage fails me."'

'Cairo will be dangerous if Gabrielle knows you're in town,' said Libby.

Remember your last encounter with him.'

She realised before she was even finished that she'd regretted stating the obvious, for AJ's sake.

'Well, it shouldn't be too bad initially,' said Jean. 'I want you to go to Nag Hammadi. That's about five hundred kilometres, three hundred and forty miles or so south of Cairo.' said Jean.

'What is it?' asked Libby.

'Everything I know about the place I've only learned from a book. It's a small city now. It was the place where a discovery was made in 1945. A collection of books – biblical texts. The Nag Hammadi Library. Lost works that show a different side to Jesus.'

'Why would I want to see that?' asked Jeff.

'A bit far-fetched.' Libby looked sceptical. 'A wild goose chase, maybe?'

'OK,' said Jean, 'but, Libby … one thing. You alone already saw what I'm talking about. The texts displayed on the walls in the museum where you met Simone, remember?'

'So,' said Jeff thoughtfully, 'there's a connection between this Nag place and Simone.'

'Long way to go,' said Libby. 'Into the desert on the whim of a far-fetched link. Sorry, lover.' She scrunched up her face.

'Lib,' Jean replied, unfazed, 'all I can explain is that every molecule of my body believes I know what the right thing to do is.'

'Be careful, though.' Aidan's voice was grave. 'Look, the case against Gabrielle, and Zimmerman … Is it proven? I mean, fully proven?'

Jeff sensed the conversation was darting all over the place. He'd made a career out of pulling divergent strands together.

'You're losing faith, team,' he said. 'Look … This Nag place … We'll have to see out Jean's … well … vision. I've no other plan. I've just bought into it's time to go again, and it has to be now. The dead aren't forgotten and don't want to be explained away.'

'It's killing me to say it,' AJ added, 'but I'm not seeing any scientific way out of this.'

'Well, even more reason to let those of us who want to go, go.' Libby was getting over her earlier annoyance. 'I'm up for action.'

'Libby,' said Jeff, 'if it could be classed as a mission, we have to just get in under the radar and do our stuff, whatever our stuff is. It's just a complete reversal of fortunes that getting into a poorer country is still an option. Egypt – the whole Middle East – is functioning to a better degree than we are.'

'When the death toll grows and grows in the Arab world, these societies will break down as well,' Jean cautioned. 'There'll be no place to land in Egypt or anywhere else.'

Jeff clapped his hands for attention. 'We're together now as a team. So, we're agreed. I'll have to ask Dale, and hopefully Beth, to have tactical and logistical control for the trip. It's a lot to ask. Let's have something to eat and a drink tonight.'

It sounded a bit too reminiscent of the Last Supper for AJ's liking. She wanted a bit of time alone.

36

Beth and Dale stayed in their room. They were struggling to get in touch with Portland. The dinner and after-dinner chat was only going to be about one place.

'Jean, before I make a final decision – can we talk more about this Egyptian village?' Jeff raised his eyebrows. 'That's a long drive.'

'My dreams all make sense now, the biblical significance of the place, I knew about.'

'Look,' he said, 'we go to Cairo, yes, but why take the risk of more travel?'

'I know it's out there,' Jean insisted. 'I've read up and seen YouTube footage of the place. I have Robinson's book on it, and I want to give you my copy. Look, I swear, this is a message.'

'Jean, what's going on?' asked Aidan. 'You're talking about dreams, but it turns out you have an encyclopaedic knowledge of the place you dreamed about.'

'Aidan, don't doubt me.' She was feeling and sounding confident. 'Now is not the time. Everything has been leading to this.'

'Right,' said Jeff, unconvinced. 'So tell me more about these books … the library?'

'They were banned back in antiquity – heretical. Buried for nearly two thousand years. The Gospel of Thomas is the masterpiece. The only copy in existence.'

Libby was looking at her proudly. Her partner was making a difference. 'Don't stop there, girl.'

'Robinson interviewed this man – don't laugh … Muhammed Ali. The man who found the Nag Hammadi Library in 1945. His book describes them visiting the find site together, in the early seventies. Robinson's only regret was that the mother of Muhammed Ali had burned a few loose leaves of the library in her backyard to light her bread oven.'

'I'm glad you know stuff, Jean,' said Aidan. 'You don't have to rely on dreams alone.' He was making a strange face, and a look from Libby soon told him to shut up.

'Can you hold on?' Jeff said. 'Dale and Beth should be hearing this. If we're going, it's them that must get us there.'

AJ got up and went to get them.

'Beth,' Jeff began, 'thanks for coming down. Any luck?'

'With what?' asked Dale.

'Getting in touch with Dylan.'

'Oh yeah, I follow you,' said Dale. 'Thanks, Jeff, we got my sister eventually. Dylan is well, for now.'

He put his arm around his wife's shoulder.

'Come over and sit,' said AJ. 'Jeff wants to fill you in.'

'Jean has done a fair bit of research on what you'd call "a target destination" – Nag Hammadi.' He gestured to Jean. 'How do you sell a seven hundred-mile round trip from Cairo? Over to you, Jean.'

The challenges were coming at her, but Jean at least was glowing with confidence.

'Thomas, the gospel starts with a show-stopping phrase. "Who so ever reads and understands the words of Jesus, written down by Didymos Judas Thomas, shall not know death."' She was the only one standing. A teacher to her core, she paused and got a supportive smile from Libby. 'Forces, good forces, are conspiring to bring us to the place where these written words were discovered.'

'"Shall not know death", intriguing,' Jeff mumbled aloud. 'Maybe that's a straw we just have to clutch at.'

The room was quiet.

'AJ, as soon as Mike confirms the transport, we'll go.'

'Honey, Dad will support you whatever you decide to do in Egypt. He'll be surprised, though. He thinks you're on a wild goose chase, I do know that.'

'I'm trying desperately not to believe that myself,' said Jeff.

37

Next morning, with the churn of making the decision to travel over, there was time to try and relax among friends amid the turmoil. Two weeks before Christmas Eve, it felt as if history were repeating itself; across the country, family gatherings had been cancelled in the face of the untreatable pandemic. The team could relax a bit more if the communications were good enough to check in with family and friends. More reported mass deaths, more reports of looting. Davina was available to do their 1332 calculation. Not everybody in the group wanted to do it. Better not to know. The team were happy to see her stay in her room, working.

'Good old Donald, he's the gift that keeps on giving,' said Aidan as he raised the TV volume. 'You couldn't make this up in the middle of a national catastrophe. Listen to the spin, it's been played over a few times already today. "We can make America even greater. Why not? We will get a vaccine. I just know it."'

'The fact that he's still alive is telling me he didn't take a vaccine. But this bullshit,' said AJ, looking incensed.

'You don't think Trump is going to let the truth get

in the way of a good story, do you?' asked Aidan.

'You see what's going on,' said Jeff. 'He's spinning trash talk. What he really wants is a stupid distraction, you know – away from him being associated with this turmoil. He probably wants the Senate stormed again.'

'Why?' asked Aidan.

'Look,' said Jeff, 'he sees the Democrats are weakened, literally by death. He sees the US military depleted. He's been stood down. Why not go for it? Anything to distract from reality.'

'But, about storming Capitol Hill, there's nobody there,' said Aidan.

'It's still a symbol,' said Jeff.

'You don't see TimeBox shutting down his account either,' said Libby.

'That said, is it time to ask – should we be advising the closing down of social media now that we're under effective martial law?' asked AJ.

'It's a point,' said Libby. 'The problem is – how? You can't track or control all the servers in all the world. Look, that's one of reasons you guys will be able to stay in touch with us over video if you can get wi-fi.'

She was more positive now; Jean had given her the 'I need you here' treatment. Love is love.

'Even if you had a signed command from the Joint Chiefs of Staff,' said Aidan, 'you know all you'll get is "we didn't know that server was operational" kind of thing bullshit, and by the way, did we want Savior

Media servers closed down?'

'Sounds like the machines have taken over,' said Jean.

AJ's cell rang. It was a short conversation. She didn't leave her seat.

'Thanks, Dad, stay safe.'

She was looking at the floor. 'What's your military language?' she asked no one in particular. 'It's a go. Tomorrow from Edwards.'

Part 4
EGYPT

38

Given the state of world affairs, the US military still had influence if it could fly into Cairo West Air Base two weeks before Christmas Day and if it could get a volunteer air crew together. Dale's network of contacts had obviously survived. It wasn't easy, but favours were called in and he had been able to procure accommodation at the edge of old Cairo. There were no frills with a US naval transport flight from Edwards Air Force base. Jeff and Aidan settled for sitting on their rucksacks and strapping themselves to lanyards attached to the fuselage.

'When do you reckon the trolley service starts?' Aidan asked.

Jeff looked at him and did his best to appreciate the joke. He thought he was nervous, very nervous. Dale and Beth were talking with the ground crew.

'Jesus,' Aidan swore. 'The last time I made this journey for you, Jeff, at least me and Libby had a drinks service to entertain us. You're reading that tome Jean gave you like a man possessed.'

'Like you say, there's nothing else to do, and Jean insists there's stuff in here. By the way, that's the second time you've made the same joke.'

Jeff held up a battered copy of James Robinson's book. Aidan saw that many of the pages were marked with coloured sticky notes, annotated with scrawls in several hands.

'Feck it,' Aidan swore again. 'When did two business hacks from Dublin become theological Sherlock Holmes?'

'I guess the answer to that is a simple one – when the fate of us all is hanging out there. I wouldn't mind a drink myself.'

'Good,' he answered. Then he produced a flask out of his baggage and handed it to Jeff. He took a swig. 'Brandy, good idea.'

'Has your little bit of research thrown up anything?' Aidan raised his voice, competing with a level of engine noise that would make an already nervous flyer even more fearful.

'The woman in the story, the mother of the boys who discovered the library, she is just a footnote in this guy Robinson's book. When we land, I want to get Jean on the cell.'

There was a sudden strong waft of fuel as the engines revved up. Dale and Beth moved quickly to strap in. Aidan grabbed his own baseball cap and used it to vomit into. They were under way.

The two Irish men were surprised when the tannoy announcement came on. It woke Aidan from a fitful sleep. Jeff was still reading Robinson, eight and a half hours later.

'Landing in Shannon in fifteen.'

'Refuelling, of course, I just didn't figure,' said Jeff.

Dale appeared and walked toward them, getting a little jousted as he went. 'It will just be thirty minutes on the ground. Then four more hours and we're there. You OK, Aidan? Look a bit green.'

Aidan didn't answer immediately.

'Sad, I'm so close to my parents' resting place but I can't pay my respects.'

Dale patted him on the back. 'You'll get their man, you'll get there.' He headed back towards the cockpit.

Jeff was also feeling the poignancy of the moment. No time to visit Anne.

Beth appeared to brief them four hours later. 'We'll drive the Hummer straight off the plane. Not stopping. Not answering questions.'

'Jean,' Jeff said into his phone, 'a bit crackly but I'm glad to get you. Tell the guys, from me, that we landed safely.'

'How was the journey?'

'Aidan looked a bit green around the gills getting off the plane. Let's just say my father-in-law got us a bumpy ride. But good old Dale had a Hummer on board and the four of us are on the road now.'

'Going to your accommodation?' asked Jean.

'Hold on till I put you on speaker …' He unbuckled his seat belt, leaned forward between the front seats and pressed the Media Pairing button on the dashboard console. A moment and it crackled into life. 'No, we're on the road to fulfil your hunch – Nag Hammadi, which brings me to the question I have.' Jeff relaxed back into the spacious back seat and re-applied his seat belt. 'The pages the old woman destroyed – burned … Why is there no reference to those pages? I mean, what might they have contained?'

'Maybe she wasn't some old crone? Now might be the time to be avoiding assumptions, not making them. Look, the mother of those Ali boys was a peasant herself. I'm sure she couldn't read or write either. Her sons were digging for fertiliser at the base of a cliff face.'

'You're right, Jean. Weren't all the Egyptian dignitaries buried in cliff faces?'

'Yes, but so what if they were grave robbers and they didn't get the loot they were looking for? You've gotten that far in the book, yeah?'

'Jesus,' said Aidan. 'Now that we're travelling, what in Christ's name are we looking for?'

'Can things not be visceral?' asked Jean. 'I know you're in the right place.'

'Big words.' Aidan sounded dismissive. 'What does that mean?'

'You have to go with your gut. The fog will clear.'

Jean was her usual calm, considered self. Aidan was starting to sound as if he shouldn't be there.

'You can do what you like,' he protested, 'but not if you're battling for your life. Can we stick with facts, my friends? Look, what are we doing in this godforsaken – not to mention dangerous – place? There'll be no one left with any memory of that old woman or her family. Come on, 1945 is a long time back – seventy-nine years, to be precise. Can we get back to reality, perhaps? Think about tackling Gabrielle. That's what we came for, yeah?'

'In time, Aidan.' Jeff tried to placate his oldest friend. 'We'll be back in Cairo late tonight. We should be able to find the location of the house where the library was first taken. After that, we'll make a stab at getting.to the find site.'

'You're right, Jeff.' Jean's voice was distant and tinny over the patchy satellite link. 'See and feel these places. You see, the Christian New Testament, as everybody knows, was made up of the allowable gospels, other books and letters – twenty-seven of them. There was a load more contemporary material. So, I was telling you that the documents that were found in Nag Hammadi … Some were known about, some were new. But the question is, why were they suppressed? Not only suppressed but banned, and buried for almost two thousand years.'

'Look, Jean …' Aidan paused to gather his thoughts. 'Apart from us being religiously educated by you, there must be a stack of biblical scholars who have figured this out. Surely the world could have solved that riddle before Jeff Bourke rocked up?'

Beth and Dale were staying quiet, concentrating on the road.

Aidan continued, 'Maybe I'm nervous. Putting off tackling Gabrielle isn't doing it for me. It's making me more nervous. Whatever about visiting this town – do we have to go out to some bloody cliff? We're not going to start digging, are we?'

They were already away from Cairo on a desert crossing highway. Seven more hours of travel ahead.

'Jean's gone,' Jeff said. 'The connection died.'

'Plenty of poverty here,' Jeff observed as they started to pass through the outskirts of Nag Hammadi.

'Yep,' Aidan agreed, 'and it's to their advantage, isn't it? Can't buy a vaccine.' He pursed his lips.

'This looks rough but the satnav pics show a modern downtown,' said Beth.

'We'll avoid that,' Jeff reached into his backpack to retrieve "Robinson". He opened a marked page and read out the street name of the original Ali dwelling. Beth mechanically typed it in to the satnav.

'How about a cup of something?' asked Aidan.

'Sure. Dale, pull in if you spot any place promising. Jeff replied, subconsciously licking his lips.

The three men had emerged from their parked Hummer outside a coffee house. Dale was first to go into the canteen for reconnaissance. Beth knew well that a woman in khaki was only a recipe for attracting attention.

'This coffee house seems like a rough and ready place for local men to congregate,' Dale reported. 'Fire away, we'll be here. Ask for *naskaafay.*'

'Bring us a takeout, will ye?' asked Beth from her window.

The boys ordered at the counter. Two cups were gruffly pushed on to the counter. The natives could reasonably be accused of not being overly friendly, though not hostile … or not yet.

Aidan wondered if there were a couple of half-empty spirit bottles underneath the counter. He certainly wasn't going to rattle any cages by asking. He was glad to have their bodyguards close by.

'Here, drink that,' said Jeff, placing the coffees on their table. 'It will do you good.'

'I'd love something stronger.' Now Aidan was licking his lips. ' Fuck, that's nearly twenty-four hours we've been in transit. Getting back to your theories, Jeff.' Aidan sipped the strong, bitter coffee and pulled a face. 'We're trying to link some obscure Bible documents to our present mess, yes?'

'It's more than a mess, Aidan. I don't know yet what the link is – or if there is one.'

'Then why are we here?'

'Ask Jean.' Jeff threw him a look that signalled annoyance. 'Why has Gabrielle been living in Cairo for over a decade? We also know that Simone is working in this … Coptic Museum. Join up the dots for me. The documents, the texts, the "Gnostic Bible" that was found here … they are all in that museum. There has to be a link.'

'I thought that was just a cover for pumping big money into the regime in exchange for brewing bad pharma?'

'Maybe … Anyway, we will have time in Cairo.

Imagine – it's six years since our last encounter with Gabrielle. I'm not exactly looking forward to renewing the relationship.'

'Zimmerman,' Aidan said suddenly. 'Since we figured this thing out, he hasn't got a mention.'

'Yeah,' said Jeff. 'The Devil's assistant.'

The word 'Devil' was spoken a bit enthusiastically, perhaps, for the few fellahin at the bar. Jeff knew he suddenly had some unwanted attention.

Aidan felt the need for support. Without standing up, he made an agreed hand signal through the window. Dale emerged from the Hummer and joined them. Jeff had picked up on the atmosphere, but he wasn't sure if Aidan's tactic was the right one. Dale took his observant bulk up to the counter.

'*Salam alaykum.*' He greeted the proprietor with a smile. '*Kaffe Americano min fadlak.*'

At least someone had learned something useful during the second Gulf war.

'No need to return to a discussion of "El Diablo",' whispered Aidan.

'You'll be telling me next that the mention of Zimmerman gets their attention as well,' said Jeff.

'No, his name means nothing. But I did think that the mention of Gabrielle got a flicker of recognition,' he whispered.

'Maybe – or maybe we're all getting a bit paranoid.'

'Where to next, Jeff?' Aidan drained his cup. 'We've outstayed our welcome.'

'Let Dale finish his coffee and we'll continue the recon.'

'Yeah? Where?'

'The Coptic Church – where else?' said Jeff. 'A priest will always talk to you. That's their job.'

'Yeah, but will he have any answers, and how long will it take?' Aidan looked uneasily out of the window. 'Who wants to be stuck in this dump? If we're going out to the desert, best get it over with.'

Temporarily geed up by the shot of coffee, they were back in the Hummer and driving with satnav engaged. Dale handed Beth her Americano in a paper cup without a lid. They passed further down the winding street.

'Just about there, I reckon,' said Jeff.

'What?' asked Beth.

'The site of the old Ali family home. All dead now.' Jeff leaned forward to speak directly to Beth. 'From what I've been reading, what was released that day in 1945 was a whole lot of speculation about the meaning of these secret gospels, and Thomas's in particular.'

This very Islamic town had a Coptic church – Jeff knew that, again from reading James Robinson's book.

A priest was standing at the portal of the building when their Hummer pulled up. A young Arab man. He was noticeably taller than average with well-groomed black hair. He greeted the two Irish men in traditional fashion.

'*Salam alaykum*. When we get white visitors, I hear about it very quickly.' He gestured towards the door. 'I am Philip. Will you come in and pray with me?'

When Beth saw her friends move towards the church, she sharply nipped in ahead of the men for the standard reconnaissance. The young priest seemed aware of what was going on. Maybe he had had similar visits before.

The interior of the building was something Jeff and Aidan were not used to seeing in Ireland. All Christians celebrate the same Jesus, of course, but the Coptic Church is way more into iconography than its Western counterpart: lots of gold-inlaid paintings of the Madonna and Child, and Apostle Mark, the traditional founder of Egyptian Christianity. It was small – maybe just comfortable enough for forty worshippers.

Beth systematically checked for access and egress routes. There was a back entrance at the side of the altar. Once she checked it was locked and the key was on the inside, she was happy to crouch up the spiral staircase to the side of the front entrance, before withdrawing to keep a vigil with Dale from outside.

'Your English is very good, Father,' said Aidan. 'Thank God, I might say, because our Arabic is non-existent. Our security people speak a bit, but … anyway.'

He wasn't sure that Coptic priests were addressed as "Father", but this young Egyptian man seemed at ease with their visit – almost as if he had been expecting it.

'Let us kneel and praise the Gospel with a passage,' said the priest, commanding his own altar.

Jeff found himself wondering if the two ex-Marines outside would have found this scene strange: three grown men, on their knees, holding hands in a circular bond – in a world being ravaged by a new pandemic. What might have seemed stranger to Dale and Beth was that the meeting had gone on for forty minutes, and that they were burning daylight if the trip to the 'find' site was to go ahead that day.

'What's taking so long?' asked Beth. 'What are the boys discussing?'

'Honey, it's like this.' Dale took her hands. 'We do planning, but it's time to do faith. Dylan needs it.'

Inside the church, the impromptu mass was reaching its conclusion.

'We will pray for the many that are dying in this world,' Father Philip intoned. 'We thank God that he has spared us, and hope that His mercy will proceed for many years yet.'

All three chorused 'Amen' and, with a warm smile, the priest indicated with a gesture of his hands that they should stand. Seemingly unaware of the time, he insisted on conducting Jeff and Aidan around the interior of the church, pointing out icons and explaining aspects of the architecture as they spoke informally.

'We have a relationship with the Coptic Museum,' he said. 'Mr Gabrielle and the lovely Simone have been here before you.'

The two Irishmen had been at ease – but not now, at the mention of Gabrielle's name. Aidan took the revelation in his stride, but Jeff literally needed to take a step back.

Obliviously, Father Philip continued. 'I was indeed mindful that other foreign visitors would be coming, as Ms Haddad was keen to ensure that "other parties" were offered hospitality. I'm guessing you and the good people outside are the other parties. Indeed, our small town is getting a lot of outside attention in recent years, which has helped my language skills.' Finally noticing Jeff's discomfiture, he smiled. 'You are versed with the personalities, I see – and yes, I am intimately acquainted with the Nag Hammadi Library. We do not have a large Christian community, but our church is placed here to recognise and commemorate the site … the find … the event.'

'You seem, Father Philip, to have been expecting us?' Jeff had found his tongue again.

'My friends, we Copts are vigilant.' His face fell. 'There have been many attacks – violent attacks. There are many enemies of the risen Christ in this country, a country that is so connected to the early Christian Church. It's wise, therefore, to be aware.'

'I'm not sure I knew anything about the Coptic faith until recent research informed me,' said Jeff.

'That is no matter, but in the world as we now find it, it seems strange to be welcoming … well … tourists.'

'I'm afraid, Father, it's a long story.' Aidan couldn't help grimacing slightly. 'And according to Jeff, it requires us to visit this site of the Nag Hammadi find, regrettably.'

'Ah …' Father Philip smiled. 'That sounds like … Oh, what's the word? Sceptic?'

'Scepticism, Father,' Aidan supplied helpfully. 'You got that right.'

'God will bless you, that is all you need to have faith in.'

The priest blessed them with the sign of the Cross.

The three men had just emerged into the entrance porch when the shot rang out. They stood temporarily motionless. In retrospect, you could join the dots: the pop; the mini explosion of the cement mortar emitted from the front wall of the church; the possibility of a second – and maybe a third – shot.

Two well-trained former Marines had been through this drill before. Jeff, Aidan and the priest were forcibly bundled back through the porch and the two open doors, with Beth and Dale cramped down and working in protective shielding mode. The second shot rang out and the round entered the porch, ricocheting off the walls, miraculously hitting nobody. Shouting commands at each other, they slammed the doors forcibly shut with an unceremonious clatter. Once the doorway was secure, the soldiers went into auto-mode. The spiral staircase in the corner held the promise of presenting a vantage point. Father Philip again made the sign of the Cross in a calm, unhurried fashion. This was a man who believed in God's will – and that will, on this day, seemed to dictate that nobody had to die.

From above their heads the three survivors heard breaking glass, but then nothing. Dale returned down the stairs. 'I smashed a panel in the oriel window to give an opportunity to return fire.

'Jesus,' was the easiest profanity that a rattled Aidan could muster.

'We just caught a glimpse of the shooter's position,' Dale explained, 'but a handgun returning fire at that range was never going be an option.'

'Thank God for that mercy,' said Father Philip.

'Yes.' Dale paused for a moment. 'I think if God had a role in positioning your church this far from the vantage point that the minaret offers, then, yes, I would be thanking Him.'

'That was a professional, for sure, to be that accurate from half a mile away.' Beth had run down the stairs to re-join them. 'The distance is the only reason we didn't receive a direct hit.' She re-engaged the safety catch on her automatic. 'Lots of movement from the sniper position. Are we pursuing? They're on the move.'

Jeff intervened. 'Guys, did you notice Father Philip has a nice Christian cemetery here, at the side?' He managed to speak calmly, but the others could see that the hand he was gesturing with was shaking. 'I wasn't planning on being in it.'

'Just an option,' said Dale.

'How safe is it to carry on to the find site?' asked Jeff.

'Depends,' said Beth. 'If our new friends have an idea of where we're headed, then a simple ambush in the desert becomes a real possibility.'

Jeff looked at Aidan; the former Marines were only offering options, but he would appreciate his friend's opinion as well.

'What do you think?'

Aidan took his time, thinking, *The two soldiers are good solid professionals – and friends. They might just be a bit unnerved at having been caught on the hop.*

'We're a long way from Cairo, did you really fancy coming back?' he asked. 'I mean, given the circumstances. Has anything changed in making you want to see the find site?'

Beth noticed Aidan was calmer than Jeff.

'That was no small event, guys,' she said. 'When it sinks in, you'll likely go into shock.'

Father Philip raised a hand. 'I can suggest you drive to the Monastery of Athanasius first,' he said calmly. 'It's roughly on the way. At least then you'll be told of any unexpected visitors to the area.'

'Can you call them?' asked Aidan.

'Contemplative monks do not require phones, I'm afraid.' If he was shocked, he was getting over it quickly. Nobody spoke for a full ten seconds while they weighed up the options.

Jeff eventually made the call. 'Let's do it.' He was afraid to make any gesture. He knew his hands were shaking.

'If that is your decision, I'll radio the abbot,' said Father Philip.

'Radio?' asked Aidan. 'What …?'

'Yes, radio communications.' Father Philip looked at him. 'They are contemplative, not stupid.'

39

It took the guts of an uncomfortable hour to get close to the co-ordinates of the monastery. The eerie but strangely beautiful smell of incense presented itself well before they got to the vault-like front doors. This was an imposing citadel. It shimmered in the far distance. That couldn't have been because of the heat – it was cool; there were maybe only a couple of hours of daylight left. It was more because the dusty golden render, contrasted with the reddish desert background, had a hypnotic effect on the eye. It was designed to be invisible.

They were met at the entrance by a startlingly thin man with a heavy grey beard, dressed completely in black and wearing the tall headdress of the Orthodox faith. He greeted them in heavily accented English

'Allow me to introduce myself – I am John, the abbot.'

John was a man in his seventies, maybe even eighties, Jeff estimated. His inscrutable expression didn't make it clear if he was welcoming his visitors, or merely tolerating their unexpected presence.

'Father Philip told me to expect you.'

'I've nothing on my mobile reception,' commented

Dale, maybe to elicit a reply to an implied question.

'Ah.' The abbot smiled. 'But you know we have radio communications with Saint Mark's and other locations. God governs all, but we must help ourselves, must we not?'

It was hard for Jeff to work out what Father Philip would have told his fellow Copt. He had to be shocked from being shot at only hours earlier. Jeff didn't know how he was feeling. Aidan was acting strange. *Calm, but he could have been killed earlier. Why wasn't he shaking? I am.* The group stood uncomfortably at the citadel's entrance in the red North African desert.

Where to next? Jeff was thinking.

'I am told you will visit the sacred library find site,' the abbot continued, 'but you will not visit it today. Instead, we will offer you hospitality.'

'You're very kind, Abbot,' Aidan answered, 'but our intention was to be on the road back to Cairo tonight.'

'My dear gentlemen, my gentle people.'

He turned and walked inside, leaving the visitors with no choice but to follow. A young monk controlled the door which took some effort to close behind them. The hallway was cavernous and cold.

'Your lives are in danger for more reasons than I can begin to explain.' The abbot paused but at least seemed to soften his tone now that he saw the dismay on at least some of his visitors' faces. 'Whatever your itinerary, you surely must say that you are acting like fools. You were shot at only hours ago. You can hardly expect me to send a novice guide with you, and unnecessarily endanger a God-given life.'

'Not at all,' Aidan tried to correct the abbot. 'We have co-ordinates, and Beth and Dale are experienced and armed.' Aidan gestured to the Marines.

The abbot's face showed a friendly expression for the first time in the conversation. 'My friends from the civilised West, you perhaps have no concept of the forces you're dealing with.' His eyes were fixed on a silent Jeff, without blinking. 'I can explain more when we break our fast. For now, I must return to prayer. You will be guided to your cells.'

The word 'cell' didn't conjure up any great imagery for the team. Dale, doing his job, advised their host that he would have to do a reconnaissance tour of 'the site', the monastery. The abbot simply dismissed the suggestion with the gesture of a hand wave. It was neither a *yes* nor a *no*, and it probably meant that many locked doors and passageways would make a nonsense of a recon. He was gone.

A novice guided them silently to their cells. He waited patiently outside. Beth had a brief discussion with the monk, in broken Arabic, about the location of the bathroom. The four got some time to settle in. The cells were two adjoining rooms, with two meagre single beds in each. Space was tight enough to make you believe that they normally held a single cot each. At least then you could kneel to pray. Jeff and Aidan sat on the ends of their cots while Beth and Dale talked standing at the cell door. She might have been ten years out of the service, but it was in Beth's Marine

DNA to monitor a couple of civilians who had just had a close call with death. She called it monitored rest. *Sit or lie on your bed. Let's keep the chat to a minimum.*

The same novice returned later and signalled with a hand gesture up to his mouth. It was time for dinner. He guided them again through the stone passageways, knowing exactly where he was to deliver them to.

The meal was a more sumptuous affair than the visitors were expecting, served with wine. The monks were assembled in dormitory fashion: young and old, and some surprisingly young. The four were led through the main dining room with its rows of communal male diners, and through a door in the mahogany-panelled partition wall. The abbot's private dining room seemed to be made to measure, in that the imposing cedar table could accommodate eight. A younger monk, Brother James, introduced himself as he and the abbot took their seats at either end of the table.

There was no mistaking that Brother James was an Egyptian. Jeff guessed that he was in his fifties; his dark brown skin matched his woollen garment and leather sandals. The abbot's lineage was a little less easy to discern. The whiteness of his all-encompassing beard seemed to lighten the skin tone of his remaining visible face – the top of his cheekbones and his forehead beneath the headdress.

They were served by their guide, who entered and left the kitchen through another adjoining door.

'Gentlemen and lady,' Abbot John began, 'I hope

you are at peace following your traumatic day. Let us join hands in prayer. Let us also celebrate our female guest – although I will speak later, I think, of another woman visitor.'

Jeff and Aidan had grown up in an Ireland where grace before meals was reserved for wedding celebrations. However, Beth and Dale were from good old-fashioned Episcopalian stock – no strangers to prayers before meals.

Serving dishes of various lamb and goat courses were brought in, all drowned with aromatic couscous. The priests and the Irishmen availed themselves of a glass of wine, while their military escorts abstained.

'There can be no room for dishonesty in a house of God,' stated Abbot John flatly. 'Tomorrow you will visit the most unassuming, the most ordinary, the blandest of desert sites. You know the history of the site already, and you approach it as if you are fooling me into thinking you are tourists whom Father Philip offered the kindness of an introduction. You underestimate us, my dear gentle people.' He leaned forward, his eyes narrowing as he focused on Jeff's face. 'Your exploits in Syria … Libya … Egypt before that, and now finally again, have long since come to our attention. It's been going on since the very beginning of time. Clichéd, I know, but it's quite simply the battle against evil.' The monotone in which the abbot spoke merely served to heighten the gravity of his words. 'You Catholics, your Pope, pronounced several decades ago that there was no Hell. No such pronouncement was – or could be

– made from the Holy See of Alexandria. Likewise, all our brother Orthodox churches, in Syria, Russia and India, quite simply not just believe but *know* the Devil and his Hell exist. The Devil exists and is always among us. The risen Christ met him in his day and in this desert, and I believe you, sirs, have met him in your day.'

The abbot had his audience spellbound with his monologue. They were eating very, very slowly.

Jeff was remembering the mantra of his old confirmation prayers: *Do you reject Satan, and all his works …?*

The former Marines had memories of their church's more graphic depiction of 'old Nick'. Beth looked mesmerised, eyed wide open, by the old man's words as the meal continued.

'Abbot …' Aidan's voice brought everyone back to reality. 'In the world as it now stands, I have to ask – what good can it be to be a contemplative monk? Like it looks, it's a case that the world is ending for many millions, billions of the vaccinated.'

'Jesus took forty days and nights in this desert to contemplate how to defeat Satan,' Abbot John replied calmly. 'If you have an accusation, then it could only be that we take a longer time than our Lord and Master. I would contend that the Devil has been here in Nag Hammadi, and has based himself in Cairo for some time. If not himself, then, more likely, one of his loyal emissaries will have pulled a trigger in the direction of you men and woman this very day. So, you see why I am reluctant to support your adventure in this desert, at least during the hours of darkness.'

Beth was looking at her husband and thinking, *Have I ever seen his jaw drop open like that?*

You should also be aware that it's not an adventure you are on, but instead, the deadliest battle that has been fought in this world in two thousand years.'

His words continued to captivate the four visitors. Only Aidan, it seemed, was overly keen to get to the punchline.

'Please, abbot … Please continue.'

The old man paused again. This time, he and his brother monk took a sip of their wine in unison. Somewhere beneath the entangled beard was an expressionless face. It wouldn't reveal if this was a man who had been waiting for many years to tell his story.

'I see you gentlemen are keen to have the mysteries of two millennia revealed in an instant,' he said eventually. 'This monastery dealt with the Devil when my ancient predecessor hid the Nag Hammadi codices, close to the time of Christ. He knew they would be needed in time, to save us – if we can be saved. I fool you not. He will come to judge the living and the dead, and His kingdom will have no end. But this earthly world will have an end.'

Seeing the need to recover from Aidan's rudeness to his hosts, Jeff decided it was his turn to speak.

'Abbot, surely the world – or at least the ecclesiastical world – knows about all this?'

'All what? I have told you nothing yet … including

what must be, to you, the dawning realisation that you were sent as a prophet. You are an emissary, a worker ... one who comes before.' The abbot hesitated. 'But remember ... Jesus also had Judas to deal with.'

The guests didn't know where to look. They continued eating. They all felt that a punchline was coming – and it was.

When the abbot had taken another sip of wine, all eyes were still upon him, but it was his subordinate, Brother James, who spoke next.

'We believe Gabrielle is the fallen angel.'

There was complete silence around the table. Nobody spoke – who would dare break the spell? None of the visitors knew where to look, or knew who would speak next.

The abbot soon brought everyone's minds back into sharp focus.

'The Austrian Devil was dead, but a new one was released upon us almost immediately in 1945. You know some of the story, I know, or else you would not be here. The Ali brothers were dupes to the Dark Angel. Those men murdered under the guise of blood revenge. They were cannibals and witless accomplices in releasing Gabrielle among us. Their mother warned them, but in the Muslim culture the woman must be subservient – even a gifted seer. They were never going to listen anyway. Their lust for gold was as heavy as the wine jar they carried. A jar the size of a man. The wonder of it was that she managed to phantom away the missing codex cover

– allegedly burned … but perhaps not.'

He left this implied revelation hanging in the air, like the golden filigree from the broken codices, eighty years before. That was in a dwelling not thirty kilometres from where they now sat.

'The three men – brothers, grave robbers – spun a tale to the Western visitors who came later,' the abbot continued. 'In fact, they ran home to their widowed mother for guidance, and then drove their mattocks through the jar, ignoring the very imploration of a devout Muslim woman. And now we all get to reap what was sown.'

'So …' Jeff was processing everything he'd heard over dinner. 'The site we are to visit tomorrow is only the place of the find, and not where the library codices were opened?'

'Simple as that.' The abbot allowed himself a slight smile. 'These fellahin could never admit that their courage had failed them, and that they needed to be shielded by a woman's skirts. It didn't matter in the end. The Ali brothers would not disobey their mother. Another of the fellahin, another grave robber, struck the blow … and the rest, as you Westerners say, is a terrible history. An ongoing nightmare, where life is taken away so easily as to render its sanctity worthless. First by the Arab Spring, a test bed for the evils of the new media, and then by the deadliest virus.'

The abbot paused, and when no one spoke, he continued.

'Except, my new friends, we're making history.

What is also at issue is that we may be the end of history. I ask you – did you ever think your catechism learning about Judgement Day would come to pass in your own lifetime? Saint Paul thought it would happen in his. Such a time was waited for, at every time since the very first decade after Jesus. But who is watching for the signs?'

Neither Jeff nor Aidan could reply. They didn't know what the question meant. Jeff knew from Jean's research that the Codices of Nag Hammadi represented an ancient branch of Christianity – the Gnostic discipline. It claimed to be about secret and sacred knowledge, but the word Apocrypha – the End of Days – was interwoven throughout it.

'Father, sorry, Abbot ...' Aidan paused, taking in what he'd heard. 'None of this version of the story is published, is it?'

'And how does that surprise you?' The old abbot took another sip of his wine. 'If you even take the world around us in the last decade, there are more fantastical happenings – dastardly happenings – made by men ... seldom women. Who would believe a simple biblical story foretold. This is a world that you, Mr Bourke, have helped to create – with your social media, where the truth is a necessary and simple casualty. Decent investigative journalists uncover part of the truth from time to time. They find out about Russian planes sent to bomb Syrian hospitals – a gross stain upon our brethren in the Holy Russian Orthodox Church. Even more have been stained by

Putin in Ukraine. But never mind them. What about all the unseen and undiscovered works of evil?'

Jeff was unnerved by the accusation. 'But, Abbot,' he protested, 'our media platform is often used to expose the heinous.'

'More evil than good, more sinning than sinned against, my friend.' The abbot's glare did nothing to soften the anger in his words. 'You yourself have investigated all the alleged good work of TimeBox in promoting the deaths from the Arab Spring. Your Congressional hearing did not go so well in protecting the truth. A price was paid. Your Congress rejoiced in findings of interference in your Trump election, but it could say … well, nothing about the carnage in North Africa, including here in Egypt, but more terribly across the Red Sea in Syria.' The abbot paused, but he was a long way from being finished. 'But now we must ask why the Dark Angel is delving into chemistry – because I think chemicals can kill more than even Assad, Putin and your Bush have managed with their bombs. Chemicals are the apocalypse.'

'But Abbot, Brother James …' Jeff's head was spinning either from the abbot's accusation or from the assassination attempt of earlier that day. 'Why Egypt? We believed our team were alone in cracking the code. Your knowledge comes as a shock to us. A pharmaceutical apocalypse is on top of us. This is a beautiful and historic country, but hardly a world leader in pharmaceutical production.'

'My friends, a young Jesus spent his childhood

years in this very land.' The abbot's pride in this fact was evident from his expression. 'The chosen people emerged from slavery from this land, having eaten the manna from Heaven. The earliest Christian churches flourished in this land even while the Roman Empire tried to extinguish them. If a battle must be fought to prepare the way for the chosen one, then it will be fought here, on sacred Egyptian soil.'

'So …' Aidan began. 'We're living … what? Some kind of biblical re-enactment?'

'Aidan, please,' said Beth. 'We're guests.'

The old man smiled politely, overlooking Aidan's interruption.

'The Muslim woman Ali made her way here on foot, injured and travelling in the dead of night.' The others listened in silence, enthralled by his words. 'It was late in 1945, nearly the Coptic Christmas – a cold night in our desert. She was received by my direct predecessor, Father Alphonsus. They spoke until before dawn, and she presented this monastery with a codex cover she had rescued from the tumult of that day. She felt that either a prized possession protected her, or that she was overseen by a protector. She told my predecessor that a supremely evil spirit had been unleashed in her own home that day. It must not be allowed to have access to the "key". She was guided to removing this most important piece. The stupid men, her sons, were in too much of a mixture of terror and disappointment to intervene. We've been watched here, and we've watched over her bravery.

What happened nearly two thousand years ago, in hiding the secret, is also a tale of bravery in the face of evil, but its detail is lost in the mist of time. Your bona fides, Mr Bourke, are not in doubt, nor those of your friends. You have put your lives in danger today – and more than once. But you have been dupes for the evils of social media, and you must acknowledge that there is blood on your hands. Beware – the Judases of this world are equally always among us. You know that before you are judged by the risen Christ, you must play your part. You think you and your small brethren – your monks, and indeed your nuns – have been alone in their crusade.'

Both Jeff and Aidan should have been aghast at the abbot's encyclopaedic knowledge of them and their exploits. Now, surprise was beyond them. The story was far from complete, but the four friends knew that the tale now unfolding was unrepeatable – because it was beyond belief: a story of stewardship of some spiritual secret as old as Jesus. There had been so many verbal punches delivered so far that the Westerners could have been forgiven for feeling dizzy. The abbot had introduced them to a whole new concept: 'chemical apocalypse'.

'You have earned a right to see the cover of the sacred script,' the abbot announced suddenly. 'This holy thing is kept securely here. It has been seen by maybe only a handful of us in two thousand years.'

Jeff felt a shiver from within his core. At that moment, he felt empty. What in God's name lay ahead?

40

'You'll come with me, after your coffee,' said the abbot.

'Just you, Mr Bourke,' Brother James added.

Jeff was suddenly feeling woozy. He was regretting taking the glass of wine. His mind was wandering.

Aren't monks kind of famous for brewing their own stuff? Strong stuff. Maybe that's it.

Dale picked up on the situation immediately and stood up.

'Not possible,' he said. Beth joined him.

The new tension in the dining room was certainly lost on the abbot.

'I will speak,' Abbot John said firmly, 'because your lives could depend upon my words. And yet, your lives could make the difference.'

'To what?' Aidan's tetchiness wasn't finished.

'To the continuance of life on Earth,' answered Brother James. Maybe he was giving the abbot's head a rest from Aidan's tetchiness.

The novice monk on serving duty re-entered the room. He placed coffee on the table. The visitors certainly needed it. The abbot seemed unruffled, though, and continued in his own time.

The monk offered to pour. The abbot declined by placing his hand over his cup. He was happy to continue sipping his wine.

'What I wish to show you is designed to help you,' he said. 'What I wish to show you is from God himself, touched by the hand of Jesus himself. Will you come with us, Mr Bourke? Just you?'

Jeff nearly couldn't help himself. Every fibre of his being wanted to say 'no'.

Not more, more, more responsibility.

But 'no' wasn't in him – not when he thought of his wife, and his friends, his family, young Dylan and the years leading up to this moment. The millions dead, and the billions more to come. *How could this day have turned out so extraordinarily?*

Jeff propped himself up and Dale stood instinctively. Beth was on her feet moments later.

'Guys, sit, please.' Jeff waved a placatory hand to the Americans. 'These aren't the people taking shots at us. These are men of God, who have given us hospitality, and who deserve our trust.'

Brother James took Jeff's cue and rose from his chair while Dale resumed his.

The three men walked as Brother James led the way through a labyrinth containing many locked doors, and with not a window in sight. Maybe it was the pace of the procession, but Jeff was feeling calm again, vaguely aware that they were descending. Their journey ended somewhere underground.

'This is the oldest part of our monastery,' Abbot

John said as they halted at the final door. 'The temperature is always constant. Very good for preserving manuscripts – the work and the word of God.'

Brother James unlocked the heavy door. Jeff wondered where and when he had picked up the impossibly large ring of keys. Such trivial thoughts at such a time. He was ushered to sit at a plain wooden table, with only two chairs available. Brother James produced gloves and approached a mounted tabernacle with a final key. What heightened the intrigue of it all for Jeff was that a solitary lit candle was already present in the room as they entered. Its meagre light was augmented by the candelabra with which Brother James had led the way.

'You may already know this,' the abbot began, 'as it's no secret, but when the Gospel of Saint Thomas was first opened and read in 1945, that was for the first time in nearly two thousand years. It started with the sentence, "These are the hidden words that the living Jesus spoke, and Didymos Judas Thomas wrote them down. Who so ever shall find the meaning of these words will not taste death." The Coptic Museum has that treasure, but we have ours.'

As if on cue, Brother James produced an ornate silver case.

'You come to Cairo and Nag Hammadi on your final journey, Mr Bourke.' The abbot's voice echoed, disturbing the candle's flicker.

Jeff tried not to show the unease he felt at hearing

the word 'final.' If he could have asked Dale at this point, he was sure the hard-bitten ex-Marine would have just given one of his down-to-earth answers: 'Treat every journey you take as if it could be your last. That's a good way of making sure it isn't.' He let the abbot's words sink in before replying.

'I believe, Father, we came because there was either nowhere else to go, or because all roads led back to Egypt.'

'How precise your words are, Mr Bourke. Gabrielle is here in Egypt, but you could go anywhere and meet a demon. But in only one place will you find the source of the vaccine poisoning, while your vaccinated Western world has now surpassed us in the dreadful count of dead souls. It all has a terrible … what's that word …? Irony about it. My Lord and Master and Saviour called for a just world and promised that he would return to establish one. The Devil is forcing that time upon us all.'

'It's that countdown that worries us.' Jeff knew it was time to explain the real reason behind their visit. 'My wife has ties with the virology community. But we cracked the code, the deadly code – thirteen hundred and thirty-two days after you were vaccinated would signal the day you die. Then it all made sense … terrible sense. The cause was in Cairo maybe, and if it was, then the answer was also here. Abbot, you say that you have the advantage of not being vaccinated, but why do you risk infection by allowing us in?'

'That, my young friend, will become clear soon

enough.' The abbot placed his hand on Jeff's arm. 'All death is certain. God will decide the when and the how. Let me explain, Mr Bourke. The missing cover you are about to see is from the only copy of the Gospel of Thomas in existence. The widow Ali always said, while she was alive, that she burned it in her bread oven. Her sons never contradicted this, either out of fear, or incompetence, or else just not knowing.'

Jeff was dumbfounded by the abbot's revelation. He stuck his tongue right into the roof of his mouth and thought, *Don't speak.*

'The reason why all this is so important is because that cover states what the Gnostic secret is.'

The abbot signalled to Brother James, who opened the lid of the silver case to reveal a worn leather book cover, as bland as could be … except for the engraved text. The lettering glowed in the candlelight.

Jeff couldn't help himself.

'Then what is it – the secret?' he blurted. 'What does it say?'

'It is a code,' the younger monk replied. 'A key – a number, written in Aramaic.'

'Abbot John, Brother James …' Jeff was struggling to gather his thoughts. 'In some way we're here because we discovered a maths pattern – the pattern of life and death. Look, there's a confirmed timetable for dying, established and proven. If the message gets out – and it will … Well, the question is – when will society break down completely? There are reports of that in America already.'

'We have had our suspicions about the poison vaccines,' said the abbot.

'But who would be listening, and how would we act?' Brother James interjected. 'We were waiting for you, sir.'

Jeff was thankful for the coolness of the room, but it was strange; there were beads of perspiration forming on his forehead and on his back. He knew that a task awaited. These men of God talked and acted without emotion. Jeff's mind was in turmoil.

Maybe this will be the last task, but maybe it will end me. Where do I stand on self-sacrifice? Would I give myself up for the lives of the world? Will it come to that? What am I now going to be asked to do?

Brother James blessed himself as he reached into the silver case with his gloved hands. He placed the ancient book cover on the white linen cloth set upon the table. The abbot also blessed himself, and placed his gloved open palm upon the writing. He closed his eyes and intoned, 'It is with reverence that I touch something that I know was touched by the risen Jesus.'

The writing looked to Jeff like a collection of symbols from some forgotten language. They were brilliantly white, even in the dimness of the little room. He might as well have been looking at hieroglyphs.

'What do the numbers mean – the symbols?'

'It's you who must find their meaning,' the abbot replied solemnly.

There was silence while the participants in this quiet drama took in the moment.

'Even the Saviour's parables needed to be decoded.' The abbot was pointing at the cover of the codex. 'I believe you will translate it for yourself, Mr Bourke. The Coptic Museum, as you surely know, must be your destination.'

41

Jeff wasn't sure how long he had been away from the dining table. Perhaps not as long as he thought, because his three companions were still sipping their coffee – though he suspected that they were on the second or third refill. The abbot had retired for the evening, and Brother James invited the four visitors to similarly retire to bed before dispatching the now familiar novice to show the guests back to their cells. He didn't wish them goodnight. He did, however, bless them with the sign of the Cross and said, 'Morning prayer will be at four o'clock. Then we break our fast before daybreak. After that, we will visit the site of the find of the sacred book.'

Jeff carried a hastily poured cup of coffee along the candlelit passageway leading back to their beds. When the four were alone, Beth spoke from the door.

'I'll take the first watch.'

Jeff knew that leopards weren't going to change their spots. But he did try, feeling calmer … tired.

'Beth, Dale, give yourselves a night's sleep.' He gave them a reassuring smile. 'This place has been well able to protect itself for way more than a thousand years. I think we'll be OK within this fortress. Tomorrow we'll be out in the open – that's a different matter.'

'No problem, chief,' said Dale, 'but it's expecting the unexpected that keeps you alive.' The former Marines were about to leave Jeff and Aidan's cramped cell.

'Stay, guys,' said Jeff. 'I think you'll want to hear this.'

'Well, tell all.' Aidan chuckled. 'Are you suddenly one of these enlightened types – Zen, like?'

'Oh, man.' Jeff sighed. 'If anything, I'm more in the dark than the light.'

'Well, come with it, come with it,' instructed Aidan.

He was trying not to be impatient and acting like he was well wound up. Jeff took a sip of his coffee, preparing what he was going to say.

'I think I know less now, not more,' he began. 'These men showed me a very unimpressive codex cover. That's this fancy word for a leather book cover that we keep hearing. You won't be surprised to hear that the special storage room was dimly lit. I did see this ornate handwriting on the front of the cover. It's written in Aramaic, the clerics told me. The writing … It's beautiful, really, you know – kind of like the Book of Kells stuff, but without the pictures.'

'Come on, though,' Aidan urged his friend. 'What did it say?'

'It was the written version of a number, or a code.'

'What number?' Aidan asked. '1332?'

'They didn't tell me,' said Jeff, 'but they repeated what Jean told us. The Gospel of Thomas starts with the words … phrase … sentence, whatever. Something along the lines of "whoever reads and understands these, the written down words of Jesus, will not know death." Probably not exactly, but you get the gist.'

'Like a two-thousand-year-old clue,' Aidan mused. 'That's what we came for, isn't it?'

'Yeah, but they pretty much said, "go figure it out".' Jeff shrugged when his friend looked at him for more information.

'Not exactly hospitable?' said Aidan.

'Yeah, but you're right. That's what we came for. Half a chance to stumble into something small or big. Something that would make a difference.'

Jeff leaned over and got James Robinson's book out of his backpack. It was the only book among the change of clothes and toilet bag.

'Yeah.' He held up the book and Aidan squinted at the cover in the dim candlelight. 'This guy Robinson, Jean was telling me, was one of those Southern Bible Belt guys. He is one of the reasons I got us – or, rather, she got us going – on this mystery tour. The Nag Hammadi Library – Jean drew me to the story. Robinson made this stuff his life's work from the sixties on. But what's happened in the last twelve hours is fantastic. Here …' The book fell open automatically to the right page; it had clearly been read many times. 'Robinson has his translation of Thomas, the fifth gospel. What I read on the plane over … He's saying that, if nothing else, this book is unique – the only full version of a lost gospel.'

'What the feck does it mean for us?' asked Aidan.

Jeff paused to mechanically sip the last of his cup, not really knowing if there was any coffee left in it. Aidan had seen this distant glaze in his friend's eyes before. Jeff spoke more slowly.

'The abbot gave me the story of how the monastery got possession of the cover of the lost gospel. It's a "key" to unlocking something.' Jeff was thinking aloud.

'No, you're losing us,' said Aidan. 'What words? A number? What key?'

The Americans were staying quiet.

'A two-thousand-year-old puzzle for unlocking something, or protecting something. You might have to have me certified.'

'Look, it's getting confusing,' Aidan prompted. 'Tell me what you've figured out in your own time.'

'There hasn't been a time in human history where the complete destruction of our world – our human world – was as close as it is now. We're here for a reason.' Jeff looked at his friends in turn, trying to gauge their reactions. Was that hope in Beth's face? Had young Dylan got at least a sliver of a chance? 'Now I see that. This book, this single surviving Gospel of Saint Thomas, is the oldest Christian document in existence. I believe we are being told it was written while Jesus was alive. It's not just another book written after the man's death. This is going to blow your mind, guys.'

'Well, if a bullet didn't do it, you might as well

take your turn.' Aidan laughed, but without any real humour, and nobody joined in.

'He's telling us that the Aramaic words – the text on the cover – were written by Jesus Himself. There's a power to be unlocked. A key unlocking … What, I do not know.'

'Fuck,' Aidan swore. 'That's a tale and a half to peddle, Jeff.'

'I know. Look, we're all exhausted. Let's bed down. If you can't sleep, rest at least.'

42

Jeff was remembering his dreams through bleary eyes. The visitors were not woken for 4 a.m. prayers, but the same quiet, anonymous novice who had shown them to their rooms appeared again at 4.30. He was carrying a tray bearing four jugs of aromatic tea when Dale stopped him in the corridor. A bit of kerfuffle and some raised voices acted as the alarm clock. Beth and Dale let nothing pass without intervention.

As Jeff sipped, he asked, 'Were you dreaming, Aidan?'

'Don't know if I got enough sleep to get to REM.' His friend grimaced. 'I suppose you had a biblical revelation?'

'Not exactly,' said Jeff thoughtfully, 'but it was strange. I was anxious. Me, you and Libby were breaking into this … Coptic Museum. It was like the old days, I suppose.'

Breakfast consisted of bread, fruit and coffee. Jeff and Aidan spoke to their host, but his responses in Arabic led them to the simple conclusion that using English was futile. They guessed that the rest of the community must have formed the habit of returning to rest after prayer. The monastery was deathly silent again. Some time passed before Abbot John appeared to wish them a good morning. He blessed the sitting group, while leaning against the door frame.

'I'll pray for you all,' he said in conclusion. 'Brother James will guide you on your journey. When you return him safely to the monastery doors, you must then proceed alone.'

While they walked along the corridor, Abbot John took Jeff to one side to speak privately to him.

'Try hard to remember your dreams,' he urged. 'The messages will guide you. The messages are from a higher power … the highest power. I can only offer my prayers and my blessing. But I know with certainty that you have been chosen and will be guided. If you succeed, we will never meet again. If you fail, we will meet – but in a transformed state of existence. You have the blessing and the prayers of us all. May God go with you.'

Jeff was hoping Aidan was within earshot, because he didn't think he could face explaining another of the abbot's show-stopping monologues.

Outside, Jeff and his companions stood in the five o'clock darkness, in front of the monastery's north-facing facade. Brother James had the hood of his woollen habit up. The winter sun, when it appeared, was not going to offer much heat at that hour – or perhaps even later in the day.

The five were as comfortably seated in the Hummer as they could be in an armour-plated vehicle.

'Drive straight on the road for three kilometres,' the monk told Dale, 'and then we will need to go across country.'

Aidan wasn't sure if the cross-country journey could be any worse than the bumpy terrain they were currently on.

'I hope you feel it will be worth it.' Brother James looked uncomfortable as he spoke directly to Jeff across the back seat of the vehicle. 'It is just a broken boulder at the base of a cliff – a brilliant marker if the original monks, my predecessors, felt their successors would need to retrieve their treasure. We will never know why it waited for the Ali family's discovery. Perhaps it was waiting for you.'

'Why do you think that was?' Jeff asked. 'People died, and the knowledge was lost?'

'No,' Brother James said firmly, 'I know it is because the prophesied time had not yet come. Now it is upon us.'

Dale and Beth might have lost the sense of the conversation, but Jeff was glad to see Aidan taking it in. He had to convince himself that he had a sane handle on his interpretation of what the abbot had said to him.

They followed the monk's directions, and a further half an hour was all that was needed. The site was bitterly cold, given that the risen sun was hidden behind the cliff, and would be for another hour or so.

Jeff was in a bit of a daze.

I've dreamed about this place, he thought. *Or have I? Have*

I seen a picture? It was as blurry as a heat haze. The imagining of a ceremony, the burial of a man-sized jar, but before that … the digging. Digging a hole in the rock, that would swallow a six-foot-tall storage jar.

He could nearly taste the atmosphere that must have been present here, at a ceremony now lost in antiquity. Sweat and incense. The ancient monks standing around, chanting incantations … burying what they believed to be the only artifact touched by the living Jesus – his own written words.

After they returned Brother James to his home, Dale and Beth upped their vigilance for the drive back to Cairo. The two Irish boys in the back had positioned themselves in the seat for a nap. Jeff noticed that the zip on his backpack was firmly closed. That bothered him, because he always left his bag slightly open – a tip from AJ about letting the air circulate among worn laundry. He opened the zip slightly and noticed the bulk of the metal case. The ornate present had been left behind by Brother James. Jeff didn't need to open the decorative lid. He already knew what was in it. He would get no sleep now.

43

The drive back to Cairo saw Aidan feeling nervous, the former Marines on full alert, and Jeff thinking, *What next?* Aidan had had his fill of whizzing bullets and puzzles to be solved. This wasn't the United States – or Ireland, even. Money spoke in Egypt. If they were stopped, a misplaced belief that an official in uniform was on your side could get you killed.

'The abbot, at least, believes in the power of this inanimate object,' said Jeff.

'It's still all a bit far-fetched,' replied Aidan.

'Abbot John knew about us,' Jeff insisted. 'All of us, and Libby as well. He knew of our work, knew of our investigations in North Africa, knew we would end up visiting him, knew my wife was part of our team.' He turned to Beth and Dale. 'What do you make of it, guys?'

'There's a lot to take in all right,' said Beth.

Dale said nothing and kept his eyes on the road.

'I know the abbot and James gave us their sacred present,' Aidan protested, 'but they're not the ones in the firing line. They're safe behind the walls of their fortress.'

'Aidan, "the present", as you call it, is the most precious thing in their possession. To them, it may be the most precious thing that any Christian has ever possessed. It wasn't given to us lightly. The abbot believes we can use it for a task. We have to pray it's the task of stopping the disease, before it stops us.'

'Jeff, if that is the case, then I hope when you show it to AJ, she can discern a chemical formula for an antidote.'

'Aidan, you're being way too smart – unhelpful.' Beth's tone clearly indicated, 'Enough – *I have a kid to worry about.*

Jeff knew it was time for him to defuse this new tension. 'Look, we'll be back in an hour or so. We'll do a conference call with Jean. She knows stuff. Maybe she can help us make sense of it.'

'We can,' Aidan replied, 'but I know the girls will think the story is half mad, I'm guessing.' He wasn't able to help himself.

Jeff exhaled two deep breaths. 'I want to check in on everyone's health, get an update on the military situation. I'll choose my words carefully.' More conciliation; this seven-hour drive was a long one.

The two-bedroom apartment had been sourced by Dale – he had his contacts. Jeff had specified the rough location and suggested provisioning it for a week. It was frugal, but nicely situated on the edge of the city – not too many prying eyes.

The team used FaceBox for video conferencing because they were sure of the product's security credentials. If they could find working servers through 4G, they would be talking in confidence.

'Jeff, honey,' AJ said after they'd all exchanged greetings, 'you have no idea how much coverage Trump is getting over here.'

'I'm only gone a wet day, love,' answered Jeff.

'Yep, but he's playing the "more people were dying of this virus when the Democrats were in charge than ever happened in my administration" card. Playing it hard. There's a few new faces from the virology community on TV. They're admitting that we're not dealing with a virus, and that's not going down well. It's the truth, but it's playing into Trump's hands. His soundbite is that a new vaccine is years away because of "sleepy Joe". Could you imagine what would go down if he knew about this Devil's Clock?'

'Yeah,' Jeff replied. 'That's what I – we – want to talk to the team about. We've had an intervention from a very unexpected source.'

'I hope it was from God.' Libby frowned.

'Look ...' Jeff said. 'It's not funny you should say that, girl, because, to be honest, one man – an abbot – believes that's exactly what's in play.'

Even over a blurry screen, Jeff could see Jean's eyes widening.

'Whatever you are going to do, doing it soon would be a good option.' Libby waved a hand towards the TV on the wall behind her. 'According to Al Jazeera, martial law is now being declared all over the Arab states.'

'Wow,' said Aidan. 'It seemed a bit more relaxed yesterday, we were in a coffee house in Nag Hammadi.'

'You made it, then.' Jean beamed at them. 'Well done. That part of Egypt was very much the birthplace of world monasticism, long before it ever made its way to Europe.'

'That's what this call is about, Jean.' Jeff turned the laptop so that the silver case that Brother James had left him was displayed for a moment. 'Our madcap trip to Nag Hammadi got us what you might call progress, that gift.' He was pointing at the case. 'I'm now just glad I followed your hunch before we're all locked down in Cairo.' But he was grimacing under the weight of the story to come.

'Or locked up in Cairo, maybe,' said Aidan.

'Is it time to try and get home?' AJ blurted out, visibly upset, knowing that a story was coming.

'Love, we're in too deep,' Jeff protested, 'and, as you say yourself, we're not in any good place. The clock is ticking. We all know when we're going to die. Dale and Beth know that better than any of us.' Jeff turned from the laptop screen to look at them. 'Are you guys up for quitting?'

The Americans shook their heads in unison.

'But what can you guys do?' asked AJ. 'This battle must be fought out in the labs. Chasing a cure for this disease is still a plan.'

'Love, that's a change from you. I'm surprised. Maybe if we weren't running out of time … But time is exactly why we must stick with it.'

Jean and Libby were shuffling in their seats, obviously uncomfortable with the pathos of AJ's domestic pleas.

'Why put yourselves in more danger? I know the disease will get us all, but a bullet would get you quicker. We'd still have time … some time together. I can ask Dad to get you out now.'

'Love, we made this amazing … unexpected discovery, in a way. We met these monks in a remote spot. They nearly knew us all by name – I mean all of us. They seemed to be expecting us, like this is mystical stuff.' Jeff was trying to reassure her and trying not to sound off the wall.

'Did he tell you what to do next?' asked Libby.

'No,' said Jeff. 'It's kind of not like that. You must find your own way. But they gave us their prized possession – a message from Jesus. I mean Jesus Christ himself.' He looked beyond the screen again at the ornate silver box which he had placed so carefully, like an important exhibit. The most important exhibit. 'Look, I nearly can't believe I've said it. The case contains the cover of one of the religious books found in Nag Hammadi, the Gospel of Thomas. A Muslim woman gave this cover as a sacred gift to a Christian monastery. According to the abbot, Abbot John, the codex cover, the book cover, holds the key to reversing the Apocalypse, the End of Days.' He paused to let his words sink in. 'There, I've said it.' He let out a sigh of pure relief.

Silence from the call. Jeff saw Jean raising her

hands and placing them on her head. He wondered if the audio had dropped; the video was still blurrily live. Once the others had absorbed the shock, Jean's impatient voice burst in from San Jose.

'Revelation.'

Jeff nodded.

Aidan filled in a few gaps from the story and supplied as many answers as he could. Jeff seemed so relieved. He drew in some deep breaths. AJ looked a bit brighter.

'To think that if it wasn't for a sniper's miss, we would never have gotten on this road.'

'What did you say, Aidan?' She didn't wait for an answer. AJ started crying.

Jeff hadn't wanted it mentioned, but of course it immediately became the focus of his wife's attention.

'Jeff, Aidan, you're bringing us into the supernatural here,' said Libby, by way of distraction. She had a sobbing AJ sitting beside her.

'So, out with it,' Jean demanded. 'What's next? What does it say on the cover? What's written on it?' She was now too excited to give AJ any attention.

'That's why we are having this talk,' Aidan replied. 'Jeff wasn't given a translation.'

Jeff stayed quiet, wishing AJ was with him, and yet glad she wasn't.

'So, what did this mysterious abbot guy say, then?' asked Libby.

Jeff gathered himself. He knew he had to speak over AJ's sobs.

'He wasn't trying to be mysterious at all, really. But he did believe in the supernatural. He thinks Gabrielle is the Devil on Earth.'

'Oh God, come home, please,' AJ said softly.

Dale and Beth had been standing behind Jeff and Aidan. Beth bent slightly to make sure her face was visible on the screen and spoke.

'I think part of the puzzle is for us to figure this out ourselves – I mean the writing, the words. To end the journey we've all been on.'

'Why don't we start helping?' said Jean. 'Let's see it.'

Jeff left the screen for a few seconds to lay hands on the silver case. He opened it, revealing a bland, drab but recognisable book cover, about one and a half times bigger than A4. When he carefully laid it upright on the wooden table, the others could see the Aramaic text emblazoned into the brown leather: beautiful script, etched into leather, a group of brilliantly white words.

'We only know the language is Aramaic from the abbot,' Jeff explained. 'He told us it's a number – strange, I know.'

Aidan pointed his smartphone camera at the text and pressed 'translate'.

'Google won't do Aramaic,' Jean said. 'You know it's the language Jesus and his disciples would have used. Now it's pretty much dead. If it's numbers, though, I'm betting a Syriac translation will do it. Try it, Jeff.'

'Jesus, this girl knows stuff,' said Libby, giving her a couple of taps on the back.

Aidan keyed in some more instructions. This time, the translate app returned a result: '"Thirty score ten", what the fuck?'

'Just be careful about the translation,' Jean warned them. 'The two languages are related, but it may be making it sound even stranger than it needs to be.'

'It's a long way to go to be filled in on a piece of math,' said Libby. 'What number is that, anyway?'

'While we're thinking about that, let me add a bit of detail.' Jean sounded as if she was addressing her class at school. 'Like, there's been huge examination of these books at Nag Hammadi in the last seventy years. We're talking now, if you believe what Jeff has been told, about the cover of the only copy of the Gospel of Thomas in existence. The book itself is kept in its home, the Coptic Museum in old Cairo. It's meant to be a masterpiece, the fifth Gospel. You should know that, Libby. You had the privilege of seeing it.'

Libby's only response was to raise her eyebrows before she spoke again.

'Great, Jean, but you're telling us all this here in San Jose. So, the boys didn't need to traipse all the way to Egypt for that snippet?'

'I know that, honey,' Jean snapped. 'I'm just talking to promote my thinking.'

There was a lot of information going through everyone's heads. A lot to take in, and Jeff was using the call to get his own thoughts straight. He was wondering about Aidan, though. His friend had gone unusually quiet. So had AJ, and Jeff was caught in the middle of them both. So, all he could do was continue the story.

'There was one other clue that the abbot was specific about. That this journey would have to bring us back to that same Coptic Museum.'

'Jesus, people!' AJ threw up her hands. 'Will you stop going on about that?'

She was feeling a sense of dread. Her husband and his mission were bringing him back into the space that Martin Gabrielle occupied. Jeff had survived a battering in Washington before, but now he was in Cairo, in a locked-down world, facing pure evil and running out of time. If AJ was feeling low in San Jose, at least she had Libby and Jean for support. Whatever Jeff and the others needed to do, they would have to do it alone. Whereas scientists working in virology and pharmacology thought they had solved the problem of Covid-19, the wider medical world was lost against the thing called Covid-24. It seemed that corporate greed driving the speed of the vaccine production system had sown the seeds for the Devil's Countdown. Jeff's tale was one where supernatural forces had to be involved. Science wasn't going to help.

'Maybe he never intended to dispatch you, Jeff, that time in Washington,' Libby suggested. 'Maybe he had set up his power base in Cairo for the real showdown. It didn't say much if the fucking Prince of Darkness couldn't kick the ass of a mere mortal.'

'What the hell?' AJ blurted into the call, sobbing.

Jeff knew Libby wouldn't stop her. She had to be allowed to feel her own anxiety. He was feeling nauseous himself.

Libby knew she had overstepped the mark. Jean grabbed her as they both grasped AJ to comfort her.

'I'm sorry,' Libby whispered.

'Look, at least the Egyptian authorities haven't done martial law yet,' said Beth, not knowing how else to respond to the emotions on the other side of the world.

'Yep,' Dale confirmed, 'we've been able to move about OK – a bit of a surprise.' Like Beth, he was trying to deal with an emotional moment through logic.

'Even if we could gain access to the book, the Gospel, what do we do?' asked Aidan. 'Chant some Glenstal-like incantation?'

Jean withdrew from their hug and addressed the screen again.

'Jeff, the book I gave you,' she said. 'You know you have been following in Robinson's footsteps in visiting Nag Hammadi.'

Jeff nodded. 'Was there anything that Robinson said that gives us a clue to … well … crack the code, unlock the key?'

Jesus, am I listening to myself? Jeff asked himself, knowing he was clutching at whatever straw he could.

'So, what are we figuring out, Jeff?' asked Jean. 'The story was that some old woman burned the cover, and with it missing, nobody had any reason to question it. You know what it was, nobody thought it had text written on it.'

'If we need to do some rapid Bible sleuthism, you best lead the way, lover,' said Libby.

'Well, there's millions of stuff on the net and YouTube,' Jean continued. 'Normally I'd say "avoid nutjobs", but now I don't know if I can completely disregard them.'

'Don't stop there, Jean, keep going.' Jeff needed her help to get his thoughts straight.

'You probably don't know this,' Jean began, 'but the Nag Hammadi Library is viewed as belonging to Gnostic Christianity. They were called heretical by Orthodox Christians – you know, seen as the nuts of the first century. Now we're looking to see if they had ... Well, as they say themselves, knowledge – *gnosis*, in Greek. But we have something that neither Robinson nor anybody else had. That treasured relic.'

'Yeah, with a few odd numbers written on it,' Aidan added.

'Where do you start?' asked Jean. 'The Bible is full of number systems and codes.'

Jeff was only half following the conversation. He couldn't keep it going, seeing AJ that upset.

'AJ, love, let me call you separately – but, team, if anyone gets a jab of inspiration during the night, let's hear about it.'

Jeff was asking more in hope than in expectation.

44

'My love,' Jeff began. He was alone in his bedroom, with AJ's tear-stained face on the screen in front of him. 'I know you're lonely and upset, but you know I must keep going. Is there an alternative?' He paused, but AJ said nothing. 'What's the word from your old man?'

'Not surprisingly, people aren't just going to lie down and die.' AJ waved vaguely in the direction of the television. The screen showed buildings in flames and groups of masked people running from the scene. 'Looters are, however, willing to kill. When he said "Four more years in four more years", we had no choice but to believe the nightmare of Trump maybe wasn't over. Dad says he's riled up the foothill militias – again – with mixed messages. But worse, the army is seeing a huge depletion. When the US military is jumping ship, you can be sure you're in trouble. Jeff, you know I can't tell him about the monk's intervention. It wouldn't help.'

Jeff was taking comfort from seeing her at least a little recovered.

'I know that, love. Just keep some faith in me before I lose faith in myself. Knowing I have your support keeps me going. You know that. Anyway, what about all those biblical plagues? God cured them, didn't he? No virologists in those days.'

'You're kidding, right? Maybe you shouldn't be. He'll end you.' AJ was crying again, softly this time.

'Not if Beth and Dale have anything to do with it. Do your best for me, love. We'll talk tomorrow.'

Jeff blew her a kiss across the screen and wondered if she knew he couldn't stay with her.

It was like being back in their monastic cell of the previous night – but a bit more spacious and comfortable. Jeff and Aidan were settling into their twin-bedded accommodation, with the former Marines next door, always on watch. This was old Cairo. On their way into the city, they had tried – as best as three white guys and a white woman could – to be inconspicuous. It was to their advantage that the locals were used to strangers as tourists, even if the circumstances were strange, and getting stranger by the day.

'If we're planning to break into the museum, we're going to need our two soldiers on message,' said Jeff.

'I didn't think they signed up for illegality,' Aidan pointed out. 'Only protection. If the word is that serving US soldiers are jumping ship, then why would you expect our two retired Joes to stay put?'

'Loyalty, decency, and now their son Dylan. If this tale about approaching the End of Days is on, then a bit of illegality is bordering on the venial side, don't you think?'

'We must have been mad to head off on that jaunt. A vanity project – "see Nag Hammadi before I die" … and we nearly did.' Aidan poured two glasses of Jameson.

'Where to now, my friend? You're not sounding completely on board.'

'Like I say, we nearly got killed, and all we got was some kind of number and a plan from Jean – "study your Bibles".'

'Look,' said Jeff patiently, 'I know we're clutching at straws, but you got to clutch at something. We've both had run-ins with that bastard Gabrielle already. He wants what we have, and he knew all along that we were his best chance of getting it.'

'Jeff, I'm not so sure that a number can be of huge significance to him.'

'Maybe … Maybe the cover itself is what he wants. But if it is, and if he knows we have it, it must be the case that he knows we are expendable now.'

'Great news.'

'Look, Jean knows a big part of the story. She's been invaluable. But before today, maybe not five living people knew about the cover of that Gospel. We know it, Aidan, and if I'm right, Gabrielle wants it.'

'Maybe our job is to reunite the cover with the book, and hey presto,' said Aidan.

'It's all in, that's for sure, and dangerous.' Jeff took a moment, knowing he needed sleep and worried he wouldn't get any. 'Yep, getting into the Coptic Museum, bringing our new possession and hoping for a miracle – the cure to the Devil's Countdown to reveal itself.'

'Not to mention getting access to the Gospel itself,' Aidan reminded him. 'I bet they do that Book of Kells thing, where one page is on display only on any given day.'

'Let's think about why the abbot wouldn't translate the Aramaic for us. What could it be about – a number?'

'Go over it again,' Aidan prompted. 'What did the abbot say to you about the text?'

'Go figure it out for yourself, like I said.'

'Yeah, for sure, that's helpful … not.' Aidan took another sip of his whiskey. 'God thinks we – or you – are the right man for the job. That's all we have to go on.'

'We must be really close.' Jeff held his thumb and forefinger a short distance apart. 'But that we just rock up and hope for the best? Not sounding like the best plan we ever had, Aidan. Better get the lads in for a chat. That drop of Irish is making you relax. I'll get a ring going on the stove.'

Aidan knocked on the couple's bedroom door.

'Guys, the "chef" is going to rustle up a bit of food and get your advice. Where are you on breaking and entering?'

They rustled their way back into the kitchen area.

'You know we had our briefing on the plane,' Dale

began, 'but that was before someone took a pot-shot at you guys. We've been under fire before, but you guys are in shock, even if you don't know it. So, let's not go getting ourselves—'

Aidan interrupted Dale mid-sentence. 'Killed.'

'I was going to say arrested.' Dale smiled. 'Getting locked up in Egypt, at this time, would probably mean being left to rot, particularly if the authorities don't like you – or if they like Gabrielle better. If we're doing something, let's do the right thing at the right time for the right reason.'

'I think I'm beyond shock.' Jeff gestured to the cooker. 'Guys, you must be starving. A simple pasta?'

Beth wasn't going to swallow this classic Irish brush-off tactic.

'We bought into the mission all along,' she said. 'Our child needs us here. We've seen difficult situations.'

'God knows Uncle Sam has been good at putting its soldiers in bad places.' Dale offered Beth his support. 'This is a bad situation, a bad place with bad karma. So, we've been talking, and we'll push it to the limit, but no suicide missions. So, you call the brief and we will call the shots – I mean, the execution.'

'This is our last chance as well,' said Beth.

Jeff found cooking strangely relaxing. That had always made for a good match with AJ. She hated cooking. He'd often rib her, saying, 'The best way into a woman's heart is through her stomach.' He was thinking about her as he opened the canned tomatoes, glad to be occupied.

This was just simple food, but always presented to look appetising. When Jeff was a young teenager mucking around in their kitchen late at night, his father had often told him, 'Go be a chef.' He was nearly wishing he had.

'Grub's up.'

Jeff repositioned his laptop on the floor. They had eaten so many times together, but everyone knew this was different.

'Let's join hands and take a pause for prayer,' said Beth.

Unexpectedly, the call to evening prayers sounded from outside. They laughed.

Thank God, Aidan reflected, *a lighter moment.*

It represented the closest thing to normality that had occurred in the last thirty-six hours. The two Americans each took a bottle of Egyptian beer.

'This is some kind of endgame,' Jeff said. 'After yesterday's events – the sniper and the abbot – I'm convinced we're not wasting our time. Have faith, Beth. That's my prayer.'

'Can we see the cover again?' asked Dale.

'Of course,' Jeff unpacked the gift again, still treating it reverently. 'Take another look – can't hurt.'

'So, as I say, and if I heard it correctly, the abbot told me yesterday that this is Jesus' handwriting.'

Dale and Beth looked at it as sharply as anyone ever trained to analyse a piece of military intelligence.

'I know what that could be,' said Dale.

Aidan was looking at him. Neither of the former

Marines made any attempt to handle the relic. Dale merely stared reverently at it while he went on speaking.

'From our Bible school, Sunday school days, the Book of Revelation was full of signs and seals and symbols being restored to their rightful place. Then the just would know that the coming kingdom of Heaven would be restored on Earth.'

'Great,' said Aidan. He didn't mean it to, but it encouraged Dale to continue.

'Like I say, this is easy. You're the two guys from Revelation – "the Prophets".'

'Brilliant – what the fuck?' said Aidan 'Our being here was predicted in the Bible.'

'Look, Revelation is probably the wildest book of the New Testament,' Dale went on, 'but I must tell you, in Revelation the two prophets are killed by the Beast. If it's any consolation, they were raised up again by Jesus.'

'Great, that's all sorted so. What next?' On another day it might have seemed funny. Aidan's light shirt was showing signs of underarm perspiration.

'I'm only telling you what a Texan Sunday school taught me,' said Dale.

'Well, how were we to know we were being protected by a Bible scholar – another one?' said Aidan.

'No, no, I'm not that,' Dale protested. 'I'm a Marine. Well, sure, I'm a Christian, I'm a believer. I mean, a lot of Texans take their Bible seriously – literally, even. Take your pick. Not like Beth's people, in pagan Louisiana.' Dale added quickly, seeing Beth's mouth open, 'Only kidding.'

It wasn't a great time for humour. They were there to work, and this work meant fighting for their son's life. Fighting for all their lives.

'Can I ask you, Dale, what else goes on in the book of Revelation?' Aidan refilled his glass with whiskey and settled back to listen.

'Well, it's a long time since Sunday school, but I can tell you that it's one hell of a ride.' Dale took a swig of his beer. 'It's good versus evil, and it's a great way to end the Bible because it's the Apocalypse. You know … "He will come to raise the living and the dead."'

'Does it tell us anything for what we do next?' asked Jeff.

'There's a Beast to be defeated, that's for sure, Jeff. I'll lend you my Bible for some bedtime reading.'

'I wish I wasn't feeling so wiped out or I'd get stuck in now.'

'Told you that's the shock,' said Beth.

'Anyway, why read it?' Aidan asked. 'We're living it.'

'Look, let's get back on track,' said Jeff. 'We need a plan to get into the Coptic Museum, if we're bringing the gift home.'

Beth was still gazing at the book cover. 'The writing sure is beautiful – hypnotic,' she said.

'What's in that Egyptian beer?' Aidan wasn't trying to be funny.

Beth ignored the comment. 'Look, if going to this

museum is the option, you'll be wearing vests. We haven't damaged you clients yet. Guess what? We're not starting now.'

'Can we reckon the parties that shot at us yesterday are pretty much waiting for us?' asked Aidan.

Jeff interrupted. 'The abbot thinks Satan will be waiting for us.'

'If you've been to war, you'd know that there's no shortage of devils around.' Dale hesitated for a moment. 'I don't know that I ever expected to meet the actual one.'

'Are you guys sure two Marines will be enough?' asked Aidan.

Nobody answered.

'Look,' said Beth, 'we drove through the old town streets earlier, to get here. We were unchallenged, not many people about. Looks like we can easily get around this part of the city. So, I guess we could get to the museum, at least.'

'I'm still mesmerised by your knowledge of Revelation, Dale,' said Jeff.

'Well, we're Bible Belters, ain't we?' He grinned.

'So, we're going to take a quote from the Book of Revelation, a biblical relic, and our life in our hands.' Aidan leaned forward, frowning. 'We're going to take on a power outside of this world, in a terrain that we're not familiar with. To use your phrase, Jeff – what could possibly go wrong?'

Jeff wasn't smiling. He couldn't suppress his awareness of the proximity of it all. Whatever they were going to do tomorrow, would his nerve hold up? He felt himself silently praying at the table when there were pockets of silence. He wondered if everyone else was praying.

'How come nobody ever pieced this together?' asked Aidan.

Beth answered when no one else offered. 'Well, it has come up. There have always been predictions about the End of Days. What you describe, what we're all involved in, has been set up for two thousand years.'

'Are we going to be protected by whoever set it up, then?' asked Aidan.

Beth was again on point. 'Our training says you protect yourself and your clients. Relying on forces – particularly unseen forces – does not sound like a plan.'

'But we'll take all the help we can get,' Dale interjected.

'Will we do a reconnaissance run first?' asked Jeff.

'Normally a good idea,' Dale said grimly, 'but too conspicuous under the circumstances.'

'So, we're just going to march into the Coptic Museum?' asked Aidan.

'Well ...' Dale looked from Aidan to Jeff and back again. 'Remember yesterday. Someone knew, or guessed, or you guys might say "had supernatural knowledge" that we would be standing on the steps of a church. Knew to the extent that the nearby mosque, with its needle-shaped spire, was the best place for a sniper.'

Beth took over. 'Yes, we're guessing our Mr Gabrielle will be expecting you.'

'It's a funny thing.' Jeff looked pensive. 'So much of life is about relearning what you already know. If you're quick at it, you have a much better chance of success.'

'What's that got to do with anything?' asked Aidan.

'I'm just remembering what AJ said. Her theory was that Gabrielle had a cut at killing me, but he never wanted to achieve that. This is the showdown. He – whatever he is – has been waiting, maybe since 1945, for this moment. Our friend Abbot John, incredible as it sounds, says that Gabrielle came into a new existence in 1945, in Nag Hammadi.'

'But that would make him …' Beth was doing the math in her head. 'What … seventy-eight.'

'Well, let's disabuse ourselves of that idea,' Jeff said firmly. 'He looks like a man of thirty. He looked like he looked when I first met him in 2003, over twenty years ago. He's a Dorian Grey.'

'Whatever he is, we have to be sure he isn't the end of us,' said Dale.

'That's the dilemma, though, is it not?' Beth's voice was quiet. 'We're all goners anyway. We've been on the battlefield. Nobody does self-sacrifice. We all want to go on.'

'That's our make-up,' Dale agreed. 'That's how God made us.'

'OK.' Aidan was nervous, and the whiskey was making him sound tetchy. 'Let's not have any talk of "we're all going to die". How about a plan like, "we're all going to live"?'

Beth was sensitive to fear. 'That's our job, Aidan, leave that to us. Every one of us gets out alive.'

'So, Jeff,' said Dale, 'your theory – or AJ's, as you say – is that this "thing", Gabrielle, has set you up for this all along. He knows you have something he wants. It looks good, the cover, but I'm not seeing a reason to kill for.'

'Dale, don't underestimate what we're dealing with here.'

'I don't,' Dale said quickly. 'We're trained as Marines to take on devils of men. If this guy presents himself as a danger to us all, I'll end him, or Beth will for sure. You can depend on it.'

Beth took her husband's hand by way of confirmation. 'Now, my advice,' she said. 'Use your full bellies to get you to sleep. This isn't a crack of dawn thing. If we are a go for tomorrow, we'll leave here at 0800. We'll be there at 0905. Might all be over by 1000. That's something positive to focus on.'

Jeff repacked the gospel cover into its case and took it with him to the bedroom. He was still recalling the words, engraved or burned on to a leather covering. Some ancient lost technique in etching. Beth's advice seemed good: use his full stomach to blast him off to sleep. They'd have no contact with the San Jose team till the morning.

45

Jeff's dreams were lucid: some kind of run over what would happen later that day.

This Book of Revelation thing … keys? But how do you open the lock? Gabrielle was in Egypt to keep away from the 'key'. To keep it at arm's length. Gabrielle's Egyptian military friends storming the Monastery of Saint Athanasius. The secret possession could be repossessed? He didn't want it, but he and Simone needed to be close, and to monitor the only relic powerful enough to stop them.

Jeff's stomach hurt, within his troubled sleep. The frustration at not being able to figure out how the cover, the relic, would work.

How does it stop Gabrielle? That's one thing. But how does it stop the world from dying?

The anxiety was too much. He woke up. It was four o'clock. Aidan was in the adjacent bunk, snoring lightly, and Jeff was glad of it. He needed to talk to Jean.

The whole city was quiet, waiting for the first call to prayer. Jean picked up on the second ring.

'Hi, Jeff,' she said brightly. 'The girls have just gone to make tea. Hold on, I'll call them.'

'Don't, Jean. The guys are sleeping here, and it's just you I wanted.'

'Good, because I've been thinking … There sure is a lot of New Testament – Revelation – going on.'

'Yeah, I was getting a bit of an education from Dale already earlier. Jean, now is the exact point in time where your … what's the word? … insight would be great.'

'You might be overestimating my prowess, Jeff. I've been thinking about that codex cover non-stop since we spoke, but anyway.'

'OK, so I didn't mention this earlier because I didn't think it was important, but the abbot, Father John, was keen for some reason and … Look, I can show you if the video will stay stable.' He held up the leather binding and indicated some residue on the underside. 'This cover was originally attached to the gospel with seven … I guess blobs of glue, or whatever the ancients used.'

'There you go, Jeff. All the Book of Revelation is about opening the seven seals.'

'This is starting to wreck my head. It wasn't me who opened the seals. It was a brave Muslim woman in the Christmas of 1945.'

'If this is the Tribulation, then there's a big shock coming.'

'Jean, Jean, slow down,' Jeff protested. 'I know our connection might break, but give my head a chance, will you? What's a tribulation?'

'It's a signal of the Second Coming. There will be … well, seven years of devastation.'

'How long has the Devil's Countdown been running?'

The connection was starting to crackle.

'Ever since the fifth of November 2020 – the day of the first trial vaccination,' said Jean.

'That, of course, leaves plenty of time for more devastation.' Jeff couldn't hide the urgency in his voice. 'Please, please, are we talking about the fulfilment of a biblical prophecy?'

'Why not? Every age has predicted it. It's going to be true one day. Why are we so knowing that we can say, "Yeah, but it's not today"? Maybe it *is* today.'

'So, you're telling me it's the end of the world, right now? Ah, it kind of begs a question. What's the point?'

'No, no, you four brave people aren't in Egypt just so you could die in a foreign land.'

'Jean, do you think you will uncover something for us to go on? Some long-lost biblical key?'

'I have an insight I'm unravelling – I need more time.'

'Not something we have a lot of.'

'Have faith and try and sleep some more,' said Jean.

46

A misty red haze hung over the city on December 13, as the sun rose close to 7 a.m. Dale's advice was to avoid windows, and Jeff was sniffing the air through the gap in a pair of slightly opened curtains. The air was moist, refreshing. Dale and Beth were up and dressed; Jeff wondered if they had even gone to sleep. Jeff ruffled Aidan into attention.

'Aidan, the signal strength is holding up. Let's get to it.' The activity was keeping Jeff's stomach calm. 'Look, we're up and have had coffee, so it's nearly show time. The connection seems OK. Should I stay, or should I go meet an old friend – not? I'm guessing you guys haven't been to bed. What is it? Ten hours' time difference?'

'Did you guys get some sleep?' asked AJ.

'Some,' replied Jeff.

'My dreams,' Aidan added. 'Beth and Dale had us playing bit roles from the Book of Revelation. Look, that's another story.'

'Well,' Libby said, 'you set us a task and it seems my girl Jean – I know you called her earlier – has an inkling.'

'What a surprise,' said Jeff. 'A pleasant surprise?'

'How will you all keep in touch?' asked AJ, trying to keep it together.

'You know we only have three people in the world to tell anything to, so you'll be the first to know,' said Jeff ,trying to be positive and reassuring.

'If there's anything to tell, of course.' Agitated, Aidan was last up but now doing a lot of the talking. 'So out with it, Jean. How do we get out of this mess alive?'

'I had a long think about it since Jeff's call.' Jean picked up her notebook and flicked through it. 'The Aramaic text, the symbols, the numbers on the cover. I know your abbot wasn't offering you much information. Even so, I checked. There are no original Aramaic writings from the time of Jesus. Probably because nearly all who spoke it were illiterate. So, this alone is a reason why the abbot thought he had something particularly special.'

'Right,' said Aidan, 'but what does quoting a goddamn number do for us?'

'I don't think that is just some number. Here goes. The age of a righteous man in the Bible – three score and ten, seventy. Remember we translated "thirty score ten", close. Suppose we lost a bit in translation. That it is the number seventy.' Jean let both sides of the Atlantic draw breath. 'Thomas's Gospel is a so-called "sayings" gospel. It claims to have— Sorry … it *does* have 114 sayings, whether you believe they come from Jesus or not. But what if "seventy" means that *saying* number seventy is the solution to the riddle, if you like?'

'Is it that easy?' asked Jeff.

'Not as easy to decipher as you might think.'

Jean paused. 'The ancient style of writing had no punctuation or capital letters. It was just one long stream of continuous writing – you know, use up every scrap of valuable papyrus. It's only modern translations that give us the structure of saying number one, saying number two. You see?'

'Well, then, the obvious question is, what does Jesus's seventieth saying say?' Jeff twisted his mouth as he said it.

AJ already know the answer and stopped looking at the screen.

Jean held up a translation of Thomas's Gospel and flipped it open to a marked page. '"If you bring forth what is within you, what you bring forth will save you. If you do not bring forth what is within you, what you do not bring forth will destroy you."'

Jeff knew then, as AJ already knew, that he would go to meet Gabrielle. The connection dropped. Jeff was glad.

47

The group travelled looking like a smartly dressed unit – mostly because Kevlar vest technology had gone extremely slimline.

'You boys look pretty,' said Beth. 'How did you all sleep really?'

'Mixed,' said Aidan. 'It's a big day, I guess. I could half hear Jeff leafing through the "Good Book", but I was too tired to ask him if he found anything.'

'Well, you did say Revelation was one hell of a ride, Dale,' Jeff commented. 'Seven seals and seven trumpets and seven bowls.'

'Funny, that,' Aidan pointed out. 'We are a team of seven.'

'Not to mention the two prophets you told us about, Dale – they were none too popular when they arrived on the scene. So apart from being killed, the Jewish public were not pleased to see them resurrected either.'

'Bummer – unpopular *and* dead,' answered Beth wryly.

Dale was concentrating on driving down streets with an alertness that acknowledged he hadn't been able to do a dry run.

'I think Dale was being a bit kind to us when he

was likening us to the two prophets,' said Jeff. 'These two boys, when they come, have the authority of God to blast as many plagues as they see fit on the Jewish world.'

'I'm not getting it,' said Dale. 'Is that not exactly what you guys were up to? Social media … it does the work of a plague in its own right. That's even before we get into a conversation about vaccine poisoning.'

'The man has a point.' Aidan was recalling his own knowledge of the Bible. 'Plagues mean locusts and frogs and all that kind of stuff. But social media, yep … I guess, when you think of it, the man has a point alright.'

'Very comforting, thanks,' said Jeff.

Beth hadn't spoken for a while. She was thinking, *It's banter but it's easing the tension.*

'Well, maybe all will be revealed.' Beth pointed through the windscreen. 'That there is the Coptic Museum.'

The museum was an unassuming two-storey sandstone building, lent a sense of authenticity by a preserved ruin on the right-hand side of the entrance. It looked as if you crossed a moat to get in – something Dale commented on.

'Only one way in and one way out.'

'A defender's dream,' Beth added.

'Let's go before I lose my nerve.' Jeff held the slimline silver case in his hand.

Beth and Dale had their sidearms neatly concealed, but accessible. It was nine o'clock local time, and the entrance door was already open. This was a quiet part of the old city.

'Too quiet,' said Dale.

'Sure you want to do this?' Beth asked.

It was Aidan who answered. 'Can we turn back now?'

Jeff knew better than to answer that question.

The four walked across the bridge in formation, guided by Dale at the front and Beth at the rear. They were disarmed to be greeted by an elegantly dressed woman. Jeff hadn't seen Simone Haddad in twenty years, but there was no doubting the recognition.

'Is that who I think it is?' whispered Aidan.

'It is,' answered Jeff.

'Fuck.' A further whisper.

'Have you come to meet Gabrielle?' asked Simone.

'Not exactly,' Jeff replied. 'I've come to see the Gospel of Thomas for myself.'

Simone frowned. 'What you must understand is that the book has been long since disassembled, and the pages protected behind individually framed glass plates. In fact, the book – the original – had no cover, but I think you know that.'

She backed into the foyer. The others followed her into the reception area of the museum. Simone stood, protected, behind the front counter.

There was a sudden, earth-shattering mechanical clatter, followed immediately by almost total darkness. A sophisticated emergency anti-theft lockdown button had been pressed somewhere. The blinding flash of a gunshot brilliantly illuminated the reception space. Beth and Dale went into automatic mode. Beth had her weapon drawn and was pinning Jeff to the ground. Dale was crouching, but he couldn't locate Aidan. They were nearly completely blind. The four panoramic window shutters were completely down, but for some reason the entrance door still let in a sliver of light from its base. Their escorts trained their weapons in the direction the flash had come from. Dale muttered 'Shush' in response to a faint moan. He knew the business of not giving your position away. There was no movement. Beth broke the silence. She could smell the close-up odour of blood, and felt the sensation of placing her hand into a growing warm pool of it. 'Jeff's hit.'

Still crouching, Dale used his phone for torchlight and fanned the space, his pistol trained on the light beam. Simone was gone, and there was no sign of a shooter. When he trained his beam on the floor, Dale saw that Jeff was face down with a gaping hole at the side of his neck – entry or exit wound, he didn't know. In the strangeness of how the mind works, Beth's stance bizarrely reminded him of that still of Jackie Kennedy draped over a fallen president. When Dale fanned 360°, the beam showed up what was left of Aidan's skull. A piece of it was preventing the entrance shutter from fully closing.

The mission was over. Dale wondered how much shock Beth would be enduring. Jeff had been shot but, soldier or not, his wife must have been inches away from taking the hit herself.

'We're in a Faraday cage,' he said. 'The phone is no good.' A shaky Beth was still sprawled over a lifeless Jeff, comforting and protecting him, drenched in his blood. She took an age to answer.

'Who were you going to call?'

'The plane – if it works.' He looked into his wife's eyes. 'We're in a bad place, Beth.'

The steel shutters began to rise slowly, mechanically.

'Jesus, Beth! Who opened the shutters? There's blood everywhere.'

'Oh God, what a mess,' she gasped. 'It's just a mechanical thing, I think. God, it's crushed Aidan's skull. That's his blood, mingling with Jeff's.'

'Have we lost Jeff as well?' Dale was still scanning the panorama with his sidearm cocked. 'It's not the way we planned it.'

'He's taken a hit through the throat – doesn't look good.' Beth was barely keeping it together.

'Fuck, what a mess!' Dale looked directly at her. 'Is our last mission going to be this clusterfuck?'

The entrance door and front window shutters continued to slowly grind open.

'Keep us covered, Dale.' Her voice quavered. 'He has a pulse but it's just being used to bleed him out. Anything stirring outside?'

'There are a few stragglers across the bridge. The blood flowing out of Aidan won't encourage anyone to come close.'

'The poor man is beyond help, but Jeff is still there,' said Beth.

'Beth, is he breathing?' Dale's pistol was trained on the inner door of the foyer.

'Whoever fired that shot is still in this building. Our next threat will be coming through that door. Where's that bitch gone? You bandage the chief up, Beth. Anyone coming through that door is going to be left with a hole in 'em.'

'But what's the plan?' asked Beth.

'See if you can stop the bleeding, bandage him up as heavily as you can. He should be dead. We're reliant on Maher loving his son-in-law. A quick extraction is his only hope – if he has any. You've seen bullets through the top of the spine before. Ever saw anybody survive?'

'Look, if he is a fighter, let's give him the best chance,' said Beth. 'He was trying to give us one.'

Dale discharged his gun twice into the inner door.

'Let's make it to the Hummer.'

'No, not till he's bandaged.'

48

Jeff was aware … looking down.

The end of consciousness. Two bangs – gunshots. Unconstrained, moving, floating. What a beautiful place. Decorated walls, even on the stairwell, monastic scripts, beautifully framed. The flow of the Coptic symbols and lettering. Pages from all the finds. The missing Gospels of the Egyptians – Philip, Truth, and the masterpiece, Thomas. Consciousness and thoughts. The Coptic monks, the Celtic monasteries. Ciaran, Clonmacnoise.

That iconic sight – the three pyramids as I last saw them, entering the city, yesterday evening. Aligned, but not in line. In the geometry of Orion. Consciousness, the end … Not the end … No body. But the undiscovered laws of nature. Maybe only temporary, before a final shutdown. How does spirit feel fear?

How does the case now stand on that desk? Two figures standing over it, beside it. Is that Gabrielle? He is changed. Who is the other figure, glowing, translucent.

'*LeLaA Nazarene,*' Gabrielle spoke, *confirmation, that's him.*

'Speak in English, our witness is present,' said a Presence. *The strangeness. Two plasma entities. What's it like? Electricity mixed with a watery mist.*

'We meet again,' Gabrielle said. There was silence.

'A humble bastard Nazarene will gain no hold on the world I have infected. Deference to an Irish pig?'

'A disciple has brought forth what is within.' Jeff heard the voice inside his skull. 'We will halt your Armageddon. The Beast will be defeated now and forever, as was revealed. One man, and a few faithful with a belief. One hundred men in a Congress, a Babylon, could be bought, but one man brought my Seal here.'

'Fool!' Gabrielle was laughing. 'You come to raise the living and the dead.'

Jeff had never heard him laugh.

'No, just one man will be raised today. I have come to halt your death march. The new Jerusalem will wait.'

'Did I not give you the sign of the world?' Gabrielle asked. 'My vaccine?'

'You've given me two thousand years of signs. Even without you, men, not women, with their technology seem well disposed to offer the sign of the world to end. For now, this Earth will be allowed its time. A world without a Satan.'

'We will see,' said Gabrielle. 'My work is then to be undertaken by the people made in your father's image.'

'Your days of offering temptation are now ended. Begone, and let us allow the righteous to claim their chance. Now see my Seal and begone, I command you,' the Presence roared.

The room began to shake, violently unstable, an earthquake.

Am I looking down at my nemesis? Recognisable, but different – Gabrielle. But who is the other figure? What *is the other figure?*

The case between the two energies shook open.

What does it matter? What is *matter?*

If they were arms, then the two figures were clutching each other like plasma combatants.

'You were undone by a mortal,' the Presence continued. 'Yes, made in my father's image. That was foretold. To get just one to stand for me, to unlock my message, then you would be challenged. Mortals without God cannot do it. God without mortals will not do it.' The room was shimmering.

'It has been a long time since we stood in this desert together,' said Gabrielle. 'Do you think I will go?'

'I know you will not. You are bloated by the depraved successes of two millennia.'

The brightness was blinding.

'Why now?' asked Gabrielle.

'You are weakened.'

'So, you think it's done, do you?'

'It is.'

The text on the codex cover glowed now, a burning white. It was burning. A shockwave blasted outwards from it. Gabrielle was rocked backwards. He couldn't maintain his grip from across the desk. Time had no meaning for Jeff, but force did. The pressures in that room pressed Jeff's 'body' back against the wall. No pain but sensation – conflict. How long had they been grappling? On Gabrielle's face, Jeff saw an expression he had never seen in his twenty years of knowing him: fear.

Gabrielle's whole being became translucent. The brightness faded, dimmed, as if the Presence was draining his energy. Jeff could see straight through him now.

Like watching burning plasma, turning to a red fog. A violent explosion blasted Jeff into blackness.

49

'He wasn't breathing, but he is now,' said Beth. 'Still has a pulse.'

The emergency lighting came on – unnecessarily, with the shutters continuing to roll back. Beth was conscious that her feet were still wading in blood. A few curious passers-by, wearing surgical masks, were outside, looking nervously into the foyer.

'Beth, I'll carry him to the jeep now. I want you to cover me from the windows at my back.'

'Please, please don't tell me that,' said Libby.

She was crying into the telephone receiver; Jean was awkwardly trying to hug her. Libby, with her free arm, responded by clutching her as tightly as she could.

'I'm so sorry, Lib.' Beth was close to tears herself. 'We did our best. It was a difficult situation.'

'Have you got him with you now?' asked Libby.

'Libby, it's difficult. I needed to tell you first. I haven't spoken to AJ yet.'

Libby collapsed into the chair beside her, losing control of the muscles in her legs. The power of grief. Jean was kneeling beside her, and she took the phone from her gently.

'How did it happen?'

'Jean, we're taking off right now.' Beth sought to reassure her friend. 'Just tell AJ … Jeff is injured, but he's hanging in there.'

'You ready, Beth?' Dale shouted. 'We have to go.'

Standing on the tarmac, Beth instinctively held the phone away from her ear.

'Yeah, let's go. What's the medic saying?'

'Pete is looking after him. He's heavily medicated,' Dale replied. 'But Jeff's eyes are open. Blood pressure is—'

'Blood pressure? Has he got any blood left— Oh shit.' Beth remembered that the phone was still live. She pressed the 'end call' button.

'Look, I don't know how either,' said Dale. 'The crew tell me Maher had enough pull to keep them on station here waiting for us.'

'Lucky us.' Beth leaned over and kissed her husband. 'We did it for our boy.'

They could hear the tannoy as they approached the steps: 'Cells on flight mode.'

Beth could see her bandaging had now been redone professionally by the medic. Jeff was lying in a cot; the drip was attached. He looked comfortable but now his eyes were closed.

'Pete, what are his chances?'

'He'll live. The wound didn't look as bad as Dale was describing.'

'What?'

'Yep, and I had blood plasma, his type, he'll live.'

'What?'

'Strap in, Beth. You're starting to sound like you need a shot yourself.

After four hours in the air, the co-pilot came up beside Jeff. He tugged him on the shoulder, being careful to avoid the heavily bandaged neck.

'We're coming into Shannon for fuel. Edwards are in contact. The colonel must be concerned for you – he's on the wire. I'll help you if you want to get the headphones on.'

Dale and Beth couldn't help it. The exhaustion forced them to sleep. They found a little private spot on an uncomfortable fuselage floor. The landing announcement roused them. A bleary-eyed Beth had to check with Dale in disbelief.

'Tell me I'm seeing things?'

'What?

'Look, Jeff is sitting up, headphones … talking.'

'Talking to who?'

'How would I know.' She turned her gaze back to Dale mostly to shoot him a bewildered look.

Jeff could hear his father-in-law's gruff voice over the crackly connection.

'Colonel? Jeff here.'

'AJ tells me you boys had a rough ride,' said Maher.

'Well, we're on our way home without Aidan,' said Jeff. He felt numb. 'I know you met him a few times, at the wedding was one time.'

'Rough, I know, and you'll know I've seen it more

times than …' The colonel's voice tailed off. 'Well, enough times,' he concluded.

Jeff's mind was wandering. *I'd better give Mike the "Yes, Colonel, no Colonel" treatment. You play the deference game with these guys, even if you are related.*

'Colonel, it's over,' he said firmly. 'There'll be no more deaths, Mike … sir. The official story is that Nature stopped the new pandemic, or disease, or whatever. The Devil's Countdown is stopped.'

'AJ will be glad to hear you're nearly home.' Maher sounded genuinely pleased to hear Jeff's voice. 'Couldn't make it all out, but this 1332 story … Well, I'll have our people look at it. Was it worth getting shot up for?'

'No more deaths, sir,' Jeff repeated.

'How do you make that out, son?' he asked. 'You wave a magic wand or something?'

'I think the "something" would cover it all right.'

'You mean you got Gabrielle?' asked the colonel.

'I mean he was got by a higher authority.'

'Son, I take it you're on meds, for that injury,' Mike paused, 'but I'm glad you'll make it back. Don't bother trying to complete the double. We've locked Zimmerman up, and I hear we've lost the key.'

'I'm just coming to terms with Aidan's death, Mike. Let me talk to you when we're back. It's over – over.'

Beth was doing something that no one on the plane would have thought possible. She was crying as she moved closer to Jeff.

'Is it over, Jeff?' she asked, as she held her hand out to take his.

'It's over,' Jeff replied softly, lying back down. 'I've never been so sure in all my life.'

He closed his eyes, and that prompted the medic to do a quick check on his vitals.

'He's asleep,' he said to Beth in a low voice. 'Let him rest.'

'How in God's name is the man even able to be alive?' asked Dale.

'Honey, I think you've just answered your own question.'

Part 5
RAPTURE

50

AJ took a lot of convincing that Jeff was recovered enough to have all the team over for Christmas Eve.

'They need to hear it from me,' he insisted. 'What happened to Aidan, I mean – and other things … important things.'

AJ agreed for one reason. It would help to put all the conjecture going around to bed.

Jean and Libby arrived first. While they waited for the others, Jean took the opportunity to have her own word with Jeff. She moved an unsteady Jeff towards the dining room. Libby had said hello, but kept her coat on. She seemed happy to give Jeff space, and went off to talk with AJ in the back yard.

'What were— Are you?' Jean asked immediately. 'A prophet?'

'The Presence called me righteous. The Hubermans called me a vessel – a carrier of … something.'

'The "something" is sometimes called hope.' Jean smiled.

'My deepest friend, your girl is my biggest supporter and my greatest critic. She's going to have none of what I have to say.'

'Not really a critic, though, Jeff. She … Well, you know she's taken Aidan's death hard. So she's not really in a good space to buy into your experiences.'

'Is that what's eating at her?' asked Jeff. 'I'm back and he's gone?'

'Jeff, come on. Her woman's perception is going to tell her that something is off. She loves both of you. You're alive and he was left behind with … you know, a shadow hanging over him. To a girl's heart, it smells off.'

'Maybe it's a small thing, but I think I was granted the mercy of not seeing my friend, broken.' Jeff had his eyes downcast, gazing at the dining room table. 'God granted me that mercy.'

'A small mercy, given that it was a large one to bring you back to life. How come no one is using the word "miracle"?' Jean tenderly touched him on his neck.

'Sure, Jean. Dale tells me I had a hole the size of a golf ball in my throat.'

'Carl Jung, as you know from Robinson's book, owned the Gospel of Truth from Nag Hammadi for a period. He did a famous interview in the sixties when he was asked if he thought there was a God. He paused on the interview and said, "I don't think, I know."'

'Yep, I guess. I know as well for sure.' Jeff paused. 'Jean, you were asking me was I a prophet. Can I ask you – are you an angel?'

She deflected the question.

'I truly believe in everything you experienced, Jeff.

You were a vessel for God's work.'

Jeff and Jean joined their partners in the back garden. The coolness of the night required a fire for warmth.

'There, I told you guys I was an angel,' said Jean. 'Jeff endorsed me, and he has met God, so he should know.'

'You are my angel, and that's enough, isn't it? He has been through a lot. Can he be expected to be thinking straight?' asked Libby sharply.

'The carnage has stopped, thank God,' said AJ.

'*Inshallah* in Arabic,' said Jean. 'God willing.' She was beaming, re-born.

'Have you seen anything like it?' asked Jeff.

'Like what?' asked Libby, sharply again.

'Like that night sky on a Christmas Eve,' said Jeff.

'Oh, here we go again,' said AJ playfully. 'Jeff and his constellations talk.'

Dale, Beth and Dylan arrived.

'Happy Christmas,' said Jeff.

AJ heralded the guys into the garden and presented Dylan with a large box in Christmas wrapping.

'Resourceful as ever,' said Jeff. 'That's my girl.'

'You're recovered remarkably, Jeff,' Dale observed, looking him up and down. 'Well done.'

Realisation dawned on Jeff: this was his world around him – minus one. A feeling of well-being welled up inside him. The Devil's Countdown Clock was no longer ticking. He stood up and hugged Beth.

'What a job you guys did,' he said, looking straight

at her. He turned to look at the others. 'All you guys. I told AJ – her dad took the trouble to radio me on the plane back home. I might have come across as a bit rude … heavily medicated. All I could express was that it was over.'

'That was good for everyone,' said AJ. 'Even if you had blurted out a story that the time of the Apocalypse was upon us – the End of Days, according to your abbot – you could blame it on the fact you were stoned out of your mind. Look, honey, you saw our best friend slaughtered. That can't have been easy.'

'I was slaughtered myself, love, and I'm here and nobody can tell me how, except maybe myself.'

'Your hunch – and Jean's – to go back to Egypt was right.' Beth smiled. 'People have stopped dying, and that's only since that Friday.'

Dylan was quiet, happy to stick to his dad once he had permission to open the present.

'Can this all be true?' asked Libby. 'I know I hadn't passed Day 1332, but it's coming up next month.'

'You're saved. Happy Christmas,' said Jean as she stole a kiss on her lips.

'If miracles are getting handed out, can I have Aidan back?' Libby still looked more angry than sad. 'Beth, Dale, you were there. Are you backing up Jeff's story?'

'It's like the man said,' Dale replied. 'A bullet wound to the throat, like the one Jeff had, just isn't survivable.'

'Yet here he is,' Libby snapped. 'The risen Jeff.' Jean was trying to put her arm around her waist, but

Libby subtly resisted the physical contact. 'Have you anything extra, Beth?'

'Nope. Lib, I'm sorry Aidan didn't make it. That's down to us for not protecting him, or down to him, if he wanted to run. We maybe don't have to buy into Jeff's incredible story. But I'll back up what Dale says. There's no way that man there can be alive. But he is. Aidan bolted for the exit even before the shot was fired. Their security door shutter springs were designed to make certain those manuscripts never left the building. He never stood a chance. And then it was over. The doors and windows opened slowly. There was light, and there sure was blood. No sight or sign of Gabrielle or Simone – and, boy, were we glad of it.'

Nobody said anything.

'Libby, we couldn't bring Aidan home.' Beth squeezed Libby's arm. 'We owed him that, I know, but we couldn't jeopardise Jeff's chances. You understand that, don't you?'

A woman's take on it was just what Libby was aching for. She was in tears now, and Jean and Beth embraced her, as a group, tightly. The grief was flowing at last.

'"The past is a foreign country" – is that the saying?' She was still trying to control her emotions. 'God knows what the new earth will turn out like,' Libby said.

'But there won't be a Satan,' said Jean.

Libby turned away from her, not wanting to go there. 'I know I wasn't with you in the museum. I know you think Aidan must have been Gabrielle's insider for the longest time. But do you give too much credit to the supernatural?'

'Libby, where's your faith, my beautiful friend?' Jeff protested as mildly as he could. ' Nobody is dying anymore. Gabrielle had all the cards. He couldn't mess it up, and he still did.'

'All I'm saying ...' Libby gathered her thoughts. 'Maybe there have been technical flaws with his vaccine ingredient. Maybe the killing machine has just slowed down.'

'You're an apologist for something, I don't know what,' said Jeff. 'What chance do I have of persuading others if I can't persuade you?'

He had clasped her by the shoulders at arm's length and was looking her straight in the eye. Jean was living out the best time in her life even while her lover was in the depth of emotional turmoil.

'There are lots of supernatural events all around us, all of the time. Egypt had been a shelter to a young Jesus. So why would it not also be a shelter for a secret that was to be stored for two millennia, then used to give mankind one more bite of the cherry of life?' When Libby didn't respond, the silence was mildly embarrassing.

'Come on, Jeff,' Libby urged him. 'Let's get back to your story – an out-of-body experience?'

'Libby, you're a sceptic – no question about it, and I welcome it. Why should all the souls who claim they've seen themselves, usually from above, be delusional nutjobs? Why can't it be true, at least some of the time?' asked Jeff enthusiastically, knowing that Beth had a story to share. 'Look, Dale, Beth – will you back me up on this?'

'Well, yep,' said Beth, 'but everyone knows we weren't in that room with you. Sounds strange, when we were tending to your actual body.'

'One of our guys had that experience, though.' Dale turned to Beth to prompt her to continue. 'Not just on an operating table or something like that.'

'For sure,' said Beth. 'A friend, Chat Campbell, got blasted against a back wall in a downtown district of Tehran – an IED. Chat's tale was that he thought … No, he *knew* he would survive, because he was observing his wounded self from a vantage point that told him there were no hostiles closing in for the kill. So, he said, there was no need to hurry up and die – you know, before somebody came around to defile you further, by ending you.' Beth noticed she had everyone's gaze. 'I'm not explaining it very well, but some of us got a lot of comfort from his story at the time. You know, even if you were in a situation where you should be dead, maybe there was … Well, what you guys call supernatural forces. Metaphysical – isn't that the word, Jeff?'

'No, these days I'll just say God.'

AJ shivered. This was like telling ghost stories at Christmas time. She asked, 'Are blankets needed?'

Dale stoked the fire.

'I thought your catchphrase was something along the lines of, "expecting the unexpected is what keeps you alive",' said Libby.

'What's more unexpected than the other world?' asked Dale.

'Look,' said Libby, 'I miss Aidan. Of course I do. I'm remembering how he kept me calm when we met Assad. All that mischievous eye contact right under that bastard's nose.'

'Do you think Aidan was turned, Libby?' asked AJ.

Libby looked at her sharply. Jeff hoped another awkward silence wouldn't explode into an argument. Libby took her time.

'Look, I've heard the whispers,' she said, 'but that's not the guy I loved.'

There was still a tremor in her voice, and she moved slightly closer to Jean.

'We never really knew what happened at that meeting with Gabrielle in Cairo,' said Beth. 'That's the unknown.'

'No, he would never say … Look,' said Libby, 'the man got a horrible death for his trouble. Isn't that enough?' Her eyes were watering again.

'Maybe now is not the time … Christmas,' Jeff suggested.

'No, Jeff,' she said firmly. 'Now is the time to clear the air.'

'Gabrielle and Simone knew our every move,' said Jeff. 'It wasn't the priest in Nag Hammadi or the abbot in that monastery that helped them. They, for sure, knew we were dealing with evil. It was the abbot himself who called Gabrielle "the Devil".'

'Well,' Libby countered quickly, 'if you're up for

believing that, then surely the Devil doesn't need any earthly assistance?'

'Jesus, I'm not trying to be argumentative here,' said Jeff.

'Sure sounds familiar,' said Beth. 'Never thought my old Sunday school days would help. You know – old Nick always trying to turn the good guys.'

Beth's intervention again at an emotional moment was no bad thing. Libby took her time, but when she spoke her tone was softer.

'So sad. No partner to mourn, no parents, no one left alive to contact … so anonymous.'

'Look,' said Jeff, 'in time to come we'll get his body returned.'

'Returned to where – Ireland?' asked Libby

'No, California, where his friends are,' said Jeff.

Libby looked a bit brighter in the glow of the fire. She, more than anyone, had soldiered with Aidan. Jeff wondered if she felt she should have been there in the end; if she felt she hadn't been in control when the end was being played out.

'Pour us a glass, will you?' Libby steered Jean in the direction of a bottle of Napa Zinfandel. 'We can toast our friend, can't we?'

'How many times in life do you get a chance to steal victory from the jaws of defeat?' Dale was allowing himself a beer, but trying to disguise the fact from Dylan.

Dylan in any event was busy with his new present, a small celestial telescope.

'I'd have thought a former professional soldier would be able to answer that better than most,' said Jeff.

'Well, sure, we have tales of taking on superior forces.' Dale smiled. 'But who has experience of taking on the Devil and winning? I thought the last guy to do that was Jesus Christ.'

Jeff raised his own glass and smiled. 'Let the world keep on spinning for another while,' he said, 'and we'll make the most of it.'

Printed in Great Britain
by Amazon

42384785R00219